October's Fear

A Larry Macklin Mystery-Book 12

A. E. Howe

Books in the Larry Macklin Mystery Series:

November's Past	September's Fury
December's Secrets	October's Fear
January's Betrayal	Spring's Promises
February's Regrets	Summer's Rage
March's Luck	Autumn's Ghost
April's Desires	Winter's Chill
May's Danger	Valentine's Warning
June's Troubles	St. Patrick's Cross
July's Trials	Memorial Day's Escape
August's Heat	Independence Day's Search

ISBN-13: 978-0-9997968-6-3

This book is a work of fiction. Names, characters, places and incidents are the product of the author's imagination or are used fictitiously. Any resemblance to actual events, locales, business establishments, persons or animals, living or dead, is entirely coincidental.

DEDICATION

This one is for all of you—Larry's fans. I never dreamed
the series would come this far—thank you.

CHAPTER ONE

"What's that noise?" I asked, rolling over in bed. A steady *thunk, thunk, thunk* was disturbing the otherwise quiet Tuesday morning outside our bedroom window.

"My guess would be that Dad's working on the piece of oak you gave him," Cara said, her voice still sounding thick with sleep as she crawled out of bed. "You might as well get up. Once he starts he isn't going to stop."

I growled, but threw off the covers and sat up. "You need to tell your parents we're engaged."

I looked down as my hand was nudged by a little tabby head. Our conversation had signaled to the other occupants of the house that we were awake and they were free to come into the bedroom and demand breakfast. Alvin, the Pug, trotted in and sounded off with one firm bark, then retreated back into the kitchen to stand expectantly by his food bowl. Ivy, on the other hand, obviously felt the need to rub herself against me to hurry me along with my morning routine.

"You need to ask Dad for my hand in marriage," Cara responded with a smile in her voice.

"I don't think I'll do it while he has an axe in his hands," I joked back. "Besides, you're the one who told me to wait."

"I know I did." Ever since her parents had arrived two

days ago, Cara had been hiding her engagement ring, placing it on the same chain with her heart pendant and keeping them both tucked under her shirt.

"I don't know what you're so afraid of. I doubt he's going to object. I did him a pretty big solid when he was framed for murder."

"The trouble is, the minute Mom knows we're engaged, she'll start pushing me to plan the wedding," Cara yelled from the bathroom.

"She doesn't strike me as a big wedding kind of mother."

Henry and Anna Laursen were an odd mix. They were both hippie types, while Henry also carried a hardcore strain of Viking. They lived in a co-op down in Gainesville that was only a few steps removed from a commune. They had arrived on the pretense of helping us clean up after Hurricane Marcy and recover from the trauma of Cara's abduction, even though we had downplayed both events. Cara in particular had made her abduction sound a lot less serious than it had been, knowing it would send her parents into protective mode. They had come up as soon as they could get away.

"She's not about big weddings so much as weird weddings. Mom and Dad have renewed their vows six times. Once at a nudist camp, once on the edge of a volcano, and another time they had a Nordic ceremony in three feet of snow. The last time was four years ago under the moonlight at a local spring and complete with a Burning Man-size bonfire."

"Ahhh, I see the problem," I said as I stepped into the shower.

Thirty minutes later, I was eating cereal and watching through the window as Cara's father chopped at a large piece of oak with an iron adze. Every couple of strokes, he'd stop and study the cuts he'd made. The wood was from part of an ancient live oak that had split and fallen during the storm. Henry was planning to carve something out of it.

There was a purposeful knock at the front door. I wasn't

surprised when Cara's mother let herself in a second later.

"That uniform makes you look too much like a cop," Anna said, looking me up and down disapprovingly. "I like it better when you wear khakis. Then I can pretend you don't work for The Man."

"Sorry, but I'm still on the road. Until things get back to normal, all of us are having to work patrol," I said, shifting my duty belt.

I wasn't overly fond of having to dress in my uniform either, but we were short-handed. Several of our sheriff's deputies had volunteered to assist in the counties to the west and south of us where the hurricane destruction had been more severe. Even in Adams County, we still had large trucks picking up piles of debris from the side of the road and several neighborhoods with homes too damaged to occupy. We'd put on extra patrols to prevent looting and help with traffic around the debris trucks, so for the past few weeks all criminal investigators had been taking shifts on patrol.

"I understand," Anna said, smiling and patting my cheek. "Is Cara up yet?"

"Yes!" Cara shouted from the bedroom. She joined us in the kitchen and her mother immediately started to explain that they needed to do a healing ceremony for the damaged live oak. I grinned and waved to Cara, then escaped out the door to my patrol car.

The green-and-white car was an older model normally used as a loaner whenever a patrol deputy's regular car needed to go in for service. It smelled of fast food, stale sweat and the industrial cleansers used to clean various bodily fluids from the enclosed backseat. Before I pulled out of my driveway, I logged onto the laptop mounted to the dash. We were skipping morning briefings for now; instead, everyone just called in and went straight to work.

My first duty assignment of the morning was in an area where a truck was clearing debris half a mile from the elementary school. Safely mingling school buses, commuters and large trucks parked half on the road required some blue lights and law enforcement presence.

I pulled up behind Deputy Julio Ortiz, who had been covering the graveyard shift. He'd picked a highly visible spot on the side of the road so folks would wake up and pay attention before passing the truck as it worked on a huge tangle of trees that had been cut and stacked in the ditch.

"Takes them about half an hour to get up the bigger piles," Julio told me. "I've just been tagging along with my lights on. We can let them do their own traffic control after nine o'clock."

"Anything exciting happen last night?" I asked, leaning into the passenger window of his car.

"Quiet. I think the storm blew away all the drug addicts and dealers."

"Suits me. Did you all have any damage?" I'd barely had the chance to do anything more than say hi to him in the three weeks since the storm.

"Nah. A few shingles off the roof, no big deal. But my neighbor had a tree come down on his truck. Had to get the jaws of life out there so he could get his stuff out of the cab. How's your dad doing?"

"He's stretched pretty thin between hurricane recovery, repairs to the office and the election," I admitted.

Dad was facing a tough opponent in his bid for reelection as sheriff. Charles Maxwell, Calhoun's chief of police, had recently been backed by a deeply pocketed PAC that had been formed by a person holding a large grudge against both Dad and me. To make matters worse, planned renovations to the sheriff's office had been complicated by extensive damage caused in a robbery attempt during the hurricane.

Julio headed home and I spent the next hour escorting the debris truck as its crew worked their way down the road. Once the school buses were off the road, I moved on to directing traffic at an intersection where the county was replacing a fallen traffic light.

I'd just been waved off by the crew as they restored power to the light when I got a phone call from dispatch. Radio codes were good for ninety-eight percent of the calls we received, but occasionally codes weren't enough to convey the particular circumstance.

"The caller reports seeing an arm sticking out of a load of debris on the side of the road," Marti told me.

"Roger that," I said, wondering if they'd found someone killed by the storm, or maybe a person who'd died of a heart attack cleaning up debris. I hoped it wasn't the former as I didn't even want to think about what shape the body would be in after this long. Maybe it was a false alarm. We'd had several dozen since the storm. Bodies can look like mannequins and mannequins can look like bodies.

As I neared the location of the call, I realized it wasn't far from the home of Horace McCune, the man behind the PAC that was tormenting Dad with negative billboards and yard signs. Was there a connection? I certainly hoped not. I didn't want to deal with him again.

I pulled up behind the huge debris collection truck. Its collector claw held a mangled mass of pine tree branches and vines. Four men wearing bright orange vests were standing beside the truck, staring at the claw. They all turned and looked at me as if I had the answer to the puzzle suspended fifteen feet in the air.

"Hey!" the oldest of the men said, waving to me as I got out of my car. He had the look of someone who worked hard every day of his life and went home to a hearty meal of steak and potatoes each night. He had grey hair, an unshaven face, a sturdy back and a respectable pot belly.

When I walked up, the man pointed to the claw. In among all the greenery was something pinkish sticking out at an odd angle. As I got closer, the sun glinted off of a man's watch on the wrist of what was clearly a human arm. Mannequins seldom wore watches, especially when they were lying on the side of the road.

"I can bring it down if you want?" the man said, making

it a question.

"No. Not yet."

If there was a body in there and they moved the claw or dropped the load of debris, it could do more damage to the victim and make it harder to determine the cause of death. It was much better to go slowly and fully evaluate the situation before doing anything that could make things harder for the investigation. I got right under the claw and looked up.

"That's a nice watch," one of the younger men said.

He was right. Even from eight feet away, I could tell that it was either very expensive or a very good fake. The arm was covered in grey hair and liver spots and it clearly hadn't been lying out in the weather for long. With a sick feeling, I looked away from the arm and stared at the entrance to McCune's estate, just two hundred feet down the road.

"You sure you don't want me to lower it?"

"I need you all to move back to my patrol car," I said, feeling my gut roll over. This wasn't good. "Now!" I added, when the men just stood there staring at me. Dutifully they followed me back to my car, seeming to finally realize that they'd actually picked up a dead man.

"Which one of you is James Collins?" I said, asking for the man who had reported the gruesome find.

"Me." The older man raised his arm.

"Tell me exactly what happened." I wanted to gather a bit more information before calling anyone else.

"We were just picking up debris like we've been doing for days, and I looked up and saw an arm sticking out of the claw."

"Were you operating the machinery?"

"No, Ty was." Collins pointed to a young, dark-skinned man who looked like central casting had sent him to fill the roll of construction worker. He wore a blue chambray shirt under his orange vest, jeans and work boots.

"Where exactly did you pick up that pile of branches?" I asked him.

"Right there, man. Just picked it up and started to swing

it toward the truck when J. C. waved me off."

"You didn't see anything?"

"No way. I sit up there in the truck and work the arm. I didn't see nothin' until I got down."

"How well do you look at the stuff before you grab it up?"

"We can't bring anything but trees, leaves and yard trash to the incineration site, so I always look. Other trucks are picking up construction trash," Collins said. That meant the body had to have been pretty well covered by pine tree branches and vines when Ty grabbed the pile.

In my heart I knew who the body belonged to, and that it hadn't gotten there by itself. If I was right, life was going to get very complicated.

CHAPTER TWO

After a moment's thought, I took out my phone and called dispatch to get the number for the Florida Department of Law Enforcement. If the body was McCune's, then Dad and I would both be prime suspects. For the last two months, we had spent a fair amount of time cursing the vicious political ads distributed by McCune's PAC. While what I really wanted to do was call Dad, I didn't want the first call I made to be to the other possible suspect. So instead I dialed FDLE and asked to speak with an agent I knew. Tom Horton would understand the situation and make sure the right person was sent to the scene.

"Damn, I see the problem," Tom said once I'd explained. "I'll get with the major and call you back in five. But you need to call your dad. We'll need an official request from the sheriff to take charge of the crime scene."

"I knew that. I just thought I should call you first."

"Say no more. You were thinking right. Give me five."

He hung up and I called Dad.

"I'm in the pasture clearing out some of the storm debris," he said when I asked him where he was. He sounded like he was in a good mood so I let him talk a bit about the work, delaying the moment when I'd have to break the bad news. Finally he asked, "What do you need?"

Feeling guilty for what I was about to hit him over the head with, I sighed. "I think some workmen have found the body of Horace McCune," I said as quickly as I could.

"What?" Dad was seldom at a loss for words, but he sounded dazed.

I described the situation.

"You have got to be shitting me," he blurted and I cringed. Stunned silence followed, then he said, "Damn it! But I agree with your decision to contact FDLE first. I'll call them and confirm the request for assistance."

There was another long pause and I knew he was wrestling with a desire to rush to the scene. As a potential suspect, anything he did could be criticized later. If he came out, then he could be accused of interfering, but if he didn't come, it could be seen as a sign of guilt. Finally he said, "Stay at the scene. I'm going to send Darlene out to take over the investigation for our department."

"I understand." Another call was coming in and I hung up with Dad to talk to Tom Horton. He informed me that he was coming out himself with a crime scene team, and that he'd already contacted our county coroner, Dr. Darzi.

While I waited for the reinforcements to arrive, I roped the area around the debris truck with crime scene tape and explained to the crew that they wouldn't be doing any more work today. We'd probably even have to impound their truck. The guys didn't look particularly upset at the prospect of watching a crime scene investigation unfold rather than spending the day hauling tons of trees to the incinerator.

They wanted to talk to me, but I didn't want to be accused of influencing witnesses, so I waved them off and went to lean against my car. I stared at the arm hanging from the claw, willing it to be attached to anyone other than McCune.

My partner Darlene Marks arrived fifteen minutes later. As investigators, we handled most cases on our own, but if a big case landed on our desk then we backed each other up.

Today, though, she was in uniform like me.

"I was almost home, shortbread," she said, walking up from where she'd parked her car.

"You worked the graveyard?"

"And chased down a hit-and-run just as I was finishing up. I'd just gotten him booked in at the jail and put in my paperwork when your dad called." She looked up, seemingly mesmerized by the arm. "You really think that's Horace McCune?"

"The watch on that wrist is worth a chunk of change. And right down the road from his driveway? Yeah, I think it's McCune," I said morosely.

"Since when did you become a jeweler? That could be a knock-off. Thirty bucks on eBay."

"Thanks for the happy thought," I said as she walked over and looked up at the dangling arm.

"Hmmmm. Not good." She glanced over to where the crew was sitting in the shade. "I take it those are the men who found it."

"James Collins called it in. Ty was operating the claw," I said as she walked toward them.

I watched Darlene question the men from a distance until the coroner's van arrived. I was surprised to see Dr. Darzi get out of a car that parked behind it.

"We get the boss today?" I asked him as he walked up with a couple of assistants I didn't recognize.

"I heard who the body might be and thought I'd take a personal interest in the case. Besides, I have a couple of medical students working with me, so I thought I would give them some field experience. This fellow is Wagner and this gentleman is Roberts," he said, introducing the students.

Wagner was short and blond while Roberts had dark skin and inquisitive eyes. The two students repeatedly glanced up at the protruding appendage while Darzi introduced them. They were clearly fascinated and anxious to get started.

"Go back to the van and get a tarp," Darzi told Wagner, who hesitated as though he was afraid he might miss something while he was gone. After a stern look from Darzi, he dutifully trotted off toward the van. When he came back, they spread the tarp directly under the claw.

"Could someone lower the body?" Darzi called over to the crew.

Ty waved and climbed back up to his seat. He lowered the claw to within a few inches of the tarp before Darzi signaled him to stop.

"We are going to examine the arm that is hanging free first. Why?" Darzi asked his students.

"Because it wasn't damaged when the claw picked up the body?" Roberts said hesitantly.

"Exactly. The crushing of the body in the claw will make examining the body for rigor mortis difficult. So we will examine the arm which is relatively undamaged," Darzi lectured as he touched and flexed the arm. Satisfied with his own examination, he let each of the students have their turn.

The scene was surreal. I watched as Darzi let each of the men reach out with their gloved hands and fondle the arm.

"So what can you tell me? You first, Mr. Wagner."

"Rigor mortis is present in the limb. So death had to have occurred at least three hours ago."

"Correct. Do you have anything to add, Mr. Roberts?"

"There is no lividity in the fingers, so the arm has not been dangling from the claw since death."

"Very good. We've been told that the body was picked up a little over an hour ago, but we should never presume anything. Is there something else?" Darzi looked at them expectantly.

"Maybe some bruising around his wrist?" Wagner asked.

"Take your glove and touch the area," Darzi instructed.

"There is some glue-like residue. His hands were taped," Roberts said.

"Exactly," said Darzi, nodding. "Now let us see what the rest of the body can tell us." Darzi looked up at Ty and yelled to be heard over the rumble of the big truck's diesel engine. "Can you please open the claw as slowly as possible?"

As the claw opened, Darzi and the students had to move back as a quarter ton of greenery fell out onto the tarp. For a moment, everyone was transfixed by the tangle of pine, oak and human body. The tree branches had punctured the victim and his clothes were torn and bloody. I couldn't see the head. I thought I could see where it should have been, but all I could make out was flesh, blood, wood and leaves. I still couldn't confirm that this was the body of Horace McCune.

I heard retching and turned to see two of the workmen throwing up in the woods. I almost felt like joining them.

Darlene walked up beside me. "That's going to take awhile to unravel," she said, shaking her head at the mess piled up on the tarp.

Darzi joined us. "I'm going to need a bigger van. Or perhaps a truck."

"How much of that are you going to take back to your office?" Darlene asked him.

"Anything that is in contact with the body." He paused and turned back to the students standing over their science project. "One of you, get another tarp." Turning back to us, he said, "We'll separate what we can and put it on the second tarp for the crime scene technicians to go through."

As if on cue, a crime scene van pulled up with a couple of cars behind it.

"These guys might have the vehicle you need," Darlene said, looking at the big blue van with "FDLE" printed in large yellow letters on the side.

Tom Horton walked over to us, looking more like a skateboarder than a law enforcement officer. I knew that he had to be in his mid-thirties, but I was willing to bet he still got carded when he bought a beer. He was wearing a boyish smile that turned to a frown when he caught sight of the tangled mess of our victim.

"Whoa! That's not pretty," he said, trying to identify what parts of the body he was seeing.

"Horton, I'm going to need a bigger van than ours to transport the body back to the morgue," Darzi said.

"Talk to the crime scene guys, Doc," Tom said, pointing over his shoulder without his eyes ever leaving the mess on top of the tarp. "Are you sure this is who you think it is?" he asked me.

"That's the McCune place over there." I pointed down the road to McCune's driveway. "And the watch on the victim's wrist looks like it's worth more than my car. Also, as best I can tell from the arm, the age looks about right."

Tom looked at the driveway. "Guess I'll head down there, knock on the door and see who answers." Then he seemed to notice Darlene for the first time. "Hey, I think we met when you were working for the city."

"A couple of years ago, yeah. You were working financial crimes and helped out with the case against Tina Ingram when she embezzled thirty-thousand dollars from the city," Darlene said.

"That's right. Good memory."

"And though I may not look the part right now, I'm the lead investigator for the county on this case."

"Fantastic. You stay here and keep an eye on the crime scene. I'll go knock on this guy's door and see who's home," Tom said cheerily.

"Is it just me or is that guy getting younger?" Darlene asked once he'd headed down the road to McCune's place.

"Maybe he's a vampire."

"Halloween *is* just around the corner," Darlene said, then turned serious. "I can't tell if that's McCune or not. For y'all's sake, I hope not."

"You and me both," I agreed.

We watched in morbid fascination as Darzi and his team pulled apart the victim's wood and brush cocoon. At one point, Roberts went to get a third tarp.

Tom was back in ten minutes. "Looking grim, boys and girls. The maid was there and said that Mr. McCune was not at home. She hasn't seen him since yesterday afternoon.

Mind you, I got all of this through the speaker at the gate. She wouldn't even open the gates for me, let alone let me in the house." He looked at the three tarps. "Three of them, Doc?"

Darzi explained. "One tarp contains the body and anything piercing it. As you can see, that includes branches that are three feet long, as well as many smaller ones. On the second tarp, we are placing anything that has blood or other secretions. Everything else is going on the third tarp for the crime scene techs to go over. For all we know, the murder weapon could be in that pile. I say murder, however," he paused, holding up a finger, "it is possible that he somehow died of natural causes and became buried in the debris. I'll know more after I examine the body. I will tell you that his head seems to be… crushed more than I would have expected. When the claw was opened, the head, or what was left of it, didn't appear to be sandwiched between any of the metal parts."

"I've been watching these crews work over the last couple of weeks," I said. "Sometimes the guy operating the claw will use it to crush the debris before closing it and lifting it up."

"I've seen that too. They'll use the claw to push down and consolidate the pile so they can get more in when they go to pick it up," Darlene agreed.

"That could explain the damage I'm seeing. If one of you would like to question the claw operator about what he remembers, that would be helpful. I'm afraid that if the victim was murdered and the crime was committed with a blunt instrument, it is going to be hard to prove which injuries were caused by the murderer and which were a result of being crushed in the steel claw. This is going to be an interesting case. A great teaching moment," Darzi said, looking over at his students.

"Glad that Adams County could provide you with a challenge," I said, hoping he heard my heavy dose of sarcasm.

"I can always count on you all," Darzi said and turned back to the job at hand.

One of the FDLE crime scene techs approached us. "I called the office and they're emptying out another van to come move the body to the morgue," she told Tom. She looked at Darlene and me, then added, "I bet Shantel is sorry she's missing out on this." Shantel Williams was the head of Adams County's crime scene department.

"Actually, she probably is. If she wasn't busy overseeing the reconstruction of her office, she'd be out here just on principle," I said.

"I heard about all the excitement during the hurricane," the woman said, shaking her head. "Tell her Deidra says hi." She turned and went back to their pile.

"Come to think of it, I'm surprised Pete hasn't stopped by," Darlene said, referring to Pete Henley, one of our other investigators and my best friend. She looked around behind her as though she expected he might be conjured up by the uttering of his name.

"He's teaching a class over in Tallahassee." Pete was our department's firearms instructor. Normally our classes were held at our own gun range just outside of town, but the bays were blocked by trees that had fallen during the hurricane and there hadn't yet been time for a workday to clear them. Talon Range in Tallahassee was owned by ex-LEOs who had offered us the use of their facilities until we had ours back up and running.

I turned to Tom. "Our victim has one good set of fingerprints. If it's McCune, I wonder if he has prints on file. He did a lot of work with the oil business out in Texas and had a few brushes with the law. Could you check with the Texas Rangers to see if they have his prints?"

"No problemo." He pulled out his phone and walked off toward his car. He was back in twenty minutes with a smile on his face. "The man was almost indicted a couple of times for his various schemes, but each time he managed to weasel his way out. However, as a young man of twenty-five, he got sauced up and went for a ride down the wrong highway. Your man has a DUI. Fingerprints are available."

He turned to the CSI team. "Deidra, see if Dr. Darzi will let you get a set of fingerprints for," he paused and took a moment to figure out which of the victim's hands was the good one, "the dead guy's right hand."

"Yes, she can get the prints. Just give us a minute," Darzi said, having overheard Tom's instructions to Deidra.

Mentally, I was saying a prayer and making promises to the Big Guy as the process worked its way along. Deidra used an electronic pad to take the prints and, at the speed of light, they were sent to Texas where they were compared to the youthful McCune's prints. Within minutes, Tom showed us a one-word text: *Match*.

I mumbled a few profanities before calling Dad.

CHAPTER THREE

Dr. Darzi and his students soon finished separating the mess.

"We are ready to transport Mr. McCune back to the hospital," the coroner told us. "I'm going to start on the autopsy as soon as we can get him downstairs. Until I remove some of the branches that have skewered his body, we won't be able to get him into one of the drawers. So if any of you want to view the operation, you'll need to follow us back. This won't be a quick one."

I shook my head.

"I think your report on Vlad the Impaled will be enough for me," Darlene said with a thin smile.

"I'm good, Doc," Tom added.

"Suit yourselves," Darzi said with a wave, calling some of the crime scene techs over to help him with the body.

After Darzi was gone, Tom and Darlene headed over to McCune's house armed with a search warrant that had been easily obtained now that there was probable cause to suspect a murder had been committed on the premises. Before they left, Tom told me, "It might be better if you didn't stay here."

He didn't want a person of interest to be left alone at the

site where the victim's body was found. I had to bite my lip and nod. As much as I hated it, he was right.

I went back to my patrol car, checking my phone before radioing myself back into service. I had missed a call from Cara and called her back.

"Go ahead and talk to Dad," she said cheerfully before I could say anything. "I'll deal with the fallout from Mom." She sounded excited and happy. I hated to ruin her mood with the news about McCune.

"Look, something has happened," I said, then told her how I'd spent my morning.

"Wow! Who could have done that?"

"The guy was an ass. I'm sure there are going to be any number of suspects. Unfortunately, the person McCune has been bitch-slapping in public for months is Dad."

"And you," Cara added.

"And me."

"No one could possibly suspect you and your dad." She paused for only a moment. "But the election…"

"Exactly. Even if most people know it's ridiculous, there are going to be enough who don't know us personally who might have doubts. Enough voters that it could sway the election."

"Do you think Maxwell will use it against your dad?"

"Maxwell can be an ass, but he's been playing fair. On the other hand, he doesn't *have* to make any accusations. They'll be out there on social media without any help from him."

"Is there anything I can do?" Cara asked.

"Solve the murder before election day."

"Are you going to be working the case?"

"As a suspect, I don't think so," I said with a little more snark than Cara deserved.

"Guess that was a dumb question." All of the joy that had been in her voice at the beginning of the phone call was gone.

"Sorry, I didn't mean it like that. I'm still in shock. And I hate the fact I can't go after the murderer head on." What I didn't say was that I was planning to do everything I could in the background to catch the son of a bitch.

I said goodbye to Cara, then radioed dispatch that I was back in service. They immediately sent me to a lunchtime fender bender that needed official supervision to keep it from turning into a physical altercation. I drove back into town to find two men glaring at each other over the hoods of their cars, both refusing to exchange insurance information.

"He's at fault. Why do I need to give him *my* insurance?" pouted the younger of the two. He was very thin and had several open sores on his face. I couldn't help but wonder what type of drugs I'd find in his car.

"I'm not giving him crap until he gives me his information," said a thirty-year-old who was wearing a shirt from Express Burgers and a name tag that identified him as the manager. I'd had dealings with him in the past. He was a jerk then and didn't appear to have changed.

"Each of you get back into your vehicles. Get your information out and I'll come retrieve it."

"He pulled out—" the meth-head started.

"He didn't stop at the sign and—" the jerk blurted.

I put up my hand and stopped them both. "Neither of you have received much damage to your cars. Maybe five hundred dollars, tops. Do either of you really want me to start looking into this? Digging around? Finding who knows what? Trust me. I've been to scratch-and-dent affairs like this where both parties ended up with felonies on unrelated charges. Raise your hand if you still want to do this thing."

Meth-head kept his mouth firmly shut and his hands close to his sides. Manager Dude looked like he wanted to say that he didn't have anything to hide, but finally he just pursed his lips and stayed silent.

"Good choice. Go to your cars, get your information and let's get this done."

Half an hour later, I told dispatch I was open again, but

before they could come up with something else for me to do, I got a text from Dad: *My office at 3:00.*

I looked at my watch and saw that it was only a little after one, so when dispatch radioed with a burglary, I told them I was on my way. After writing up a report on the phone, TV and Blu-ray player that had been stolen while their owner was at work, I headed to the office and found Darlene sitting in her patrol car and working on a report.

"Where's your new partner?" I asked as I leaned in the passenger window.

"Don't even joke about that. He's inside. And I thought *I* was perky. No, I'd much rather carry your sorry sourpuss self around. And it's creepy how he looks younger than he did a couple of years ago," she said, shaking her head.

"I take it you all got invited to Dad's office for a three o'clock meeting?"

"We did. Though I'm a little surprised *you* were invited," she admitted.

Assuming it was a group meeting about the murder of McCune, I was a bit surprised myself. I'd assumed I'd be frozen out of the investigation since I had a solid motive.

"What's *he* doing here?" I said, seeing Chief Maxwell pull into the parking lot.

"This is going to be some summit," Darlene said, raising her eyebrows. "Guess we better go in so we can get a good seat."

Desperately wanting to ask her what they'd found at McCune's house, I kept my mouth shut as we walked into the building. I didn't want to put her in the awkward position of telling me to go fish.

Tom Horton was waiting for us outside of Dad's office. "He said he'd be ready in a few minutes," Tom informed us, wearing a smile that seemed decidedly out of place.

As we waited, I wondered if Dad had brought Mauser into work with him today. Mauser was his three-year-old, black-and-white Great Dane of unusual size. He was a burly one-hundred-and-ninety pounds with floppy ears and a serious drool problem. I thought that if Tom was scared of dogs then he was going to have that smile wiped off of his face rather quickly.

Maxwell joined us and Dad's assistant gave us the all-clear. Dad stood up as we came into the office. At the same time, Mauser scrambled up from his bed beside the desk and trotted over to greet everyone. Maxwell gave Mauser a perfunctory rub on the side of his head without much emotion. I'd heard he wasn't a huge fan of dogs. Mauser, for his part, sniffed Maxwell up and down both legs and moved on. Darlene and the dog were old friends and she gave him a few solid pats on the side while he leaned into her. Tom was definitely not afraid and was already gushing over Mauser before the dog even got to him.

"Wow! Now *that's* a dog. What's he weigh?"

Dad told him while Tom vigorously scratched Mauser on his side and tried to get a hug from the dog. I finally saw Tom's smile falter a bit when Mauser begrudgingly accepted his attention, then ignored him and came over to me. I gave the dog an extra-firm ear rub as he leaned against me.

"Have a seat," Dad told us. "I'm going to get your supervisor on speaker," he said to Tom, who nodded and looked over at Mauser as though he was hurt the dog had rejected his overtures of friendliness. I gave Mauser another pat on the side as he settled down beside me.

Dad put in a call to Andrew Warren, who served as deputy director of investigations for FDLE. Once he was on the phone, Dad explained who was in the room and brought him up to speed on the investigation.

"Dr. Darzi is completing the autopsy on McCune to determine the cause and time of death. Your crime scene techs have searched both the site where the body was found and… well, I'll let Tom fill us all in on the search of the victim's house."

"Deputy Marks and I secured a warrant for the victim's residence and did a preliminary search. We turned up a number of items which we left for the crime scene techs to secure. Among them, we found blood evidence inside and outside the garage, as well as in a maintenance shed at the rear of the house where a tractor is stored. Based on that, we believe the victim was killed at his house. Of course, our opinion could change based on our CSI team's analysis of the scene." Despite the grim nature of his report, Tom's smile and good nature were now firmly back in place.

"Thank you, Tom," Warren said. "Sheriff Macklin, I understand that you have a personal connection to the victim which might cause any investigation conducted by your office to be seen as compromised. I appreciate your prompt action to ensure there's no question about the integrity of the investigation. How do you want to proceed?"

"Excuse me," Chief Maxwell interrupted. "I don't understand exactly why I'm here. The victim lived outside of my jurisdiction, the body was discovered near his home, and the investigators on the case feel there's a good possibility the murder occurred at that home, which I again point out is outside the city limits."

"I think we'd be foolish to pretend we aren't coming down to the last weeks of an election," Dad said, looking Maxwell square in the eye. "For the record, you've been a stand-up guy through all of this… stuff with McCune's vendetta and smear campaign against me. I asked you to attend this meeting so you can voice your opinions on the way forward with the full realization that, in the near future, this might become your responsibility." Dad's expression was somber.

Whatever Maxwell was expecting, it certainly wasn't that. After a moment's silence, he said, "The only reason I'm running for the office is because I feel like you've had your time and that I might be able to bring some new ideas to the department. I appreciate you keeping me in the loop and I'll be happy to give you whatever input I can on the investigation."

"Good," Dad said and started to go on, but Warren cut him off.

"We would be willing to take over the investigation."

"No. I want to have your help, but I won't turn it all over to FDLE. My suggestion is that Deputy Marks stand as the lead investigator. She worked for Chief Maxwell for many years and they've remained friends." Dad looked at Maxwell. "Do you have any doubts that she'll conduct herself in an honest and fair manner?"

Maxwell looked at Darlene. "No. I've never had any reason to doubt her integrity. If the sheriff is willing to give her a free hand, then I'll fully support her efforts."

"I'd like to keep Special Agent Horton on the case too," Dad continued. "And, of course, since we're in the middle of rebuilding our crime scene department after last month's events, we'd very much appreciate FDLE's technical support."

My eyebrows went up. Dad seldom kissed ass that much. It was a testament to how quickly he wanted the murderer of Horace McCune brought to justice that he was willing to do whatever was necessary to leave no doubt he'd taken advantage of any and all resources available.

"That sounds reasonable to me," Warren said. "Tom, is your work schedule clear?"

"I've got a couple of pending cases, but they're all on the back burner at the moment. There's nothing I'd like better than to stay over here and help these folks out." Tom sounded as happy as a pig in swill. I forced myself not to roll my eyes, knowing that my annoyance at his upbeat attitude had more to do with my own frustration and worry than it did with him.

"Then it's settled," Dad said. "Tom and Darlene will act as partners on the case. I'm clearing Darlene's schedule so she can devote all of her time to the investigation. Recognizing that I have one of the most public motives for wanting to see harm come to Mr. McCune, I will consult with FDLE before making any decisions concerning the direction of the case. However, let me be clear. I am not recusing myself from the investigation."

"Understood. I've got a meeting to go to, if that's all," Warren said, then we heard him hang up.

"We'll know more after the autopsy results come in and all the evidence collected at the house has been examined," Dad said, standing up and signaling that the meeting was over. "Darlene, Larry, will you stay for a moment?"

He came from behind his large desk and stepped between Maxwell and the door. "Thank you," he said, putting out his hand.

"Good luck with the investigation. If there is anything that I or the police department can do to help, let me know," Maxwell said, shaking Dad's hand and sounding almost friendly.

Dad turned to Tom after Maxwell had left. "I'm glad you're here."

"Absolutely. We'll catch this killer. Don't you worry."

Once everyone else had gone, Dad turned to back to Darlene and me. "I don't have to tell you how important it is to catch the son of a bitch who did this. Darlene, I know how good you are and I'm going to stick to my word not to interfere with your investigation. However, I do want to see regular reports. Larry, I don't want you talking with Darlene about the case, but I want you to read the reports as well."

"That's a very fine line," I said, thinking about how hard it was going to be to read the reports and not discuss them with Darlene.

"If you are seen to influence the investigation in any way, it could be used by a defense attorney in the future. He or she could claim that you or I are better suspects and that we steered the investigation toward their client because we were the actual murderers."

"I know. You're right. I'm just used to shooting my mouth off about cases," I said in a moment of raw honesty.

"We've all got some tough times ahead of us," Dad said, scratching Mauser as he leaned against him. The dog's eyes seemed sadder than I'd ever seen them and, watching them together, I fully realized just how much of an impact the election, the hurricane and now this murder was having on my father.

I heard a small voice in the corner of my mind vow that *I* would catch the killer. No one was going to do this to my family and get away with it.

CHAPTER FOUR

An hour later, I sat at my desk working on my backlog of reports. With the murder hanging over our heads, I was finding it impossible to concentrate on all of the petty crimes and misdemeanors I'd logged in over the past twenty-four hours.

I saw Darlene approaching and looked up. She passed her desk and came over to stand beside mine, looking down at me thoughtfully before speaking.

"I'm probably going to regret this," she said, looking over her shoulder as though she was afraid someone might be listening, "but I'm having a conference call with Dr. Darzi and Tom Terrific in a minute, if you want to listen in."

"Tom's not here?"

"He had to go back to Tallahassee to clear up his calendar, so he'll be on the call from his office at FDLE. But," she said, holding up a finger, "you can't say a word. They can't know you're listening."

"You got it!" I said eagerly, hopping up out of my chair. "And thanks."

"We'll do it in the conference room," she said, shaking her head as I followed her down the hall. "This is a dumb idea."

"I'll be a good boy," I promised.

Before dialing the speaker phone on the conference room table, Darlene looked at me and put her finger to her lips, emphasizing the gesture with a squinty look. I put my hand over my mouth to assure her.

"Dr. Darzi, Darlene Marks here. I'm going to get Tom on the phone now."

"Sure, sure," Darzi said while Darlene tapped some buttons to connect Tom to the call.

"Tom?"

"Here," he answered.

"The autopsy of Horace McCune has been a challenge," Darzi began. "But I can give you a few preliminary results that might aid your investigation. First, the time of death. Assuming the body was exposed to the outside air for most of the time since the victim expired, I would be willing to say that he died sometime between six in the morning and six in the evening on Monday."

This was good news for Dad and me. I had been on patrol almost the entire time and Dad would have been in the office or at meetings most of the time. With luck, we might both be able to account for our movements during the entire twelve-hour period.

"What about the cause of death?" Tom asked.

"That is more problematic. I found no definitive cause of death. Of course, he had multiple wounds from the tree branches that were forced into his body by the machinery, but all of them were postmortem. I think there is a good chance the fatal wound was applied to the victim's head. However, I cannot determine that with any certainty because the head has been pulverized by something large and flat. The object used to destroy the head was considerably larger than the head itself." Darzi was being more cautious than usual.

"Are you saying someone smashed his head after killing him?" Darlene asked.

"The crushing of the head could have been the cause of

death or, yes, it could have been done shortly after he was killed."

"Wow! You didn't find any evidence that he had a fly's head, did you?" Tom asked.

"What?" Darzi asked, sounding very puzzled.

"Like David Hedison's character in the original *Fly*," Tom said with a smile in his voice.

"No, no," Darzi said, sounding mildly annoyed either by the frivolous nature of the comment or by the fact that it had gone over his head.

Tom's comment suddenly made me think of my mother. We'd watched the old black-and-white film together the summer when I was ten. After that, we'd often mimic the high-pitched voice of the human-headed fly as he cried, *"Help me, help me!"* at the end of the movie. It had always made us smile.

Thoughts of Mom had been very near the surface ever since I'd asked Cara to marry me. I was wishing Mom could be here for the wedding and I was also wondering what she would think of the current election. Mom and Dad had always joked about him running for sheriff and it had been her death that had finally spurred him to do it.

I was jolted out of my memories when I heard Darlene ask a question.

"We found a bit of blood in the bucket of a tractor on McCune's property. Do you think that could have caused the type of damage you're talking about?"

"I am not familiar with tractors, but I would think so," Darzi answered.

"Though, if he was killed with the bucket, I'd think he would have had to be tied up or medicated," Darlene said thoughtfully.

"There was evidence that his hands had been taped at some point during the murder or the disposal of the body. However, there were no abrasions or bruising to indicate that he was restrained prior to being killed," Darzi said.

"I guess the killer might have taped the hands to make it

easier to transport the body," Tom suggested.

"As for drugs, you all know the routine. It will be weeks before the basic toxicology report comes back. With the condition of the body and the circumstances under which it was found, I did go ahead and order more detailed lab work. I indicated all of the usual suspects used to incapacitate a victim."

Tom and Darlene asked a few more general questions, but Darzi didn't have any more wisdom to offer.

"I did manage to contact his next of kin," Darlene said. "A daughter, Meredith McCune, who lives out in Texas. She's flying to Tallahassee tomorrow. She sounded like a chip off the old block. Headstrong would be putting it lightly. It took her a few minutes to process what I told her, but then she was talking about how we better make this the case of the century and devote all of our resources to finding the killer."

I was surprised that Darlene hadn't mentioned the daughter to me earlier, but of course she wasn't supposed to be telling me anything. I was reminded of the risk she was taking by letting me eavesdrop on the conference call.

"We will be ready for her," Darzi said, and I heard a smile in his voice when he added, "I will put on my deepest accent. She won't be able to understand a word I say."

"That ought to light her fire," Darlene said with a laugh.

Once Darlene disconnected the call, I grinned at her and said, "Miss McCune is going to love it when you start asking questions about her background and where she was during the murder."

"I'll make sure that Tom's with me. Though as heir to what I would imagine is a sizeable fortune, she shouldn't be surprised when she gets wind of the fact she's showing up as a bright green blip on our radar."

Little did we know.

I answered a few more calls for service on the road, then

signed off with dispatch. It was after six and I started to head home, but decided instead to swing by Dad's place. I couldn't help worrying about him, and my earlier thoughts of Mom weren't helping. For the first time, I fully understood what it meant to love someone so much that you could never imagine losing them. How do you deal with the loss of someone who has become a part of you? While Dad had managed to find love again with his girlfriend, Genie Anderson, it would never be the same as what he'd had with Mom, and I knew that he would have given anything to have her with him now.

I passed Dad in his driveway where he was using the tractor to push a pile of pine and oak branches into the ditch by the road. At the house, I was greeted by Mauser, who came galloping across the lawn. He was obviously enjoying the first cool weather of fall and tagged me with a bump to my hip before zooming off in the opposite direction. I braced myself for his return, having experienced more than one crash when he'd misjudged his brakes.

Dad came back on the tractor and drove it toward the barn, gesturing for me to follow him. I helped him lay out a few piles of hay in the paddock for Finn and Mac, his twin Quarter Horse geldings, who were waiting patiently in their stalls to be let back out after dinner.

"Why the hell do I feel guilty?" Dad said, opening Finn's stall and watching the horse trot toward the hay.

"Because you're doing the right thing and letting other people handle the investigation," I said, doing the same for Mac.

"You've got a point. I'm treating myself like a suspect. Doesn't help that I've wished the asshole would drop dead a dozen times over the last month," he grumbled.

"McCune went after both of us in a very personal and public way."

"I shouldn't have let it get to me. By doing that, I was just feeding into his plans. Now he's dead and we're in the crosshairs."

I wanted to tell him what I'd heard during the conference call, but that would mean letting him know how Darlene had skirted his rules for keeping me away from the investigation, even though he'd said I could read the reports. We were all walking some very thin lines. Instead I said, "Nobody believes we had anything to do with the murder," hoping it was true.

"Even if we're cleared, it's still gonna be used by folks who don't want to see me reelected." He turned off the lights in the barn as we walked out, then looked at me. "Maybe I've had my run as sheriff."

The sun was low on the horizon and it shone a golden light on his face, highlighting all his hard-earned wrinkles and scars. Before answering him, I thought about what his winning the election would really mean: four more years of dealing with all of the hard work and stress that went along with a job where your day-to-day decisions had life-and-death consequences and a thousand armchair quarterbacks waited to criticize your every move. I had to ask myself if wanting him to remain sheriff was selfishness on my part. Maybe I just didn't want to deal with a new boss. Perhaps I really was enjoying a few perks of nepotism, though I'd always thought he was harder on me than anyone else. But was that true?

"I don't think I can help you make that decision," I said lamely.

"That's the same crappy kind of advice I used to give you," he said, then a smile spread across his face at the sight of Mauser. "You're not starving."

The dog did not agree, whining as he stared at us and tried to force us toward the house with his superior canine mental powers.

"Why don't y'all come over to the house tonight?" I suggested. "Henry would love to see Mauser. He likes the big lunkhead almost as much as you do."

There was a long pause before Dad answered. Finally he said, "Sure, why not? Let me feed him and we'll follow you over. Speaking of Henry, have you told her parents that you're engaged?"

"Technically, I still need to ask his permission. Cara has been hesitant to let her mom know, but today she finally gave me the go-ahead to talk to her dad. But for tonight, mum's the word."

CHAPTER FIVE

When I got home, Cara came out on the porch and gave me a hug.

"Will you ask him tonight?" she asked with a smile before she saw the lights of Dad's van pulling up behind my patrol car.

"I asked Dad to come over. He's… taking everything pretty hard."

I could see a brief flash of disappointment in Cara's eyes. Now that she'd worked up the nerve to let her mother in on our plans, I couldn't blame her for wanting to get it out of the way. Having Dad there was likely to delay my conversation with Henry.

"No one can seriously think you two had anything to do with McCune's death," she said.

"We have to be considered as suspects. We have a pretty obvious motive. Besides, public opinion is a fickle beast." I shrugged.

"Mom fixed dinner. I'll set a place for your dad," she said, rallying.

"Thanks."

I followed her inside and was greeted by Alvin sniffing my leg and Ivy glaring at me from the back of the couch. She was ready for Cara's parents to go home.

By nine o'clock, we were all sitting outside around the fire pit by the Laursens' yurt. Mauser had pressed himself between Henry and Anna, sitting with his head lolling on Henry's knee while the big man massaged his ears. The evening was cool and the small fire felt good, scenting the air with pine smoke. Cara and I were sharing a bench. I put my arm around her and she laid her head on my shoulder with a small, contented sigh.

Dad sniffed and mentioned that his sinuses were bothering him. This set Anna to digging inside a large hemp bag for a bottle of syrup she'd mixed up herself containing honey, mint and a half dozen other herbs that she swore would fix him right up. While she was sorting through the bag, she pulled out a small leather holster and the nickel plating of the gun inside reflected the dancing fire.

"What do I spy with my little eye?" Dad said. He'd visibly relaxed as he'd chatted with Anna and Henry around the fire.

Anna looked up at him. With a scary grin, she pulled out the small Colt Detective Special. For a moment I was afraid she was going to sweep herself or us, but I needn't have worried. She handled the weapon with surprising care, keeping the muzzle pointed in a safe direction and her finger off the trigger.

"My sister gave this to me when I left home," she said. "We grew up in Middle-of-Nowhere, Missouri and did a lot of plinking as kids. I was determined to make my way out to California and Peggy knew that I might hitchhike or get in with the wrong crowd." She stared at the revolver for a moment.

"Go ahead, tell the story," Cara said in the begrudging manner of a child who's heard a story a hundred times but knows that their parent can't resist telling it again.

"It's really not my story," Anna said, oddly hesitant.

"But it's why Aunt Peggy insisted on you taking the gun."

"That's true. Peggy is five years older than me. When she was young she had a wild side that our little town couldn't handle. This was the early '70s, a few years post-Manson, so once my father realized that he couldn't keep Peggy down on the farm, he took her aside and gave her a lecture about how dangerous the world could be. When he was done, he gave her this gun and told her to come home when she'd seen all she wanted of the world. A week later, she took off in an old pickup truck with a boy from high school. She'd just turned eighteen."

Anna stared at the fire, seemingly lost in her memories. "Peggy came home four years later, having been across the country a couple of times. She was my hero and when I turned eighteen I was determined to hit the road on my own adventures. Like Dad had done with her, she took me aside and told me about some of the bad moments she'd had roaming the country. And she pressed this gun into my hand." Anna held up the revolver again. "I didn't want to take it. That's when she told me about a time when she was hitchhiking in Washington state.

"The weather had turned cold and a light rain was falling. Her last ride had left her at a diner that was fixing to close. She was wondering what to do next when a man came in and ordered coffee at the counter. When he saw her sitting alone in a booth, he asked if he could join her. The young man's smile was genuine and he was neatly dressed in preppy clothes. His clear blue eyes looked friendly, so she nodded. They talked about politics and the sad state of the country until the waitress came over and told them they'd have to leave so she could close up. The man paid for both of them and asked if she needed a ride. Peggy didn't see any reason not to accept. Ten minutes later, they were in his Volkswagen Beetle driving down a wet Washington highway.

"She said he grew quiet as they drove, then he told her that he needed to stop and relieve himself of some of the coffee he'd drank. They pulled over, but instead of getting out of the car, the man lunged out of his bucket seat at her. Shocked, she didn't have time to keep him from getting his hands around her neck. Somehow she managed to bring her knees up, which kept him from getting all the leverage he needed as he attempted to strangle her. Peggy tried to use her arms to push him away, but there was no way that she could overcome his weight and strength. Almost without thinking, she dropped her right hand down and began to search for something to use as a weapon. As soon as she felt her knapsack, she knew what she needed to do. She said her vision was beginning to blur when she finally grasped the handle of this gun. She fumbled a moment getting it out of the holster and her purse, but as soon as it was free, she rammed it into the man's stomach. He must have known what it was because he released his grip almost immediately. Gasping for breath, she spit out that she'd blow a hole in him if he didn't get away from her. Sure enough, he sat back in the driver's seat and blathered about being sorry. She just got out and ran."

"Bundy," Dad said softly.

"To this day she swears it was," Anna said, nodding. "So I took the gun and I've carried it with me ever since."

"I won't even ask you if you have a concealed carry permit."

"She does, and it's the scariest picture I've ever seen of her," Henry said.

"Ted Bundy," Dad mused. "I've got my own Bundy story."

I turned and looked at him. I'd heard him mention Bundy, of course. You couldn't live in Florida without the serial killer's name coming up occasionally, but I'd never heard him mention any personal connection to him.

"When I was a junior in high school, I played on the football team. Heh, play is about right. We were two and seven for the year. After football season and the holidays were over, a group of us from the team still hung out together. Actually, those were the best times. We could boast and brag about being on the team without having to face reality on Friday night. Anyway, it was a Saturday night in January when a group of us decided to go to a party on the outskirts of Tallahassee. We felt like we were going to the big city though, honestly, the house was just across the line in Leon County and just as country as our neighborhoods in Calhoun. But there were girls and some alcohol. We got buzzed. Not drunk, mind you. We all had a solid sense of responsibility. We didn't do anything crazy, just had a great time. I got home in time for my midnight curfew feeling amazing. At that point, I would have called it the best night of my life. There was a girl at the party who I'd idolized and that night we sat and talked and even made out a bit."

"You're making me queasy," I joked, and got an elbow in the ribs from Cara and dirty looks from everyone else. Dad ignored me and went on.

"With a little bit of a beer buzz, I thought I was on top of the world. I slept that night in a warm bed with thoughts of pretty girls and good friends and great times running through my dreams." Dad paused.

I had no idea where this was going. I honestly believed I'd heard every story that Dad had to tell.

"When I woke up in the morning, I strutted down the hall to breakfast, ready to dig into the pancakes and bacon that my mother was making. Dad was already at the table, reading the *Tallahassee Democrat*. I glanced at the headlines, then picked up the sports section. That's when Mom turned on the radio. She liked to listen to Casey Kasem's countdown on Sunday mornings. It was the top of the hour and the news came on. The main story was about the horrific murders of sorority girls at the Chi Omega house in Tallahassee.

"It took a minute for the words to sink in. Then, as if a switch had flipped in my brain, my mood went from lighthearted to a dark, introspective feeling that I didn't like at all. A voice inside my head was pointing out to me that while I'd been having the time of my life, these poor women were being brutally beaten to death only a few miles away. I'd learn later that the murders had taken place hours after I was home safe in bed, but that didn't make any difference to me. In my mind, I'd been drinking and laughing while helpless people were being killed. All week, I would come downstairs and grab the paper so I could read whatever new information the police had released. I was slowly realizing that I wanted to be a watchdog. I wanted to be one of the people who protected the innocent. Within a month, I'd made up my mind to join the sheriff's department when I graduated. From that moment on, I think my destiny was set."

"So you're saying Ted Bundy is the reason you're in law enforcement," I said, trying to joke about it to lighten a mood that had turned very dark with the image of Bundy and his crimes.

Dad just nodded.

"He was as close as a man can come to pure evil," Henry said, poking the fire with a stick.

"I believe in forgiveness and redemption of the spirit, but there are some people who have immersed themselves in so much darkness that the light can't ever reach them," Anna said, putting the gun back in her purse.

"Dad, I think you and Larry should go somewhere and talk," Cara suddenly blurted.

My mouth fell open and I looked at her, horrified, as Henry turned to me with a quizzical expression.

"You want to talk to me?" Henry said. The red and orange light of the fire highlighted some of his bearded face while leaving others parts in shadow. The overall effect made it look like he was wearing some kind of odd devil mask.

"I guess," I said as my body rose off of the bench of its own volition.

I walked away from the fire with my mind scrambled by the sudden turn of events. After the sort of conversation we'd been having, I wasn't prepared for this. I wondered if I could come up with a phony premise and put the talk off for another day. What the hell had Cara been thinking?

"So what do you want to talk to me about?" Henry asked when we were well away from the others. The moon was full and, as our eyes adjusted to the darkness away from the fire, I could see Henry's face clearly. It was open and friendly.

I hesitated for just a second, then plunged ahead. "I asked Cara to marry me. I mean, I want to ask Cara to marry me. Well, I guess I'm asking you for her hand or… something."

I hadn't felt this awkward since ninth grade when I'd gone to pick up Tina Sullivan for my first real date. Dad had waited in the car while I went up and knocked on her door. Her dad was the best carpenter in the county and one of the biggest men I'd ever seen. He was easily 6'5" and weighed more than three hundred pounds. I don't remember what I finally managed to stammer, but I never forgot what he said to me. He'd leaned in close to my ear and said, "I ever see one tear in her eye, I don't care if your father is a deputy, I promise that you'll cry a thousand tears for every one she sheds because of you." I'd almost pissed my brand new J.C. Penney slacks. Standing in front of Henry now, I was feeling the same way.

It seemed to take Henry a very long time to answer, which did nothing for my nerves. Eventually, he said, "I like you, Larry. I owe you a lot for helping with the murder investigation when I was in the hot seat down in Gainesville. But I worry about Cara. She was abducted last month. We haven't really had a chance to talk about that, but I'll tell you that I was pretty disappointed you didn't call me as soon as you knew she was in danger."

"In all fairness, it was in the middle of Hurricane Marcy. There wouldn't have been anything you could have done from Gainesville."

"I hear you. But what I want you to understand is that, if you become her husband, it doesn't mean I'm done being her father." His voice was firm and determined.

"I understand. And if the circumstances had been any different, I would have called you right away," I said, wondering if I really meant it.

Henry smiled. "You're a good man. If Cara will have you,

then it's okay with me. I think Anna might want to talk to you about a couple of things, but she likes you too." With that, he gave me a bone-rattling clap on the shoulder. "We should go for a weekend in the woods. I bet there are a few things I could teach you."

My stomach churned, wondering what that experience would be like. "Sure," I said, not sure at all. *And what did he mean about Anna wanting to talk to me?* I wondered as we made our way back to the fire.

"You really want to marry this guy?" Henry asked Cara in a booming voice.

"I *told* you," Anna said to Henry, then she looked at Cara. "I knew you all had something up your sleeves. I was hoping it was a baby, but I'll take a wedding."

Cara covered her eyes in embarrassment as Dad raised his eyebrows at me, his expression highly amused.

"What type of wedding are you thinking? A friend of ours, her daughter had a… well, sort of an elvish goddess wedding. Very earthy."

"We have plenty of time to decide on the details," Cara said in her best animal trainer voice.

"If you were pregnant, that would be even better. I love a pregnant bride," Anna said, and I saw Cara bite her lip.

The rest of the evening was a strange blur of congratulations and talk of our pending nuptials while the two rather large elephants of the election and McCune's murder seemed to stomp around just outside the glowing ring of the campfire.

"It's been a long day," I said when Cara and I were finally alone in our bedroom.

"That's what I'd expect to hear from an old married man," Cara said, poking me lightly in the ribs. "I'm sorry about throwing you under the bus out there. The mood had just gotten so dark, I wanted to do something to lighten things up. The words just popped out before I could stop them."

"It's okay. I'm glad it's done. Your dad took it pretty

well."

"Mom was certainly at her cringe-worthy best."

"I can't disagree with that," I said as I crawled into bed beside Cara.

"You're dad seemed to cheer up as the evening went along. I'm glad you asked him to come."

"We'll see what tomorrow brings," I said and gave her a long kiss before turning out the light.

CHAPTER SIX

I spent the next morning handling more routine calls for service, which had an unexpected upside. I was able to lose myself in the work and forget about everything else for a while. I listened attentively to the woman who was pissed that her neighbor always set his trash can on her property by the road when it was trash pickup day. I explained to the man who wanted to report his car stolen that, since he'd given his keys to the woman at the bar so she could go buy a pack of cigarettes without specifying when she needed to return the car, what he really had was a contractual disagreement, not a theft.

I was just thinking about a lunch break when I got a text from Darlene asking me to meet her and Tom Horton in the conference room at the office.

Tom's good humor was still in force when I joined them. "We just want to ask you a couple more questions before we move you over to the cleared list," he said, waving me to a chair with a big grin on his face.

"That's what I always tell the prime suspect right before I trap him in a lie," I said half seriously.

"Nah, if we were going to do that then I would have taken your gun when you came in," Darlene said with a wink.

"With the doc's rough estimate and a preliminary interview with the maid, we feel pretty confident that we have the time of the murder narrowed down to about two hours."

"We also have the scout vehicle's account," Darlene added.

"The what?" I asked.

"The debris contractor that picked up the body has a guy who scouts the route for the trucks the day before. He makes a list and estimates the size of each pile, which equates to how long it should take the truck to pick it all up. Long and short of it is, he's pretty sure that the pile looked the same at five o'clock the day before as it did yesterday morning. So that would mean the body was already in the pile by five on Monday. The maid said she saw McCune around two that afternoon. If all of that is true, then the murder happened between two-thirty and four-thirty on Monday, which fits with Darzi's estimated time of death." Darlene rattled all of this off in her most professional manner.

"Which leaves me in the clear since I was on the road all day," I said, feeling better about life.

"*Voilà*, you're golden!" Tom said with a flourish. He was a goofball, but I decided I liked him. "Your dash cam and dispatch's GPS records on your patrol car confirm it. You were never closer than five miles to McCune's place between two and six the day he was killed."

"Soooo…?" I asked.

"We're going to ask Deputy Director Warren and your father to okay you consulting on the case," Darlene said, not giving away the fact that she'd already let me listen in on the phone call with Darzi.

"And there's more good news. We're making progress clearing your dad," Tom said.

"There's just an hour between three and four that we haven't nailed down," Darlene said.

"Solving the murder is the only way to really clear us," I said, as much to myself as to them. "I appreciate y'all doing this."

"Let's get'r done," Tom said, taking out his phone. Within five minutes, he'd spoken with Dad and I was cleared to read reports, sit in on interviews and even voice my opinion.

"Just in time." Darlene smiled and looked at her watch. "McCune's daughter should be storming in here in about half an hour."

While we were waiting, I got lunch from the vending machine then sat down with Tom to review a few notes about McCune while Darlene went back to her desk to wait for his daughter.

Right on time, the conference room door flew open and Meredith McCune came striding in. Darlene followed a pace or two behind, trying to keep up. Tom and I scrambled to our feet while Meredith dropped a file folder onto the table and fixed us with steely eyes.

"Gentlemen, I'm Meredith McCune." She stuck out her hand toward Tom while her face remained neutral.

"Special Agent Tom Horton, Florida Department of Law Enforcement," he said, giving her his best high-beam grin. She pumped his hand quickly then turned to me, shaking her blond head.

"I know you, Larry Macklin," she said, keeping her hand to herself. "Dad thought you were a jackass."

"Opinions vary," I said, and immediately regretted the smart-aleck reply.

"What I've got here," she said, tapping the folder, "are statements from witnesses and evidence of where I was and what I was doing over the last couple of days. If you need more, I can get it for you. To summarize, I've been in Houston and the surrounding area for the past week. Also included in the folder is the last will and testament of my father. I'm his chief heir. I've added a very rough estimate of his net worth and contact information for his financial consultant and tax lawyer. I had it all on a flash drive, but then had second thoughts, not knowing if this rinky-dink cop shop would need hard copies, so I killed a few trees and printed it out. The reason I did all of this was to save time. The heir is a natural suspect. I get it. I didn't do it and this is the evidence. Check it out. I know you will, but then get on with finding whoever killed my father!" She'd been on a tear, barely stopping for breath, but she managed to shout this last line.

"We're working on doing just that, Miss McCune," Tom said.

"Don't blow air up my skirt." She was actually wearing a pantsuit that had probably cost more than my first car. "And why is this man even here?" she asked, pointing at me. "Dad had been harassing him and his father for months. Seems to me *he's* a prime suspect."

"He's been cleared," Darlene said.

Meredith turned to her with blazing eyes. "His alibi better be as solid as the Rock of Gibraltar, 'cause if this isn't solved in a month, I'm going to bring in my own team to scour the landscape and double- and triple-check everything you've done."

Darlene bowed up and moved in close. "It's solid," she said, matching the woman stare for stare. I glanced at Tom, who had wisely decided to stay out of it. Meredith looked away first and I caught a glint of victory in Darlene's eyes.

"Look, I know my father was an asshole. He wasted time and money on stupid, petty grudges. He left a string of enemies that would have made any dictator proud. If you all can prove yourselves capable, I'll provide you with any information I can that doesn't compromise our businesses."

"What *was* your business relationship with your father?" Tom asked, and I silently applauded him for trying to take charge of the situation.

"We had some shared interests. Not many. We didn't have the same… style. We were both interested in expanding oil exploration in the Gulf, but it was a no-go. Too much of a political powder keg here in Florida. That's another area where we disagreed. I avoid any political controversies. My businesses make money. That's the point. But Dad was looking for power. I think he liked pushing people around more than making money. You see where all of that got him." She spread her hands. "Lost in this backwater. Of course, his other problem was women, which is how he wound up here in the first place. If there was a gold digger within a hundred miles, he'd find her. Men are pathetic." She snorted. For someone who claimed not to care about power, she sure liked being in charge of the conversation.

"We'll need a list of anyone who you think might want to harm your father or who would profit from his death," Darlene said in a no-nonsense tone.

Meredith nodded. "Do you have email?"

She knows *we have email*, I thought, finding it very difficult to feel any sympathy for her as the grieving daughter.

We all handed her our cards. She looked at mine with particular scorn. "Are you really going to be involved with the investigation of my father's murder?"

"Sheriff Macklin and Deputy Macklin have done everything they can to ensure the investigation isn't tainted. They called in FDLE immediately," Tom said, earning more points in my book.

"Calling you all in is a good thing?" she said, barely toning down the sarcasm.

"Bad guys, who you gonna call?" he answered with a smile.

"I'll get you the list of Dad's enemies," Meredith said and turned as if to leave.

"We have some more questions," Darlene said, stepping between Meredith and the door. Definitely a power move.

For a moment I thought Meredith was going to reach out and brush Darlene aside, but then she relaxed and turned back to us.

"I've got a lot to do. I have to bury my father and start settling his business affairs. He had several lawsuits percolating. You guys," she said, looking straight at Darlene and then tapping the folder on the table, "are going to have enough to keep you busy for a week with my whereabouts and the list of Dad's enemies. I'll be at the best hotel in Tallahassee, whatever the hell that is, for several weeks. Get done with this, then call me back and I'll come answer your questions.

"You think I'm being a hard-assed bitch. Not even close. I could have waltzed in here with a dozen lawyers whose combined salaries are more than the yearly budget of this office. Do your homework, then call me."

She headed for the door. For a moment I thought Darlene was going to block her again, but she didn't make a move. Meredith walked out of the room and left a wave of a-thousand-dollars-per-ounce scent behind her.

"That was impressive," I said ten seconds after the door banged shut.

"I'm going through all of this with a fine-toothed comb," Darlene said, reaching for the packet of information that Meredith had brought with her. I resisted the urge to make cat-fight noises. Obviously feeling the need to defend her animosity, Darlene continued, "She came in with a pat alibi and was more than glad to start pointing fingers in other directions. That's suspicious behavior."

"You won't get any arguments from me," Tom said, raising his hands in surrender. "It did seem a little contrived."

"I'm not going to say anything since one of her fingers was pointing in *my* direction. But you're right about one thing, she's certainly a piece of work."

"So where do we go from here?" Tom said, then went on to answer his own question. "Since you all have a history of working together, I suggest you continue that partnership. I'll freelance and oversee your efforts, as well as coordinate the evidence until your crime scene team gets their facility back in order."

"Works for me," Darlene said, still frowning at the folder

Meredith had left. "I want to get started on Meredith's alibi."

"Before you do that, why don't you take me out to the house so I can see the murder scene? Or at least what you think is the murder scene," I suggested.

"Okay, hotshot. I wouldn't mind taking another look around."

Darlene and I were heading across the parking lot to her car when I saw Pete heading our way. He looked uncomfortable with his almost three-hundred pounds crammed into a uniform that was at least one size too small.

"If I'd known I'd have to go back out on the road, I'd have ordered new uniforms," he said, picking at his waistband. He looked at me for a moment, then shook his head. "I really want to make a joke about you killing McCune, but it just isn't funny. Not with the election coming up."

"Got that right! Besides, he looks to be in the clear," Darlene said, tilting her head toward me.

"Just as well. We need all the deputies we can get. I got to get off the street."

"It won't be much longer now. Dad said all of our guys will be back from the coast by the end of the week."

"Glad to hear it. I'm not cut out for the road. I was giving some woman a ticket this afternoon when her ten-year-old kid asked me if I was too fat to be a cop. You know what I told him?" He paused for dramatic effect, then gave a rueful grin. "I told him I was."

"Come off it," I chided. "You're on the SWAT team."

"I'm the designated sniper. I find a nice comfortable spot where I can see the bad guy, then I lay down and wait for a thumbs-up or down. No heavy body armor or busting through doors for me." Pete gave us a quick salute and headed into the office.

CHAPTER SEVEN

When we pulled up to the gate outside McCune's property, Darlene punched some numbers on the keypad. "We had the code changed to the department's main number. I'm surprised Meredith didn't ask to come out to the house."

"I'll admit she isn't acting like a normal victim's daughter, but if you didn't notice, she isn't exactly normal."

"A thousand-dollar suit and an attitude doesn't impress me," Darlene said with a bit more venom than I thought was called for. *She really doesn't like the woman*, I thought.

The house was a sprawling mansion on a large tract of land. The lawn had been recently mowed, but the rest of the landscaping was lackluster compared to the house. I remembered from my earlier encounter with McCune that the house had been built at the insistence of his last wife, who had quickly become an ex-wife. Once she was gone, his interest in keeping up the house and grounds had faded fast.

"The regular staff is comprised of the maid, Red Hills Security and Pops Davis, who comes in once a week to tend to the grounds." I knew Pops. He'd run the best lawn service in town since I was a kid.

"Was there anything on the security cameras?" I'd seen several since we drove onto the property.

"The system isn't working. According to the maid and Red Hills, something went wrong with the computer that did the recording. Supposedly, McCune told Red Hills that he didn't like the damn things anyway. They tried to get him to upgrade the system, but he just accused them of trying to bilk him out of more money, so they let it drop. The camera at the gate works and can be viewed from the house, but it isn't recorded."

"And being this far out in the country, there aren't any other cameras to catch cars driving by."

"Not for miles."

"What about the gate?"

"There were three different codes that would open the gate. One was the master code, the second was used by Red Hills and the third was used by Pops, pest control, the pool service and any other maintenance service he employed. None of the codes have been changed for years."

"So pretty much anyone could have gotten access to one of the codes to get in."

"There's also another gate at the back of the property, but the good news there is that it doesn't look like it's been opened in more than a year. Seriously overgrown with vines."

"So whoever killed him was invited in or used a passcode."

"And used one of the codes again to get out with the tractor."

"You're pretty sure he was killed here?"

"Don't take my word for it, Doubting Thomas."

"No, Tom's the other guy," I joked.

"He's really a pretty good investigator, but all that positive energy gets to me after a while," Darlene said, shaking her head. "I'm glad to have you back, my pouty friend. Come on. I'll show you where the blood was found."

We walked to the back of the house where a door led into the three-car garage. There were dozens of evidence flags around the door and on the concrete skirt that extended for four feet in front of it. Most were located along the edges of the concrete.

"This all blood?"

"Blood and other tissue." Darlene pointed to the hose attached to a faucet a dozen feet away on the side of the garage. "Someone sprayed the blood off of the concrete, but they didn't try too hard to clean up. Looks like they just sprayed off the obvious bits."

She took an evidence envelope from her pocket and pulled out a ring of keys. After a moment's search, she found the right one and unlocked the door. We walked into the garage where a BMW and a new black SUV with darkly tinted windows were parked.

From the black dust, flags and markings on the floor, walls and shelving, it was clear the FDLE crime scene techs had thoroughly processed the garage. Darlene took out her phone and pulled up a photo, then held up the phone so I could compare it to the corner of the garage. The photo showed the luminol test. I didn't need to have a doctorate in forensic science to see that someone had been hit and bled all over the area. In the photo, I could make out blood splatters on the walls and another area on the floor where the blood had pooled. She pulled up another photo which showed smears of blood on the knob of the door leading back outside.

"He wasn't killed right away?" I asked.

"That or he'd gone zombie." Apparently all of the Halloween decorations around town were getting into her head.

"So he makes it outside and the killer finishes him off," I said, opening the door and looking outside. Across the yard I could see a large metal shed. It had two garage doors that could have easily accommodated a full-size RV. "Where's the tractor?" I asked, already having an idea.

Sure enough, Darlene pointed at the shed. We walked over to it, passing more evidence flags as well as a spot where a plaster cast had been taken of a tire track.

"Seems like the killer wasn't in the mood to carry McCune. Apparently they drove the tractor over here," Darlene said when she saw me looking at the tracks.

At the shed, Darlene led me around to a side door and pulled out the bag of keys again.

"Are the doors normally locked?"

"According to everyone we talked to, no."

"Doesn't that all seem odd? This was a man who worked hard at making enemies, yet he didn't take any serious security precautions? I know that when we were here two months ago he buzzed us through the gate, but all you'd have to do is get the code from one of the people who've had access to it over the last couple of years."

"Which could number in the hundreds, counting all the maintenance services he used. Red Hills said that McCune would even give it out to limo drivers if they were going to pick him up. I agree it was pretty stupid for a man who churned out enemies, but I think the explanation is clear enough. McCune was one arrogant son of a bitch. He didn't think anyone would dare screw with him."

"You have a point. I think that's why he was so aggressive. He attacked everyone who offended him as a way of saying 'Don't mess with me.' Like a rattlesnake flicking its tail."

Darlene unlocked the door to the shed and swung it open. When she flipped on the light, it illuminated a huge area filled with maintenance equipment that looked almost new. The large orange tractor was parked in a bay on the opposite side of the building. It had a bucket attached. Nearest to us were a couple of professional-grade, zero-turn lawnmowers. There were various attachments for the mowers and tractor lined up on the floor and several power tools hung neatly on the wall.

"There was a little blood on the tractor's bucket," Darlene told me. "Everything else was neat and orderly."

I looked over the tractor. The key was in the ignition. "Was the key here?"

"Yep. We had FDLE check the whole tractor for prints. They picked up a few, but I imagine it was wiped. Plus there's grease and oil on most of the surfaces. The prints they got were mostly smeared."

I climbed up onto the seat of the tractor and turned the key to the first position, giving it a second for the glow plug warning light to go out before turning it the rest of the way. The diesel engine came to life.

"Look at you, farm boy," Darlene said.

I raised the bucket four feet off of the ground, checked the brake and then, leaving the engine running, I jumped back to the floor. Darlene joined me in inspecting the underside of the bucket. I pulled out my phone and took a couple of pictures, not that there was anything to see other than cold steel.

"I'd say the killer drove the tractor over to the garage, crushed McCune's skull with the bucket and then rolled him into the bucket to take him out to the road."

Darlene thought about it for a second, then nodded. "There's not much traffic on the road, so it's possible. They dropped the body and covered it with brush to make sure it wasn't found right away, then headed back. There's a hose on the side of this building too. So they could have washed the bucket off out there and then just backed the tractor on in."

"The bucket is big enough that once the body was inside and it was raised above eye level, no one would have been able to see it, even if they had driven by before the killer finished dumping it."

"We've got public works coming out to put a sign up on the road requesting anyone who might have seen something to give us a call."

"With all the clean-up going on, no one is paying much attention to heavy equipment on the side of the road," I said, climbing back on the tractor, lowering the bucket and turning off the ignition.

"What did the maid have to say?" I asked once I was

back on the ground.

"Not much, but I wouldn't mind pushing her a little. She's staying out at the Roads Best Motel while we have the house closed off," Darlene said.

"I thought he didn't have a live-in maid."

"Maybe he felt threatened by you and your dad and wanted protection," Darlene said with an evil grin. "Seriously, though, apparently she started with a service and then he brought her in full time several weeks ago."

I shrugged. "Whatever. I want to walk through the rest of the house before we talk with her."

"That's a journey in tacky excess. Ten thousand square feet of expensive crap."

Having seen just a bit of the inside of the house myself, I knew that Darlene was right. It was a like a museum to consumerism. I imagined most of it had been bought by the ex-wife. That thought made me ask, "What about the ex?"

"There are three. The last one is living down in Naples. Apparently, she walked away from McCune with some cash and then found herself another rich husband. I've seen pictures. At some point in her life, she invested heavily in her breasts and it appears to have paid off. We talked to her briefly, but she doesn't seem to have a motive and she has a pretty solid alibi. According to her, she was hosting a bridge party for twenty of her richest friends."

"And the other two?"

"Tom offered to track them down. I think he was hoping to view more pictures of large-breasted women."

After an hour of traipsing through the house to no good purpose, we locked up and headed for the motel. Darlene had called ahead to make sure that the maid, Cary Trent, would be there.

I hadn't asked for Darlene's impression, wanting to approach Trent with a clean slate, though it was impossible to know someone's name and occupation and not form some type of image in your head. I had pictured the maid as an older woman who most likely smoked cigarettes and was supporting an adult son. I couldn't have been more wrong. While the woman who answered our knock was probably in her mid-sixties, she looked fit and focused.

"Come in," she said, moving back from the door. Her expression bore a mixture of sadness and boredom. She sat on the bed while waving us to the two chairs in the room. "Mr. McCune could be difficult to deal with, but once I got to know what he expected, it was one of the best jobs I ever had. The pay was great." Her eyes narrowed as she looked at me. "You aren't the same guy who was with her last time."

"I'm Deputy Larry Macklin," I said, handing her one of my cards. Her face lit up with recognition.

"Of course! The billboards! I thought I recognized you. You know, for the last couple of months, Mr. McCune hasn't done much but grumble about what an ass you are. Sorry."

"I know what he thought of me," I said dismissively.

"And your father. Mr. McCune never let up. Of course, I've worked for him for almost a year and you're not the first person he's gone after."

"We'd like you to give us a list of any of those people that you can remember. Ones he targeted and any who you know held a grudge against him."

"There was one for sure. She came to the house a couple of weeks ago," Cary said.

"What happened?" I prompted, though I could see by her eyes that she was bursting to tell us about it.

"Her name was Cecilia or something like that. Mr. McCune refused to let her in, but she kept hitting the buzzer until he called the security people."

"Maybe she was just a persistent saleswoman or a process server," I said, thinking that McCune had probably attracted a lot of both with his money and penchant for lawsuits.

"No, it wasn't that 'cause I could hear what she was saying over the intercom. The woman was shouting that McCune had something to do with her son's disappearance."

I leaned forward. The death of a child could certainly lead

someone to revenge.

"Did you hear any details?" Darlene asked.

"Not much. Mr. McCune saw me listening and told me to quit being a snoop." Cary paused for a second, then her eyes lit up with a memory. "Wait, I remember she told him that she was going to be here for a week if he wanted to talk to her. She told him he'd be sorry if he didn't."

"Here? In Calhoun?"

"In this motel."

Darlene's eye widened. "Did you get a look at her on the monitor?"

"No, I wasn't close enough to the door."

"I don't suppose you got a last name?" I asked.

"No, just Cecilia… or maybe Sissy. Something like that."

We couldn't get her to lock down the specific date this had happened. The closest she could come was two weeks before the murder.

"Yesterday you told us that you heard the tractor on the day Mr. McCune was murdered. Where were you in the house?" Darlene asked.

"I was in my room. I usually worked all morning. You know, making the bed and picking up Mr. McCune's clothes. The man was a slob. I'm sorry he's dead, but honestly, I don't think he ever picked up after himself. I cleaned the kitchen and dusted the library, then I took a break until about five."

"What were you doing on your break?"

"Lying on the bed reading a book. It feels good to get off my feet for an hour or two."

"And you heard the tractor running?"

"Yeah, just kind of in the background."

"What did you do after your break?"

"Normally, if Mr. McCune was home, I'd fix him a light dinner and then get out of the way if he had any… women over." Cary looked down at her lap.

"Women?" I remembered him making some comment about getting rid of his last wife and settling for the services of working women.

"Yeah, jeez, it was embarrassing. Really the worst part of the job. There were women, working women, that he brought to the house. I guess I ought to be glad he didn't make passes at me. I've had a few guys…. But, no, he just brought those… prostitutes to the house, about two or three times a week. I'd go hide in my room as soon as I could so I wouldn't hear them going at it. It was kinda sick."

"But he wasn't around that night?" I asked.

"No. I assumed he'd gone somewhere. He never tells… told me what he was doing. When he wasn't there, I'd usually do about another hour's work then call it a day. That night I cleaned the guest bath upstairs."

"When was the last time one of these women came by?" Darlene asked.

"I guess a couple of days before the… murder. It was Candy. Can you believe that name? Of course, I'm sure that's her working name. She's cute too. I don't know why she'd do it with him. Never mind, that's dumb. She did it for the money. He paid me well, so he must have paid her a whole lot."

She gave us nicknames and descriptions of several other women that he'd used, then said, "I guess you think I was stupid to work for him, but the pay was really, really good."

"When you heard the tractor on Monday, what did you think? Weren't you curious about who was driving it?" Darlene asked.

"Not since Mr. McCune was home. Besides, Pops has come by and worked on the yard a lot since the hurricane. Normally, he'd just come once a week, but with all the storm debris he's come out a bit more often. Anyway, Mr. McCune didn't like me being nosy, like when that woman was trying to get in. If I came downstairs when I wasn't working, he'd ask me why I was sneaking around."

I had no doubt she was telling the truth about that. I was sure that a man like McCune had plenty of secrets he wouldn't have wanted a maid to know.

We asked a few more questions, then stood up to leave.

"I don't know what to do now. Do you know who I should talk to about my last check?" Cary asked as we walked to the door.

"The estate will be handled by his lawyer." I remembered the packet that Meredith McCune had given us. "I'll see if I have his name. If I do, I'll call you."

"I'll need to get back in my room soon. I only brought enough clothes for a couple of days."

"If we aren't able to open the house, we can have someone escort you in," Darlene said.

"I think I'd *want* an escort. I'd be too creeped out to go there alone after what happened."

CHAPTER EIGHT

We left Cary Trent and headed up to the motel office to see if we could track down the woman who had come out to McCune's house. "Cecilia or maybe Sissy" wasn't much to go on, and the time frame was pretty loose. On the other hand, the motel wasn't very busy this time of year unless it was a college football weekend and the Tallahassee motels were all full.

Roads Best was owned by a Pakistani family. The oldest son, Tarek, was manning the front desk. "Uh oh," he said when he saw us.

"Nothing to worry about today," I assured him.

"Last time she was here, there was damage to the motel. Father was not impressed," Tarek said with a broad smile.

About a month ago, Darlene had been driving past the motel when she saw what she thought was a drug deal in progress. When she pulled into the lot, the man in question had grabbed the woman he was talking to and run into a motel room. Darlene, worried that it could turn into a hostage situation, had brashly run up and kicked in the door. She'd found the guy stuck in the bathroom window as he tried to escape, while the meth-addled woman was completely unaware she'd been in any danger. Darlene had limped around for a week after the incident.

"I appreciate you having flimsy doors that are easy to kick in," Darlene said, grinning back at Tarek. "And the fact that you have narrow bathroom windows."

"You laugh. I had to clean the man's urine off the wall from where you dragged him out of the window."

The pleasantries out of the way, we asked Tarek about our mystery woman.

"Maybe. Though we've had a lot of people in here lately. The hurricane was very good for business," he said, tapping a few keys on a keyboard.

"This would have been a week or two after the storm, we think," I said.

"Yes, maybe… how about this one? Celina Pappas. Very nice lady. Stayed…" He looked at the reservation information on the screen. "…eight nights. And she's coming back in two days."

I raised my eyebrows and looked at Darlene before asking Tarek for a printout of her information. I called her number as soon as we were back in the car and got lucky with an answer on the third ring. I explained who I was and why I was calling.

"I'm not sorry that bastard is dead," Celina Pappas said flatly.

"We'd like to speak with you about your conflict with Mr. McCune. I understand you're planning to be back in Adams County in a couple of days."

"I'm in Tallahassee now. I can come meet you at the sheriff's office in the morning," she said, sounding confident.

Is she really eager to talk to us, or is this the cockiness of a murderer who thinks they're smarter than the cops? I wondered. Giving Darlene a thumbs-up, I told Celina that we'd meet her at nine.

"Interesting," I said after ending the call.

"No love lost there." Darlene had been able to hear most of the conversation. "I wonder if she was staying in

Tallahassee when the murder occurred. Just a forty-five minute drive."

"According to Cary Trent, the woman was determined to confront McCune."

"I'll put her on the list. Though Miss Meredith is still at the top. Even with a solid alibi, she could have hired someone to do the job."

"A woman like her would be used to hiring people to do her dirty work."

"Exactly. Then she comes strutting in here with an alibi in both paper and digital format. Humph!" Darlene growled.

"I've never seen you dislike someone this much."

"I've got a cousin like her. Always strutting her stuff. And it was never enough for her to brag about what she was doing; she had to run me down at every opportunity. Paula Ponytails made me miserable every time we got together with my aunt and uncle. Spoiled more holidays than I care to count."

"Paula Ponytails?"

"Yeah, that's what I called her. She was proud of that hair. One time she made some derogatory remark about *my* hair, so I grabbed those ponytails and dragged her around the house."

I was used to Darlene saying almost everything with a smile in her voice, but not this story. I didn't need to have a psychology degree to tell that there was some deep-seated animosity still festering below the surface.

"Meredith might remind you of Paula, but she's not the same person," I said, not knowing what kind of reaction I was going to get from a very tense Darlene. I waited until she turned to look at me.

"You got a point, Short Round. By the way, I hate it when you point out my faults." She started the car.

"What happened after you pulled Paula's hair?" I asked as we headed back to the office.

"I got sent to my room, then my mother came in and gave me a rough talking-to. She told me I was grounded for a week, but then she winked at me before she left the room. Paula never came to our house again. The lesson I learned was that violence sometimes solves problems."

I laughed, then thought about it for a minute. "I hate to admit it, but that *is* kinda true in law enforcement."

"Yep. Sometimes you got to knock the bastard down and sit on him," Darlene said, her good humor completely restored.

We both headed to our desks to answer a few emails before knocking off for the day. We were greeted by Lt. Johnson, our supervisor in CID, who informed us that all regular patrol deputies would be back on the road tomorrow and we could return full time to investigations. Finally some good news.

As I was getting ready to leave, I saw Tom Horton coming out of Dad's office. He caught up with me and walked with me to the front door.

"Hey, Larry. I was just telling your dad that, as far as I'm concerned, he's in the clear. I've found at least three corroborating witnesses who can vouch for his whereabouts during the time we think the murder occurred." For a minute, I thought he was going to high-five me.

"I appreciate your thoroughness," I said sincerely.

"Now we just have to find the murderer."

I filled him in on the rest of our day and Darlene's focus on Meredith.

"Hired killer," he mused. "That's a movie trope. In real life, it seldom works out the way they want it to."

"Meredith has the money. Yet there's something about this murder that doesn't feel professional."

"There aren't many real assassins. Most hired killers are amateurs trying to make a fast buck. Though it had to have been somebody bold to attack McCune while the maid was in the house." Tom thought for a moment. "I remember her mentioning that it was her habit to go up to her room in the afternoon. Which could mean the murderer was someone who knew the maid's habits."

"Good point. I wonder how often Meredith visited her father."

"And when was the last time?"

"She didn't give the impression that they were close. Business-close maybe, but not family-close."

"I'm following up on the ex-wives, though none of them stand to gain monetarily. In fact, I think they're going to lose alimony payments."

I waved goodbye to Tom and headed out into the parking lot, glad to be taking my old unmarked car home.

Cara gave me a big hug when I came into the house.

"I'm really glad you've been cleared to work the case." I'd called her earlier and given her the good news. "Umm, let me know when you've been home long enough that I can bombard you with my list of complaints," she said with a sardonic smile.

"Uh oh. What's wrong?"

"I warned you. Mom is talking about a druid ceremony under the oak trees."

Barely controlling a shudder, I said, "Speaking of which, where are your parents? I didn't see them when I drove up." They were usually very hard to miss.

"Mom wanted to get some Halloween decorations."

I didn't like the sound of that at all. "Halloween is still a couple of weeks away."

"I know. She said they were buying them for us, but…"

"Shouldn't they be getting back to the co-op in Gainesville? They kind of run things down there." I was searching for help here.

"Don't talk to me. I said the same thing to Dad. His answer was that he's turned over a lot of the work to Teddy and the board."

"Ivy can't take a couple more weeks of company," I said, nodding to the tabby who was strutting around her food bowl, waiting for us to quit talking and feed her. Alvin had given up and was lying flat out on the kitchen floor, looking like he'd lost his best friend. Sometimes I thought food *was* his best friend.

"I'm with Ivy. Love my parents, but they drive me crazy. We may have to push a little."

"Be gentle, though. They're a little crazy, but I owe them for you," I said, giving her a long kiss.

We had a peaceful dinner, then Cara's folks showed up just as we were washing the dishes.

"I found some very nice materials to make traditional Samhain decorations," Anna said, bringing in several bags of herbs and different fabrics. "I was able to find a few things in the woods around here, but the rest came from a friend who lives just north of Tallahassee."

"Let's work on these later," Cara told her, taking the bags. "I'll put these in the back room so Ivy and Alvin don't get into them."

"We should start collecting wood for the bonfire too," Henry told me.

"Bonfire?"

"Always have a big one on All Hallows Eve. Weather permitting."

"Yeah, okay," I said, seeing our chances of getting them to leave early rapidly evaporating. "How's the carving coming?" I asked to change the subject from Halloween.

Henry frowned. "Puzzling. The wood is quiet. I've been waiting for the oak to reveal its inner self, but so far…" He shrugged. "Sometimes it takes awhile."

Not too long, I hope.

Cara and Anna came back into the kitchen. "I want to talk to you," Anna said, giving me a small frown.

"Okay," I said, wondering if this was what Henry had warned me about.

"Let's go for a walk."

I wanted to point out that it was already dark, but I kept my mouth shut. Throwing one desperate glance at Cara, I followed her mother out the door.

The air was cool and the moon was rising above the tree line, casting quite a bit of light in the yard. I'd almost decided this wouldn't be too bad when Anna said, "I'll grab a lantern," and ducked inside the yurt.

She popped back out with her lantern in hand and beckoned me to follow her into the woods. Shaking off images of witches luring their victims, I went after her.

"I want to talk to you about several things that are bothering me," Anna said, stopping and turning so suddenly that I almost bumped into her. If this was an interrogation method meant to put me off my stride, it was working alarmingly well.

"Sure," I managed to say.

"First, I've always known that you're a cop. Henry and I are so grateful to you for catching those murderers down in Gainesville, and I also can't forget what happened last May. But it wasn't until Cara's abduction during the hurricane and seeing you in uniform this week that it really started to worry me. You're a smart man. You could do something more… productive." She held up the lantern. "Don't get me wrong. I'm not one of those hippies who yells 'Pig!' whenever they see law enforcement. I know that most officers are fine people who are just trying to help folks. But, having said that, you can't deny that it's a dangerous profession. Plus, I've seen men and women beat down by the constant interaction with bad people in bad situations… and good people in bad situations."

The way she rattled this off made it clear to me that she'd been working on it for a while, so I took my time before answering her.

"Everything you say is true. If you had asked me a year ago, I probably would have agreed with you that I should try another profession. Trouble is, I'm good at being an investigator. I've even come to enjoy the work.

"But I understand your concerns. I worry about Cara too. Last month terrified me. Honestly, that's what motivated me to ask her to marry me. But I don't think it would be a good idea to give up a job that I like and am good at out of fear."

Anna looked at me closely. "You're a good man, Larry." Then she grabbed me by the arms and said firmly, "I want you to stand right there."

She positioned me in the middle of the small clearing we'd stopped in, with my back facing the moon. I didn't have a clue what she was going to do. *Go along to get along*, my inner voice suggested.

"Is there something else you want to talk—"

"Just be quiet for a moment."

Anna raised the lantern and blew out the flame. After a few seconds, my eyes adjusted to the moonlight and I could see her clearly. There was a quizzical expression on her face as she peered at me, moving a bit left and then right, up and then down.

More than a little weirded out, I starting counting in my head to stay calm, hoping that she'd finish whatever she was doing before I reached twenty. I made it to fifteen.

"Your moonlight aura is a deep red. You're a very grounded and realistic person. A person of action with a strong will to survive. Cara's aura has always maintained a soft blue color, indicating that she is intuitive, communicative and has clarity of vision. You will make a strong couple, much as Henry and I have," she said softly.

I tried to get a good look at her pupils to see how dilated they were, then decided it was uncharitable to attribute her spirituality to drugs. Instead I said, "Thank you. I promise you that Cara and my relationship with her will always be my top priorities."

"I know they will. If they aren't, Henry will come up and clunk you in the head with his favorite bronze axe," Anna said, laughing softly.

I couldn't decide if her last comment was a joke or not, but it didn't matter. Anyone who didn't treat Cara right would deserve a little realignment.

We walked back to the house while Anna extolled the virtues of an outdoor wedding with, as she put it, light pagan overtones. I avoided commitment, telling her that we really hadn't had the chance to think about what type of ceremony we might want.

"And don't wait for the wedding to start working on the baby. Like I said, a pregnant bride makes for heartwarming wedding pictures."

Stifling a cough, I said, "You have a very interesting way of looking at the world."

"It's served me well," she said, and tapped the side of her nose.

CHAPTER NINE

The early morning sunlight was streaming through the windows as Cara and I got ready for work on Thursday morning.

"I should have known she was getting ready to do that old aura trick with you when she dragged you out into the moonlit woods."

"She's actually kind of endearing in a witchy way," I said.

"Don't let her fool you. She can be devious when she wants something."

"She wants two things. A pagan wedding for her daughter and a grandchild, and not necessarily in that order."

"We'll see if she gets either of them," Cara said dryly and gave me a quick kiss. "I need to get going. Angie called in, so I've got to walk the dogs this morning." She'd recently been promoted to office manager at the veterinary clinic, but she still pitched in from time to time with patient care.

I arrived at the office an hour before Darlene and I were scheduled to meet with Celina Pappas, which gave me a little time to polish off some reports. Then I headed down to our once-and-future crime scene office and evidence room.

"That's not a happy look," I told Shantel.

She was seated at her desk, frowning at her phone.

Behind her, the office was covered in canvas tarps and plastic covers. A temporary wall had been erected while the contractors worked on the addition that had been planned months before a miscreant had driven a bulldozer through the wall during the hurricane in an attempt to steal evidence, almost crushing me in the process.

"If you find any dead contractors, you might as well come and arrest me. I swear they have more excuses than most of the crooks we arrest. The plumber isn't going to make it today because he lost half his crew to a raid by the INS. Don't even get me started on that. But why in the world wouldn't you check… Never mind… Leave it in the pew, as my momma used to tell me." I suspected that under her dark mocha skin, her face was flushed with anger.

"This too will pass," I said, trying to sound hopeful.

"Your father better get reelected. I don't want to have to get used to a whole new boss," she grumbled. "I've already lost my right hand man *and* my office."

Her old partner, Marcus Brown, had recently taken a job with FDLE and she still hadn't forgiven him. Though I knew that what was really killing her was not being able to be out in the field. Dad didn't trust anyone else to oversee the construction and was keeping her tied to the desk until the building was more secure.

Shantel seemed to shake off some of her dark mood. "Sorry I wasn't there to handle the McCune crime scene."

"Dad probably wouldn't have let you anyway. He is trying to be above reproach with this case. Until we were cleared by FDLE, he didn't want anyone too involved."

She nodded. "Still… I know the FDLE crime techs are good, but this is my job."

"Trust me, we'll all be glad when you're back out in the field."

"Then go kick some construction workers' behinds."

We gossiped a bit longer before I headed off to the conference room to meet Darlene.

"What approach do you want to use?" I asked her.

"I say we go light at first. If it looks like she's a viable suspect, I'll tap my phone on the desk and we'll push her a bit and see where that goes. I ran a check on her. She's from Texas, so if we make a mistake she can just hightail it back to Galveston."

"And if she did that, we'd have a hell of a time getting her back in an interrogation room."

"That sums it up, sport. So let's not disturb the neighborhood without just cause."

We got a call from the front desk that Celina Pappas had arrived, so I went up meet her.

"Deputy Larry Macklin," I introduced myself.

She was a short, sturdy-looking woman in her late fifties. She had blue eyes that were sharp as daggers and she pinned me with them as soon as she saw me. A wicked smile appeared on her face. "I've seen the billboards. He sure had it out for you. Tell me you killed him and I'll give you a hug."

I gave her a noncommittal smile and we walked back to the conference room. After Darlene introduced herself, she explained that while this was an informal conversation, it would still be recorded. Celina gave her consent and we got down to business.

"We understand that you were out at Mr. McCune's house a couple of weeks ago, trying to gain entrance. We're interested in what your business was with Mr. McCune."

Almost before the words were out of Darlene's mouth, Celina's hand had whipped down to a pocket of her jeans. I wondered for a second if the metal detector at the door was working, but all she brought up was a crumpled piece of paper which she unfolded and slammed down on the conference table. "I'll tell you and everyone in this county what I was doing at McCune's house."

I picked up the paper and looked at it. It was a missing person flyer with a picture of a smiling young man who held a strong resemblance to Celina Pappas.

"My son has been missing for ten years and McCune

knows…" An odd expression crossed her face and she corrected herself. "*Knew* what happened to him. He's been lying for years."

"You think McCune had something to do with," I looked at the flyer again, "Ryan's disappearance?"

She sighed deeply. "I'll start at the beginning. Ryan worked as a derrick hand on an oil rig. One of McCune's many oil industry-related businesses involved managing rig crews and Ryan worked on one of those crews. He would spend two weeks on and one week off. He was twenty-five and had worked on derricks all around Texas ever since high school, so when he went to work for McCune's crew he was promised a job as a manager if he stuck with them for six months. He was told it was a probationary period. Anyway, this was Thanksgiving, and he'd come home to spend the week with us in Galveston. We had a wonderful holiday." Her face glowed with the warmth of the memory.

"He left to go back to work on Sunday. The rig they were working on was an older one and there wasn't any cell service of any kind. They had a satellite phone, but they discouraged the guys from using it. So we didn't expect to hear from him for a couple of weeks. He said he'd call as soon as he was back on dry land. Two weeks came and went. No call. We knew that bad weather could delay the transfer of shifts, but the weather had been fair. We called Gulf Coast Energy Resources. They told us that he'd never shown up for his shift."

"Gulf Coast Energy Resources was McCune's company?" Darlene asked, writing it down.

"Yes. He sold it when he left Texas several years ago. Ryan was working out of their Pascagoula office, so my husband drove over there to see if he could find out anything. Everyone said Ryan hadn't shown up for the shift so Sam—he's my ex, Ryan's father—drove all over Pascagoula looking for Ryan's car. Of course, at that point we didn't know if he'd even made it over there. Something could have happened anywhere from Galveston to

Pascagoula. The police wouldn't do anything 'cause we didn't have any proof that he'd made it to their city, plus they said he was an adult and could disappear if he wanted to. It was awful. We felt scared and alone.

"Credit card companies and the cell phone company wouldn't give us any information either. But my other son, Todd, is very clever. He does IT work and knows how to get around things. We were able to get into Ryan's apartment and Todd hacked into his computer. After that it was easy for him to get access to Ryan's accounts and get all the information we needed. I won't bore you with the details. The point is, we found out that Ryan had definitely made it to Pascagoula. Eventually, his car was found in a field about twenty miles outside the city. It had been burned up, but it was pretty clear it hadn't been a robbery. He had some expensive tools that he always carried with him to work on the rigs and they were still in the car."

"So if his equipment was still in the car, why do you think the company was responsible?" Darlene asked.

"Ryan had been upset with the way the rig was run. On top of that, most of the people who were on his shift wouldn't talk to me. Those who did were very evasive. I wanted the cops to question them or make them take a lie detector test or *something*, but even with the car being found, they wouldn't take on his case. I did finally talk the Galveston police into listing him as a missing person so we could at least get him into some of the national databases." She shrugged.

"So you came here to talk to McCune?"

She looked down at the table. "I came here to hassle him. I've tried for years to talk to him. His lawyers have sent me numerous letters accusing me of harassing him, and they aren't wrong. I've talked to a few ex-employees of McCune's, and they all said the same thing. If something happened to Ryan while he was working for Gulf Coast Energy Resources, then it was McCune who issued the gag order. They told me that he ran a dangerous operation, skirting as many of the regulations as he could. A few years before Ryan went missing, a couple workers had been killed and a several were injured when part of the rigging collapsed. That's why they would have wanted to get rid of Ryan. He wouldn't have put up with dangerous conditions."

"That gives you a very strong motive for McCune's murder," I said, looking at Darlene to see where she wanted to go with this.

"I don't deny it."

"Where were you on Monday?" Darlene asked.

"I was in Tallahassee. I've been working with a lawyer trying to file a wrongful death suit against McCune."

"That's going to be hard without a body or any evidence."

"We just wanted to force him to disclose information. I know I won't get very far without something concrete that connects Ryan's death to McCune. I just thought that, if we can get a suit filed, then we'd be able to question some of the other guys who were working on the rig at the time. Maybe, since McCune doesn't even own the company anymore, they'd be more willing to talk."

Celina gave another big sigh. "I've lost my family. My husband and I divorced a year after Ryan went missing then, six months ago, Todd told me that, until I can talk about something other than Ryan, he doesn't want to see me. But how can I give up? Ryan was my son."

A dead or missing child can often dominate the emotions and focus of parents. Nothing could be more natural, but it often leaves survivors feeling adrift without part of their family. Parents sometimes grieve differently, causing them to drift apart. I felt sympathy for Celina, but it didn't change the fact that she had a very good motive for murdering McCune.

"You need to help us out. We need to know where you were from noon to six o'clock on Monday," I said.

"I met with the lawyer downtown that morning, from nine until a little after ten. I'm sure his office can give you the exact time down to the quarter of an hour, since that's how they charge. After that, I went back to the motel, one of those on the north side of town by the interstate. At some point I wandered over to the Cracker Barrel for lunch. Then I went back to the motel and worked at pulling together all of the information the lawyer wants. Oh, yeah, I also filled out a loan application online, since I'll need to come up with a ten-thousand-dollar retainer for the lawyer."

"Was anyone with you during any of this time?" Darlene asked, casually tapping her phone on the table.

"No. I mean, when I was in the Cracker Barrel there were people around and the waitress, but no one specifically with me."

"Do you have the receipt from the restaurant?" I asked.

"Yes, I keep all of my receipts. Maybe someday a judge will make McCune… or I guess his estate now, reimburse me for all of my expenses. I've already spent over a hundred-thousand dollars trying to find out what happened to my son," she said, her chin pointing up with stubborn pride.

"We'd like to examine your computer and your phone," I said, and watched her eyes narrow. "It could help us confirm that you were doing what you said you were doing during the time of the murder."

"No," she said flatly.

"We know you had a motive for killing McCune. We need to know whether you had the opportunity or not," I explained.

"I'm sure that you both are nice people and are good at your jobs. But you need to understand that I've spent years trying to get cops to do their jobs. All I've gotten is stalling and lip service. Now I'm supposed to roll over and give you anything you want so you can investigate the death of the bastard who was covering up my son's disappearance. No."

She clutched her purse and stood up. "I have learned a lot about the law in the last few years. You can't make me give you access to my things unless you get a court order." She turned and headed for the door.

"When we're searching through McCune's house and

records, we might come across something that pertains to Ryan's disappearance," I said as she started to open the door.

That stopped her for a second. Without turning around, she said, "I'll think about it."

After she'd gone, Darlene looked at me. "The lure of information on her son was well played."

"Even if she killed him, she obviously didn't find out what she really wants. Proof of what happened to Ryan."

"Maybe she confronted McCune and he told her that he knew Ryan was dead."

"Possibly. Though I'm not sure I can see her driving a tractor." I thought for a second. "Not that a middle-aged woman can't drive a tractor."

"It might be a line of inquiry. What's her background? Did she grow up on a farm?"

"There's plenty of room to dig around in her life and Ryan's disappearance. If she *isn't* the killer then maybe we can help her out when we find the person who did it."

"You're such a good little do-bee," Darlene said with a smile. "I'll let you take the lead on rummaging through her baggage."

"No problem," I said, then felt my phone vibrate in its case on my side. A glance at the screen told me it was our supervisor, Lt. Johnson, and I answered quickly.

"Macklin, I've got a death investigation for you," he said.

Normally, dispatch would have called me directly, but since we had all just returned to our regular shifts, I figured they hadn't yet received an updated duty roster.

"I'm just getting up to speed on the McCune case," I said, though I knew I wouldn't get anywhere by claiming a prior commitment. Darlene, Pete and I were the only investigators who handled violent crimes, so each of us always had a number of cases on our desks.

"Marks is the primary on that case and, besides, you have FDLE to back you all up. This one looks like an accident. Shouldn't take a bunch of your time. Not that I give a damn if it does. Just be glad you aren't running patrol anymore,"

Johnson snapped.
    "I'm on it," I said.

CHAPTER TEN

Johnson instructed me to contact dispatch for the details. Once I got them on the line, Marti said, "I didn't want this one going out on the radio. According to the caller, a man named Ray Haggard, the body is Eli the Veggie Man. Haggard went out to his place and the gate wasn't open, but Eli had told him he'd have a dozen pumpkins for him. The guy does carving demos. Anyway, he went around the gate and found Eli lying at the foot of the stairs to his house."

"I understand why you didn't want this out on the radio," I said.

"So many people know the Veggie Man that the lurkers who listen in on their scanners would have the news spread all over the county in five minutes. There'd be a dozen people out there before you could get there."

"Appreciate it. Is Haggard at the scene?"

"Yes, I've still got him on the phone. I've also called the coroner. According to Haggard, there isn't any doubt that Eli is dead."

"Tell him I'm on the way."

I wasn't surprised that they hadn't dispatched a patrol car. Normally, patrol would get there more quickly than an investigator, but since this was a suspected accident and the person was obviously deceased, it made sense to let an investigator respond and cut out the middleman.

Eli Waters had owned and run the Veggie Man Stand for decades. Getting your pumpkin or your Christmas tree from Eli the Veggie Man was a tradition for most county residents. When I pulled up to the parking area by the stand, Ray Haggard was pacing back and forth by the gate.

"There wasn't anything I could do," he said as I walked over to him and introduced myself. Haggard was wearing a crew neck sweater over a slightly rounded belly, making him look like a young and out of shape Mr. Rogers.

"Did you touch the body?"

"Just… I just felt his hand. I knew he was dead when I saw him. But I felt like I had to, you know, check." He looked embarrassed. "I called 911 right away."

"You did the right thing. Wait here. I'm going to look at the body. Can you point out where you walked?" The ground was sandy clay that held footprints well. I wanted to follow Haggard's path as much as possible to avoid disturbing any evidence if the death appeared to be anything other than an accident.

"I went from the gate. I had to squeeze through the gap. From there I went straight back to the trailer behind the stand. I went on that side," he said, pointing to the right of the stand.

The vegetable stand was a large, open-air pole barn, eighty feet long and twenty-five feet deep. It was decorated for Halloween and was filled with pumpkins and other produce. One large sign reading "The Veggie Man" hung over the front of the stand, while dozens of little signs marked items for sale, including honey, pecans and every manner of vegetable. Behind the stand was a nicely kept singlewide where Eli lived.

As soon as I rounded the end of the stand, I saw Eli lying at the bottom of the steps leading down from a small deck on the front of his home. He was sprawled face down on the stone walkway. A pumpkin lay smashed about a foot from his head. A puddle of blood had spread out from under his forehead, stopping just short of the pumpkin. The tableau looked like an illustration for a morbid fairytale.

Haggard had been right, though. I didn't need a doctor's opinion to know that the man was dead. His skin had a greyish-blue tint and his left eye was open and staring blankly. A spec of sand rested on his milky grey iris.

I noticed two unusual things right away. The first was the smell. Not the bad kind, though there was some of that, but the heavy, cloying scent of cologne. The second was that Eli wasn't wearing the jeans and work shirt that I was most used to seeing him in. Instead, he was dressed in a pair of slacks and a light blue dress shirt.

I backed away from the body and tried to picture the scene. The deck was about four feet off the ground. Eli was lying with his feet on the last two steps, meaning that he probably fell from the third or fourth step. I pulled on the railings lining both sides of the stairs. They seemed sturdy. The steps weren't covered in wet leaves or algae. Of course, I knew that it was possible for a person to trip over their own feet. Who hasn't gone to the ground a time or two without there being a specific cause?

The pumpkin. He would have been carrying the pumpkin. I tried to imagine what would happen if I tripped down the stairs carrying a pumpkin. The first image that came to mind had me falling on top of the pumpkin. That clearly hadn't happened here. In the second image, I cast the pumpkin away from me as I fell, but the pumpkin was too close to the head of the body for that to have been the case with Eli.

Reluctantly, I headed back to my car to get some crime scene tape. I could be wrong, but this didn't look like an accident. Dad wasn't going to be happy. With everything else going on, he didn't need the murder of an institution like the Veggie Man.

I called Shantel. "If you think you can get away from your construction project, I've got a case I'd like you to work."

"Perfect timing." I could hear the light in her voice. "The crews have finally secured the old part of the building, so they can get back to work on the addition while we resume doing a little business. I've even got a special assistant on loan from FDLE. You out at the Veggie Man's stand?"

I wasn't surprised that she knew where I was. Not only did she monitor the radio, but she had a sharp ear for anything going on in the department. "Yes, and I think it's something other than an accident."

"Of course you do and God bless you for that. I'm on my way."

As I was festooning the area with yellow tape, the coroner's van pulled up. Linda and Anne were in the front seat and Anne waved brightly from the driver's side.

"Remember, we aren't talking to him," I heard Linda say after Anne had turned off the ignition.

"Why aren't you talking to me?" I asked good-naturedly.

"Because you didn't call us to come pick up your human porcupine," Linda said. "Most unusual corpse in months and you don't think about us."

"Hey, blame your boss, not me."

"He *is* always grabbing the interesting cases," Linda allowed as they got out of the van.

"I think this case could have some... different angles," I said, trying to get them interested in Eli's death. Not that the women needed much encouragement. Their enthusiasm for dead bodies rivaled Dr. Darzi's. "You will have to wait until Shantel gets here to take pictures and videotape everything."

Before they could answer, Shantel pulled up with her old partner, Marcus Brown, riding shotgun. I gave him a bro hug when he got out of the van.

"It's good see you!"

"Your dad and I talked FDLE into letting us borrow him while we get back on our feet," Shantel said.

"Man, that dozer sure did a number on the office," Marcus said, shaking his head.

"At least we got the place secure and the security cameras back up and working. I was going crazy being locked up in there," Shantel said.

"How do you like your new job?" I asked Marcus as he and Shantel got their cameras and equipment ready.

He gave me a frown. "It's all right, but it ain't home, if you know what I mean."

After they'd made a record of the scene, I walked to the body with Linda and Anne. "Before you start, I want you to smell him," I said, not wanting to tell them what I was looking for.

Linda gave me a narrow-eyed look. "Dead bodies always smell like… You know, what with the evacuation and—"

"I know all that. I want to know if you smell something else," I explained.

Linda got down on her knees and gently sniffed the air. She made a couple of ugly faces before she signaled for Anne to give it a try.

"There's the smell of… cheap cologne under the other odors," Anne observed.

"What was that old man stuff? My grandfather used to use it. Old… something."

"Old Spice?" I asked.

"That's it. Smells like that. Grandpa would use it when he was going out to dinner with Grams."

"Exactly. From his clothes and the cologne, I think Eli was planning to go out on the town."

I left them to work on the body and walked back to where Shantel and Marcus were beginning to tag and photograph items that might be evidence.

"You really think someone killed him?" Shantel asked as she put a flag down next to a crushed Express Burgers cup.

"Yes and no. On the one hand, the scene looks staged. On the other… weird things can happen. I'm not going to form an opinion just yet."

"Liar, liar pants on fire. You've made up your mind," she said, looking for the next item to tag.

"It's the pumpkin that gets me. I just don't think it would land like that." I frowned.

"But the pumpkin does explain why he wasn't holding the handrail and couldn't get his hands out in front of him soon enough to keep from cracking his head open on the stones."

"See, I can agree with that. But why was he coming out of his house with a pumpkin? All the pumpkins he was selling were over at the stand."

"What are you doing with this case anyway? Aren't you and Darlene working on McCune's murder?" Shantel stopped and looked at me. "You know, McCune's place is just a mile farther down the road."

"My mind already went there. But I can't see any connection except for the proximity. Assuming this was a murder."

I went back to my car to do a little research. I had a love-hate relationship with the laptop mounted on my dash. On the one hand, it allowed me to run background checks and follow up on witnesses and leads. But on the other hand, it was a distraction from the real world. I found myself being lured by its one-touch answers when I was supposed to be out talking with real people and gathering evidence in the real world. With a sigh, I ran a background check on Ray Haggard. I'd sent him off to work after getting his vitals and telling him that I'd want to interview him in more detail within the next couple of days.

Haggard had no wants or priors. Not even a traffic ticket. He lived in Calhoun in a nice mid-century neighborhood. Nothing fancy. A quiet neighborhood that saw the occasional burglary or domestic issue, but nothing more serious.

Next I plugged Eli Waters into the system. He'd been arrested for lewd behavior back in the '80s and again for soliciting a prostitute in Tallahassee ten years ago. There weren't any details regarding the arrest in the '80s. Back then, a lewd behavior arrest often involved nothing more than going a little too far in the backseat of a car. The arrest had been made in Adams County, so I might be able to dig up the paperwork or court records. My victim profile was going to be a little more interesting than I'd imagined.

I looked up to see Anne getting the gurney from the back of the coroner's van and I went over to help her.

"What's the verdict?" I asked.

"He's dead," she said with a smile.

"Want to take a guess on when he died?"

"Dr. Darzi gave us a stern lecture about speculating on the time and cause of death. He said that cops take anything we say as gospel, no matter how many qualifiers we put in front of it."

"You don't want to be the teacher's pet, do you?" I joked. Anne was an intern and her mood varied between being a little bit flippant and being deadly earnest about her work.

"Ask the boss," she said, indicating Linda as we got close to her and the late Eli Waters.

"Let me guess. You want to know the time and cause of death. Come on, Macklin. Be original."

I shrugged. "Inquiring minds want to know."

"This is preliminary, so don't hold me, Dr. Darzi's office or the profession of pathology responsible if different results come up during the autopsy."

"Promise, cross my heart and hope to jump over a four-leaf clover."

"He appears to have died sometime between two in the afternoon and midnight yesterday. You can probably narrow that down a bit if you consider his business hours."

"I haven't talked to anyone yet, but the stand is usually open until six o'clock to get the commuter traffic."

"Cause of death... head trauma. It looks like he bled for a while after he cracked his skull open."

"Could a fall from the steps have caused that much trauma?"

"Now you're pushing it, buster. You'll have to wait until

Dr. Darzi does the autopsy before you'll get any more detailed information," Linda said with the stern look of a disappointed teacher.

"Didn't mean to presume. You're just so good... I expected you'd have all the answers," I said with an innocent look on my face.

"Flattery won't get you anything this time. It's going to take some detailed X-rays and examinations to give you more," Linda said as Anne unzipped a black body bag and set it down next to Eli.

The body looked odd with its feet, head and hands bagged to preserve evidence. I watched as they shifted the body into the bag before hoisting it eight inches onto the gurney. Anne raised the gurney and they rolled off toward the van. *What an odd way for Eli to leave the business he's loved for so many years*, I thought.

I yelled for Shantel to join me. "Get your camera and let's go through the trailer."

Marcus was still working the area around the stand. They'd already marked dozens of items. Since this was a place of business where people got in and out of their cars and trucks several times a day, there were more than a few pieces of trash on the ground. Any one of them might have been the clue that linked our killer, if there was a killer, to the crime. Of course, there was a big problem with evidence collected in a public parking lot. It would be almost impossible to prove that any specific item had been dropped at the exact time of Eli's death.

"I'm ready when you are," Shantel said, her video camera on and ready to roll. She had me state the date, time and who was present then, wearing gloves, masks and booties that made us look like alien invaders, we walked up the steps to Eli's home.

I'd used the keys in Eli's pocket to unlock the door before dropping them in an evidence bag. I'd also already checked the back door and found it locked, as well as all of the windows shut and in good condition. No one had fled out the back or through a window.

"He was neat. I'll give him that," Shantel said while filming.

The trailer had an open floorplan combining the living room, dining room and kitchen. The living room was furnished in a mix of different styles, but everything was clean and well cared for. In one corner of the living room, a large oak office desk was piled with neatly stacked invoices, bills, mail and ledgers. Above the desk hung a pin-up calendar from a farm machinery company.

We went into the master bedroom next. It took up the entire north end of the trailer and included a master bathroom. Again, everything looked neat and tidy. The clothes in the drawers were almost military in their neatness.

"No sign of a female companion," Shantel pointed out while filming the master closet.

I randomly checked the sizes on the clothes and found them all to be consistent—medium shirts and 32x30 pants. "Doesn't look like he had anyone, male or female, sharing this room with him," I agreed.

We headed to the other end of the trailer where there was another bath and two more small bedrooms. The first bedroom was made up as a guest room. There was a twin bed with sheets and a comforter, and a wardrobe containing a few odds and ends, but nothing to suggest that anyone had used the room in months.

"Wow!" Shantel exclaimed as she entered the third bedroom. "You have *got* to see this. I'm going to have to give this film an R rating… or maybe even an X," she said in awe.

I have to admit I was taken by surprise, even after her warning. Inside the room was a vast collection of mainstream men's magazines from the '50s through the '80s. I'd have to leave it up to others to decide how pornographic they were, yet none of them would have been rated hardcore. There were boxes and boxes of *Playboy*, *Penthouse* and a variety of lesser known titles.

"He was a serious collector," I said, looking at the neatly

labeled boxes and stacks of magazines stored in plastic collector's sleeves.

"The volume is what takes your breath away," Shantel said.

"He had a couple of arrests on his record. One was for soliciting a prostitute."

"I think he might have liked the ladies… to pure distraction. There must be thousands of magazines in here."

"My wife would *not* want me searching this room," came a voice from behind us. We turned to see Marcus looking at the collection with raised eyebrows. "Man, he was really working this," he said, taking in the detailed notes on the boxes that were stacked all around the room.

"Maybe he was killed for a *Playboy #1*," Shantel said in a tone that left me not knowing if she was kidding or not. "I'm being real. Collectors can be seriously crazy. I had a boyfriend who was into all that comic book, graphic novel stuff. Those people can be cut-throat."

"I was going to laugh, but you've got a point. Somehow we'll have to figure out if anything is missing," I said.

"Ha, you'll have a dozen deputies volunteering to go through this collection," Marcus said.

"Men, whether it's cars or women, they're always looking at ones they can't afford," Shantel huffed.

"I've got just the man," I said, thinking of Julio Ortiz, who'd been interested in getting off of patrol and into the criminal investigation division for a while now. He'd helped me out on a couple of cases and was smart and enthusiastic. I pulled out my phone.

"You at work?" I asked when he answered the call.

"I'm scheduled to come in at three."

"Perfect. I need some help on a case. It might have to be off the books, but I'll talk to Dad."

I knew that the department was already in deep with overtime costs due to the storm. FEMA had promised to reimburse the department for up to seventy-five percent of our hurricane-related expenses, but the big question was how long it would take for them to come through with the money.

"No problem," Julio said.

I told him where to find the crime scene.

"Oh, the Veggie Man. Wow! I buy stuff from there regularly. Nice guy."

"He had his secrets," I told him, looking around the room again.

CHAPTER ELEVEN

We'd just finished up with the house when Julio arrived.

"Here are some pictures of the body," I said, showing him a few of the photos I'd taken with my phone. "What do you see?"

"You wouldn't think he'd die from that short of a fall." Julio scrolled through the pictures. "That pumpkin. Was he carrying it?"

"That's what it looks like. There weren't any pumpkin guts on the stairs."

"Something doesn't seem right about the position of the pumpkin. Somebody pushed him, maybe? Still, if he was carrying the pumpkin then you've got the same problem. Do you think the pumpkin could have been put there after the guy was dead?"

"That's what we need to find out." I was glad that he'd had the same questions I did. I had been very careful not to prompt him.

"Was anything stolen?" he asked, causing me to grin.

"That's the first job I've got for you," I said, and waved him toward the trailer.

"Wow. He sure did like the ladies," Julio said, impressed with the collection of magazines.

"We need a rough inventory to determine if—" I was interrupted by the sounds of shouting from outside.

We ran out to find Marcus on the ground, wrestling with a large man who was yelling something about his brother.

"Hey! Break it up!" I called as I trotted down the steps, followed by Julio and Shantel.

I pulled out my cuffs as I approached the pair rolling on the ground. I dropped down onto the man, followed by Julio.

"That hurts!" he complained as I held my knee firmly planted in the middle of his back.

"Then settle down," I told him.

"I want to see my brother!" the grey-haired man shouted. He must have been in his early sixties, but he had the strength of a man much younger.

"Who are you?" I asked.

"I'm Micah. Micah Waters," he said. "Eli is my brother."

Some of the fight went out of him. Even though he had relaxed, the three of us holding him down did not. I'd learned long ago not to relax my grip just because the suspect seemed to have given up.

"We're going to release you. But you have to promise that you won't try to enter your brother's house. I'm sorry to have to tell you, but he is deceased." I felt him tense up again. "His body has already been taken to the morgue. I'll tell you whatever I can and help you in any way I'm able. Do you understand?"

"Yes," the man said, his voice subdued.

I nodded to the others. As we released our grips and stood up, Micah tried to get to his knees and slipped. Julio and I reached out and helped him to his feet. He was dressed in work clothes and wearing a nametag that said: "Micah Waters, Owner, Empowerment Printing." I had a vague memory of a large building in an industrial park on the west side of Tallahassee.

"What happened to him?" Micah asked, his eyes downcast. All of the fight seemed to have gone out of him.

Before I could answer, he turned to Marcus and said, "I'm sorry. I should have listened to you."

"It's your family. I understand," Marcus said as he wiped the dirt from his clothes. He'd lost a rubber glove and his booties in the melee.

"Eli was found at the bottom of those stairs this morning," I said, pointing toward the house. "When was the last time you talked with your brother?"

"Thanksgiving five years ago," he said.

That certainly wasn't the answer I was expecting. Hiding my surprise, I said, "Seems like a long time for brothers not to talk."

"It was his choice, not mine."

"You all had an argument?"

"Ha! Since we were kids we've had arguments. Not just me. He argued with Mom and Pop all the time."

"What were the arguments about?"

"He thought we were too prudish... that we judged him. Eli always wanted to have everything his way. He wanted to go off and party, but then to come home and go to church on Sundays."

"You all had a problem with his lifestyle?" I asked, and Micah gave me a small smile.

"No, that's the sad part. My parents never said a word to him. He'd be out partying, then come home smelling like booze and women, and my parents would give him a hug and tell him they loved him. But it just made him mad. I think he wanted them to get angry with him, but they never would. So he'd get mad himself, knocking things over and telling us that we were judging him." Micah shook his head.

"What happened five years ago?"

"It was the start of Thanksgiving week. Mom went into the hospital. I called Eli, but he told me he couldn't come over until Thanksgiving because the three days before the holiday were big days at his stand." Micah looked around and shrugged. "Mom had been in the hospital before. I guess he didn't think it was a big deal. I tried to tell him that she was really sick. Pneumonia. She died Tuesday morning. I called Eli again. He said he'd be there as soon as the stand closed that evening. But at three o'clock, Pop had a stroke. By the time Eli showed up, it was too late. Pop lingered for a couple of days, but he was never conscious again. Eli blamed me, though he was really angry at himself. He stormed out of the hospital and told me never to talk to him again. I've called dozens of times, but he never answered. I thought I'd have time to wear him down. Sooner or later, I'd come out here and he'd have to talk to me. How's that for irony? Now I'm angry with myself. I should have come sooner."

He looked down at the ground, then up at the sky. I could see him clenching his teeth in an effort not to cry. Still a tear rolled down his cheek.

"Come back to my car," I said, gently guiding him to the parking lot. I nodded to the others, who went back to work.

"What happened to him?" Micah asked as we walked.

"He hit his head on the stone blocks at the foot of his stairs. That's all we know right now."

Micah seemed to think about this and he still hadn't said anything else by the time we reached the parking lot.

"I know it's been a while since you talked with your brother, but did he have any enemies that you know of?"

"Me, Mom and Pop. We were the only people I ever saw him argue with. He was perpetually fifteen years-old when he was with the family. The last time I came out here before our big fight, I remember watching him talking and laughing with everyone. That was Eli. A big kid. Even at his age."

Micah leaned against my car and I thought about the times I'd stopped at the stand. Eli had seemed to love bantering with everyone. He'd called most people by name and would give out samples and talk about who had grown the fruits and vegetables. I remembered that he claimed to have grown some of them himself.

"Where is his farm?" I asked Micah.

"He owns ten acres down the road." Micah pointed to the south. "It's only a quarter of a mile or so. He'd pull his farm wagon down here sometimes."

"Are there any out-buildings on the land?"

"Just a barn and a well house."

"Did your brother have much money?"

"Ha, no. Don't get me wrong. He was a good businessman, worked hard and kept his books like a New York City accountant. But he liked to spend money too. He…" Micah seemed embarrassed.

"He spent the money on girls?" I suggested.

"Bars and strip clubs. I never understood it." He paused. "Maybe I did. See, like I said, Eli was a big kid. That doesn't make for long-term relationships. When he was younger he was always with a new girl. He'd wine and dine her, buy her gifts. But he'd never get serious, so the women would get tired of him and go find a guy who *did* want to settle down. Of course, those were the good ones. There were a few of the other kind."

"The other kind?"

"Yeah, you know, the ones that would milk him for everything they could get until he caught on and kicked them to the curb."

"Where there any girls five years ago?"

"Nah, some of that changed when he turned fifty. This is going to make him sound worse than he was, but…" Micah paused.

I sensed his hesitation to talk about his brother's habits and I did my best to reassure him. "For me, one of the hardest parts of an investigation is putting together the victim profile. No matter who we are, we all have flaws. Digging them out and exposing them seems like a violation of a victim's privacy. But we have to see who the victim was. We're more than the sum of our actions. Blended in with our actions are our intentions and all the mitigating circumstances. While I have to uncover his secrets, I'll treat him and his life respectfully. You have my word on that."

Micah nodded, then looked at the ground. "He went to prostitutes. Eli said it was cheaper in the long run. Told me that at his age, he could buy a prettier girl than he could pick up."

I remembered hearing something very similar from Horace McCune. I knew that he used prostitutes, and now here was Eli. Killed a mile away, two days later, and also a customer for sex workers.

"I know he was arrested for soliciting once. Do you know where he found the prostitutes that he hired?" I asked the question while realizing that the business of sex work was changing fast. Years ago, men picked up women at spots around town. There were always those seedy areas that a bartender or cab driver could direct you to. But these days guys went online. There must have been hundreds, if not thousands, of websites dedicated to helping men find women, and women to find customers.

"No, I don't. Really, I just found the whole thing disgusting. I tried a couple of times to convince him that he was degrading the women and himself. He'd get mad and tell me to quit preaching at him."

"You own your own business?" I said, nodding toward his shirt.

"Mom and Pop started it. Eli and I were supposed to run it someday. It's just me now. We publish educational and spiritual books and films. Good books at fair prices. That was Pop's motto for the business and the creed that we lived by."

We spent another ten minutes talking about how his brother's body would be handled and who he'd need to contact at the morgue. I assured him I'd be in touch through the whole process to make sure that he could lay his brother to rest as soon as possible.

After Micah left, I walked back to the house, unable to stop myself thinking about the connections between Horace McCune and Eli Waters. *Stop it!* I ordered my brain. It was way too early to become obsessed with a trail that might only be a mirage.

"This is too much," Julio said, sorting through the

magazines in the back room. "At least he was organized. There's a list of the magazines inside taped to the lid of each box."

"How much is this stuff worth?" I wondered.

"There are collectors for everything. Most of them are in good condition. Actually, you could probably call them near mint. I got into collecting cards and comics when I was a kid," Julio said.

"Bet you still buy them," I said.

"I still have my collection." He looked at his watch. "I've got another hour before I'm supposed to be on the clock."

I held up my finger and called Lt. Johnson.

"You're turning this into another homicide?" Johnson asked with more than a tinge of irritation in his voice.

"Would you rather I just rubber-stamp it as an accident?"

"Watch it," he warned. "What do you want?"

"I'd like to be able to use Julio on this case."

"That's up to patrol."

"I wanted to check with you before going to another department or the higher ups for help," I said, trying to sound sincere, though I doubt I succeeded.

"So now you care about the chain of command." It wasn't a question. "If they'll let you use him, then I'm fine with it," he said and hung up.

I called the lieutenant in charge of patrol, who said they could let him go half-time. Then I speed-dialed Dad.

"Tell me the Veggie Man wasn't killed," he said when he answered the phone.

"The jury's still out."

"Great," he said with a lethal dose of sarcasm.

"I called to see if I could use Julio on the case. Patrol said they'd be willing to share him."

"Whatever it takes to solve this. Did you see the billboard on Jefferson Street? Across my face, someone's painted 'Who killed McCune?' in giant red letters."

I knew the billboard he was talking about. This one simply had a picture of Dad and a one-word question:

Favoritism? McCune had been an expert at skirting the libel laws.

"Rock and a hard place. If you have it taken down, then people will think it's true."

"On the other hand, if it stays up through the election, how many thousands of voters will see it?" I couldn't tell if he was depressed or angry. I was hoping for anger. That would be normal.

"We're working as hard as we can to solve the McCune murder."

"I know. Without a clear suspect, it's going to take time. Unfortunately, I only have a few weeks before the election."

"We'll get through this," I said, thinking back to the many times Mom had used that very phrase. It had been one of her go-to cheer-me-ups.

There was a long silence from Dad and I felt sure he was sharing my memories. Finally he said, "Go ahead and use Julio."

I hung up and told Julio that he was temporarily half of an investigator.

"I'll take half," he said with a smile.

"I found a laptop," Shantel shouted from the front door.

"Where?"

"In his truck. He had it tucked under the center console," Shantel reported as I followed her outside. "I've bagged it up. I'll get Lionel to do a forensic examination of it." We'd been told to not play IT-guy with electronic devices after a couple of our burglary investigators had screwed up evidence.

"I'll send him Eli's phone too. I've got it bagged in my car." Linda and Anne had found it when they'd examined the content of his pockets.

"I'm scared to think what might be on the laptop after seeing his magazine collection," Shantel said.

"The big question is, was he meeting someone last night? Was he supposed to meet them here or somewhere else?" I wondered.

"With an older guy, it's hard to say if he would have done a lot of texting or email."

"Just about everyone under eighty emails these days, and only a few non-tech types don't text. Don't try and destroy my hopeful vibes."

"I won't rain on your parade. I'm just glad to be out in the real world and not cooped up watching workmen who make more money than I do take lunch breaks and talk about how difficult it is to patch a roof."

We looked through everything else in the truck, a 2010 Dodge that was in great shape.

"This is the cleanest truck I've ever seen," I said.

"Shame everyone doesn't keep their vehicles this clean. It makes searching and processing them a lot easier. Two years ago, we had a van that had been used in an armed robbery and we took three thirty-gallon trash bags worth of garbage out of it. When I vacuumed it for trace evidence, I ended up with ten vacuum bags full of hair and every other kind of filth you could imagine."

"I remember that one. Someone had been taken hostage."

"That's why the van had to be so thoroughly processed. I told Lt. Johnson that we'd be lucky to find anything useful among all that trash. Turns out I was right."

I realized that we should probably do something with the produce stand. There were a lot of fresh fruits and vegetables that would just rot if we taped it off and left them sitting there.

I'd gotten the name of Eli's lawyer from Micah, so I gave him a call.

"Yes, he has a will on file with us," Mr. Hastert told me. "I'm sorry to hear about this. Eli seemed like a great guy. But before we go on, I'd like to verify your identity. I'll call the sheriff's office and get back in touch with you."

Prudent, if annoying. I waited impatiently and five minutes later my phone rang. We picked up the conversation where we'd left off.

"So no enemies that you know of?" I asked.

"No. There weren't any lawsuits or land disputes, nothing like that. I just handled some routine matters for him."

I explained the situation with the produce stand and asked if he had any suggestions.

"Those are assets and, technically, they should be sold and the money put into his estate. However, logistically, by the time we got someone over there to work the stand and paid them, there wouldn't be much financial benefit. As the executor of the estate, I think I can authorize the donation of any perishable items to a registered charity. Fruits and vegetables, that sort of thing. Any items that have a longer shelf life, such as honey, should be held over until their value can be estimated and sold for the benefit of the estate."

"The First Methodist Church runs a food bank for needy families," I suggested.

"If you want to call them and supervise the distribution, I'm good with that. Take pictures and document it."

"Who is the chief beneficiary of the will?"

"Funny you should mention that. It's his brother, but a week ago I met with Eli about a letter he'd gotten from the IRS. While we were talking, he mentioned that he might be making a change to his will."

"Did he say what changes he was thinking of?"

"No, it was just an off-hand remark at the end of our meeting. Sort of an I-might-be-seeing-you-again-soon sort of thing."

"Did Eli talk about his brother?"

"Now you're getting into client-lawyer privilege."

"Your client is dead."

"Yes, but I now represent the estate and my duty is to oversee the distribution of the estate as laid out in the will." He paused for a moment, then went on, "I'll say this much. Eli had some strong, often negative, feelings toward his family. However, they were of a very general type with no specific actions mentioned that particularly angered him."

"I guess that answers my question. Do you have a rough

estimate of the value of his estate?"

"Assuming that he hadn't made any radical changes without informing me, I'd say it's around a quarter of a million dollars, plus the value of the business, if I can find a buyer for the name."

I thanked him and asked him to let me know if he discovered anything new.

CHAPTER TWELVE

The prostitute angle still bothered me. Eli's laptop and phone might answer those questions, but they might not. Plus, it would probably be a few days before Lionel West could get to it. He was our only IT guy and there was usually a waiting list for his attention.

So I called Eddie Thompson, my primary confidential informant in all matters related to the dark underbelly of Adams County. He was becoming noticeably less helpful as he got his life cleaned up. I tried hard not to begrudge him a better life, but it was hard to find a snitch who was in the gutter enough to be useful while still being trustworthy.

The call went to voicemail. I left a message for Eddie to call me the first chance he got. Just as I hung up, I got a text from Linda telling me they were going ahead with the autopsy on Eli Waters in a couple of hours. I texted back that I'd be there.

My next call was to the First Methodist Church to ask if they wanted the produce. The woman in charge of the food bank sounded beyond grateful and had a van sent out in less than fifteen minutes. Marcus and Shartel helped me oversee the loading of the van, cataloging all items that went to the church.

"I'm starving," I said, watching the van drive away and then looking at my watch. It was two-thirty. Julio had just left and I'd need to head over to Tallahassee for the autopsy in about an hour.

We closed down the scene before heading to the taco stand. The Guatemalans who ran it made good food and gave law enforcement a twenty-five percent discount. How could we lose?

The stand was located near the courthouse, with several picnic tables set in front of it in the shade of a large live oak. We sat in the warm October sun, enjoying our tacos and watching cars drive by. I hadn't even finished my first taco before Darlene pulled up with Pete in the car.

"What are you two doing driving around together?" I asked.

"Jealous?" Pete lobbed back. "I had to leave my car at the garage."

"Anything new with the McCune case?" I asked Darlene when they joined us with their food.

"I've spent most of the day trying to hunt down security cameras within a mile of the house. Public works got the sign up on the road asking for witnesses, and I did an interview with a news crew who's going to air a request for information. I've already received a couple of voicemails. I'll follow up on them this afternoon."

I filled them in on Eli's death.

"Does sound odd," Pete said. "He was a great guy. Sarah and I bought stuff from the stand a few times a month. Little weird about the porn collection, though."

"Most people have secrets," Darlene said.

"That's what I learned from the Dick Tracy Detective Correspondence school," I said with a grin.

"My second year on the job," Pete said, "I responded to a home invasion call. A woman had answered her door only to have a man force his way in. Bad dude. I mean, he had a rap sheet that included assaults, rapes, you name it. He'd escaped from an Alabama prison. Anyway, when I got there, the woman was outside the house, crying and saying that her attacker was still inside. I knew her. She worked at the bank, was always nicely dressed and had a kind word for everyone. A state trooper had shown up, so I had him go around back while I went in the front door.

"The inside of that house was unbelievable. This woman had to have been the biggest hoarder in the county. There was junk piled all the way to the roof. The only ways to get around inside were these narrow corridors through the jumble of trash. Luckily, I was thirty pounds lighter back then, but even so it was a tight squeeze. As I wandered through the maze, I could hear someone else moving around in the house. Ten minutes into my search, I heard screaming. Turned out the bad guy had disturbed a nest of rats. When he tried to scramble away from them, he knocked over a wall of boxes and was buried. Took us two hours to get him out. He was hysterical, and we finally had to have him sedated. He got sent back to Alabama to spend the rest of his life in jail, but what stuck with me was the woman. I never imagined that anyone 'normal' could live like that. I don't see how she could even function in the house. That was my first introduction to the secrets that people keep."

I stood up. "Catch you guys later. I've got an autopsy to go to. We'll see how many more secrets Eli was hiding."

I took my trash to the can and headed for my car. As I opened the door, I looked up to see that Pete had followed me.

"What's up? I mean, I know about McCune's murder and the elections, but you seem unusually quiet," Pete said.

I leaned against the car and sighed, then unloaded on him. "It's just a bunch of stuff. Cara's parents are staying with us, Dad's taking the situation with the murder and the billboards hard, and now I've got this other murder that might not be a murder. If it *is* a murder, then that has me off on another case when what I want to focus on is the McCune investigation. The worst part is that my mind is trying to come up with links between Eli's case and the

McCune murder which may or may not really be there."

Pete looked thoughtful. "I was out at Talon Range at seven this morning, so I'm done for the day. You want me to ride over to Tallahassee with you? Be like the good ol' days when we were partners."

What I wanted was to be by myself to brood over my problems, but what I *needed* was a friend to listen to my crap and give me some feedback. I nodded. "Sounds good."

"Darlene, I'm catching a ride with Larry!" he shouted. Darlene waved and went back to her conversation with Marcus and Shantel.

"So lay it on Uncle Pete," he said once we were headed out of town. I described the Waters case and gave him a run down of the McCune murder.

"I don't think you're imagining the similarities. You're just confusing similarities with links," Pete said.

"Exactly. There are more things that are dissimilar than similar."

"A fingerprint or shoe print match is a link. The fact that they both preferred prostitutes is a similarity. But you still want to compare evidence found at both crime scenes since the deaths are closely related in time and space."

"What I don't want to do is to screw up Eli's death investigation because my mind is really focused on McCune and the election," I said.

"You're not wrong about that," Pete agreed, rummaging around in the glove box. "Didn't I leave some Mike and Ikes in here?"

"Darlene made me thoroughly clean out the car when she became my partner. Something about not riding in a dumpster."

"That was an unopened box of Mike and Ikes," he grumbled.

"Then there's all the getting engaged stuff. Don't get me wrong. I love Cara and I'm glad I asked her, but now with her parents camped out in the front yard… It's just that much more stuff I've got to think about. You have a wife and two daughters. How do you deal with all of your responsibilities?"

"I prioritize. Most people don't understand how prioritizing works. About six years ago, I was freaking out. Both girls were in elementary school and Sarah was trying to go back to work. In the middle of that, I'd just been moved to persons crimes, so I was being called out at all hours of the night for serious crimes."

"So what'd you do?"

"I read a book. I've still got it. It's called *The Boulder on Your Shoulder*. Stupid title, almost like a kid's book, but after I picked it up and started to read it, I realized it included a lot of helpful advice. For instance, do what you need to do when you need to do it and forget the rest. That was one of the pearls of wisdoms I discovered. It also explained that getting your priorities in order doesn't mean that you just take all of your challenges and make a single priority list.

"The book explained that your priorities should change throughout the day. If you're at home, then you should use the set of priorities that you've decided on for that day at home. Forget everything else. And when you're at work, you focus on your work priorities. It sounds simple, but it took awhile to put into practice. Sometimes I have several separate priority lists running around in my head. And you should constantly assess your priorities. Sometimes when I'm going to spend the day at home, it's all about Sarah. Another day, I might concentrate on spending time with the girls."

I took my eyes off the road and looked at him. "I never knew you were that organized," I said suspiciously. Pete had always seemed to have a laid-back, drifty sort of approach to life.

"How do you think I can be such a good marksman?"

"Natural talent? A lot of practice?" I hadn't thought that much about it, though I knew Pete was one of the best shooters in North Florida. He could drill holes with his Remington 700 at a thousand yards. Plus, he was a great handgun instructor.

"Focus. Priorities. When I'm behind a rifle, I have to let everything else go and prioritize my focus on the scope, my breathing and the pressure of my finger on the trigger. With a handgun, it's the same only with changing priorities. On a course of fire, I might be standing in one place, in which case the sight, my breathing and trigger finger are my priorities. Or I might be moving, in which case not tripping over my own damn feet is uppermost in my head."

"You're almost making sense," I said as we passed into the Tallahassee city limits.

"You just have to learn how to compartmentalize your life. In each compartment, you focus on the most important task. Also beer and food."

"What was that last part?"

"I have a few beers when times are getting me down. Also, if you hadn't noticed, I eat my share of comfort foods. Speaking of which, why didn't I get a taco to go?"

In the morgue, we found Linda already working on Eli's body. Except for the depression on his forehead and the abrasions around it, you could almost believe that he was only asleep.

"This is your lucky day," Linda said as she took samples from Eli's hands. "I will be your captain for today's incredible journey with our deceased. Never fear, Dr. Darzi will review the autopsy tapes and data and sign off on the final report." She smiled at us.

"A few initial observations." Linda's voice had slipped into a professional tone. "You will notice that there is symmetrical bruising around the knees on both legs. Also, there are only light abrasions on his hands."

"Did you find any trace of pumpkin on him?" I asked.

"No. At least nothing that's identifiable with the naked eye. What were some of the items we found on the clothes?" she asked Anne, who was assisting her.

"Hay, grass, sand, two types of animal hair. All the samples were in expected amounts and places," Anne said, reviewing an electronic log.

Pete and I watched while they proceeded with an external examination of the body.

"Now this looks interesting," Linda said, when she got to his face.

She took some pictures, then gently wiped an area on his forehead until it was clear of dirt and dried blood, then took a few more pictures. Next she swung an overhead X-ray machine over the body. She looked at us after she had the machine pointed at his head and said, "Y'all might want to join us behind the screen for this."

We stood behind a six-by-six wall with a window in it that I presumed was lined with lead. Linda snapped an image with a wired remote, then she went out, changed the position of the X-ray, came back and snapped a few more images.

"At least we don't have to worry about the patient getting too much radiation," she said as she pulled up the images on several large LED screens mounted to the wall around the autopsy table.

"Here," she said, using a laser pointer to highlight an area of fractured bones in Eli's forehead. "I doubt it could be proven, but if I had to guess I'd say that his head hit the pavement twice. You see, here is an ellipse of fractures." She highlighted an area. "While over here, slightly off center from the first group, is a second impact. It's like a Venn diagram with the heaviest fracturing in the overlap."

"But you couldn't swear to there being two blows?" I pressed her.

"No. It's just an interpretation of the evidence, and I'm sure you could find a number of pathologists who would come up with another explanation for what we're seeing on the X-rays. The abrasions and marks on the skin don't clarify the situation. Also, remember I won't be the pathologist of record. Dr. Darzi might look at the evidence and see something different. If that's the case, then the report will reflect Dr. Darzi's opinion."

"But you think he was killed?" Pete asked.

"I think his head hit the stone pavers twice. Both times with considerable force. Two other pieces of evidence might point to something other than an accident," Linda said, and walked to the other side of the body. I had only seen Linda at crime scenes where she was usually bantering with everyone. But performing an autopsy, she was a different person. Impressively professional.

"The first is the knees. You can see that the damage to both areas around the knees is pretty similar. Usually, if a person trips then they're likely to try and catch themselves. This almost always results in the body twisting, causing more damage to one side than the other. Now, imagine if someone shoves you from behind. You have less time to react, which means you're more likely to go straight down onto the pavement… or, in this case, down the stairs."

"Maybe he passed out," Pete suggested.

"That would explain the symmetrical damage to the areas around the knees. However, we have some minor scuffing of his hands, which suggests that he made an attempt to get them out in front of himself. He just didn't have time to brace himself enough to keep from slamming his forehead against the walkway."

"You mentioned something else?" I said, unable to decide whether I was happy that my hunch had been right and this was likely homicide, or depressed that it was turning into another investigation that none of us needed right now.

"We collected half a dozen hairs in the blood surrounding the body," Linda said as though I should understand the significance of that.

"And…"

"They had been pulled from his head. Assuming they are his hairs, which I'm going to do since they were lying on top of some of the blood and matched the length and color of the hair of the deceased. Point being that, if someone picked up his head and slammed it down on the pavers, they might have pulled out a number of his hairs in the process."

Suddenly I could see how the murder had taken place.

The killer was behind Eli and had shoved him as he went down the steps. Then he had come down the stairs and grabbed Eli's head, slamming it down for the *coup de grâce*.

The rest of the autopsy proceeded without any other revelations.

"I don't see any outward signs of intoxication. We'll submit the samples for a typical toxicology screening, unless you have any evidence of a specific toxin," Linda told me.

"None. He didn't even have a bunch of prescription drugs. Not bad for a man his age."

We were back in the car and headed for Adams County by six. I called Cara.

"I'm really not avoiding your parents," I told her.

"*I'd* like to. You should have picked me up at the clinic. I would have been glad to sit in on an autopsy rather than have Mom badger me to walk around our place looking at woodland settings for the wedding."

"We haven't even set a date."

"Try telling her that. The word 'ceremony' messes with her head."

I took a deep breath before launching into the real reason I'd called. "I need to stop off and talk to Eddie on my way home."

There was a long silence from Cara. I waited it out.

"I know how important these cases are. But after the election, you are going to owe me… big time." I didn't question whether she was serious or not. I knew she was.

"I accept your terms," I said and glared at Pete when he made whip-cracking motions with his hand. I told Cara that I loved her and wished her good luck with her mother. Then I hung up and half turned to Pete, keeping one eye on the road. "You're one to talk. Your three women have you wrapped around their fingers."

"Ain't denying it," he said and, as if on cue, his text alert sounded. He smiled and checked it.

Something caught my attention in the rearview mirror. We were on the main four-lane highway that led from

Tallahassee to Adams County. You get used to recognizing unusual driving patterns when you've been on the road as much as most LEOs. There was a car several lengths behind me that was driving oddly. That didn't always mean much these days, but after watching it for a couple of miles, I decided the car was hanging back on purpose.

"There's a car acting squirrely behind us," I told Pete. "Doesn't want to pass."

"Bad guy or do-gooder?" Pete asked.

Even though we were in my unmarked car, most people with a little practice could spot the nondescript Dodge Charger as a cop car, and there were a number of people who didn't like to pass cop cars, regardless of whether they could do it legally. Sometimes it was a bad guy who didn't want us to run his tag. The old ladies and do-gooders didn't like to pass cops because they were too afraid of being ticketed for speeding, even if they weren't.

"It keeps creeping out from behind other cars to peek at us. Looks like they're up to something."

"We're only about five miles from Lake White Circle," Pete said.

"Sounds like a plan."

Lake White Circle was a short loop with a public boat ramp at the center of it. The turn would be to my right and, if I was quick and had a little luck, I could pull through it and come out behind our hanger-on. I put on a little speed, thinking that I would be able to catch up with him in a couple of miles. If he ran, then I'd have my answer and could flip on the lights and give chase.

I suddenly wished I had on my ballistic vest. Of course, the odds were that it was just someone who was being extra cautious around a cop, or someone with a minor warrant out on them.

After I passed the first turn onto Lake White Circle, I slowed down and put on my turn signal, pretending as if the second turn onto the circle had been my intended destination all along. The car had to slow down almost to a crawl to stay two car-lengths behind us. I pulled into the circle and, as soon as I was out of sight of the main road, I accelerated. A quarter of a mile later and I was ready to turn back onto the main road. I expected to have to chase the car down, but instead I caught sight of it coming back toward me.

"That's it!" I said to Pete as it rushed past us, headed back toward Tallahassee.

"That's odd," Pete said, making the words sound like an accusation.

"That son of a bitch was following us." I said, spinning around in the grass median and pouring on the gas.

CHAPTER THIRTEEN

I caught up to the car within a few minutes, only to find it dutifully following the speed limit. I could see that a male occupant was driving. I ran the tags and they came back registered to a Sean Briggs out of Destin. No wants or warrants. The car was a new BMW. Destin and a fancy car… this wasn't a poor guy.

"Help me find something to pull him over for," I asked Pete.

"I'm looking. Could be his taillights don't work," he suggested.

"I'm afraid they do. Whoever is driving is smart. I don't want to give him a chance to object to our stop." Contrary to popular belief, you can't just pull anyone over. Of course you *could*, it just wouldn't hold up in court without just cause.

"Damn it, he's heading for the interstate. Quick, do a search of his name. We need his cell phone."

I handed my phone to Pete, told him what app to use, and he had Sean Briggs's cell phone number in under a minute. I had subscribed to a search service a few months ago and had found it to be pretty handy and a lot quicker than some of the more professional searches.

"All hail the Internet. What now?" Pete asked.

"Text him this: *I have an urgent message. Are you alone? Can I call you now?*"

"Why…"

"Just do it," I told Pete as the other car came even closer to the interstate.

"Done. Oh, I get it," Pete said with a smile.

We watched Sean through the window. Sure enough, he leaned forward and tapped something on his dash. I had no doubt that it was his phone. A second later, my text alert went off.

"He wants to know who the hell I am. Guess you better introduce us," Pete said, chuckling.

"Can do."

I flipped on my blue lights and siren. Briggs hesitated for only a moment before he slowed down and eased off onto the shoulder. I thought again about the ballistic vest in my trunk and remembered a training officer at the academy who had told us that every officer has a ballistic vest. The living ones are wearing them while the dead ones have them in their trunks. At least I had Pete with me for backup. I got out of the car and Pete did the same. The worst spot for an officer to be in a gunfight is the seat of a car.

As I walked to the rear of the BMW, I could see the driver's hands on the top of the steering wheel. He wanted me to feel safe. I looked in the rear windows, making sure there wasn't anyone else in the car. Everything looked okay.

"Keep your hands where I can see them," I said as I continued to approach the driver's window. He'd already rolled it down.

"You have nothing to worry about," he said, which only made me worry.

"May I have your name?" I said, standing beside the car just behind his door. If he went to throw it open, I wouldn't want it hitting me or forcing me into the road.

"Sean Briggs. I'm a lawyer. Though don't hold that against me," he said. "I do have a concealed weapon on me. I also have my license and concealed carry permit in my wallet."

"Where is the firearm?"

"Under the seat," he said, still keeping his hands on the steering wheel.

"And your wallet?"

"Jacket pocket."

"Without turning your head, remove your wallet and hold it out the window."

"You texted me," he said, realizing what had happened. With a sigh, he retrieved his wallet and held it out the window. "It would be interesting to see if that would hold up in court. I'm afraid you'd be in the right having not requested that I answer your text, but rather making it compelling for me. Bravo, officer?"

"I'm Deputy Larry Macklin," I said, though I had a feeling he already knew who I was. I was certain that he'd been following us. I looked at his driver's license and concealed carry permit. According to his license, he was fifty years old and lived on Gulf Shore Drive in Destin. I didn't need to look at his registration since I already knew that the car belonged to him and the odds that he didn't have insurance were less than nil. "Why were you following us?"

"I beg your pardon?"

I was looking in the car, trying to find an excuse for searching it or for arresting him. Better yet, both. The BMW looked like it had just come from the showroom floor.

"I saw you behind me when I was traveling toward Calhoun. When I turned onto a side road, you turned around and came back. Again, why were you following me?"

"I'm mystified. I got off the interstate and was looking for a gas station. I couldn't find one, so I turned around. Now that you mention it, I *did* see your car in front of me. Really, officer, I was just—"

"There's a gas station at the exit," I interrupted.

"Not one that I have a credit card for."

"What is your business in Adams County?"

"None. I just got off the interstate to look for gas."

"Where are you headed?"

"Tallahassee."

"Business or pleasure?"

"Business."

"What kind of business?"

"Lawyer business," he said with a smirk. "That's enough. I'm not going to answer any more questions. If you want to give me a ticket for texting while driving, please get on with it," he said with a slight edge to his tone.

"I'm going to let you off with a warning this time, Mr. Briggs." I wanted to tell him that I'd be looking into his background, but I was getting older and wiser and was learning how to hold my cards close to my chest. I handed his wallet back to him. "You're free to go."

He took the wallet without a word. I stood there for a moment and watched him drive away.

"What do you think that was all about?" Pete asked. He had stayed behind his door while the exchange went on.

"If I were to guess, I'd say he works for Meredith McCune. Just the type of slimeball I'd expect her to hire." I got back in the car and sat there for a minute, searching the Internet. "Bingo! He's not only a lawyer, but ex-military who works as a private detective."

"Nice work if you can get it," Pete said. "With those credentials, he can get a pretty penny for his troubles."

"No doubt. Now why has she hired a private detective to follow me around?"

"She either doesn't trust you to find out who killed her father or *she* killed her father and wants to know if you're getting too close."

"Miss McCune has just asked to be put under the microscope for real now," I said, and called Darlene to fill her in on the latest.

"That's mighty interesting. Good job, speed racer, on catching the little sneak," Darlene said. "I've spent the day running down a dozen people who had a grudge against McCune. I also have several names of men who worked on the oil rig at the same time that Ryan Pappas did."

"I'll tackle that in the morning after I fill you in on Eli's… I'm hesitating, but it really is looking like a murder. I'm going to follow up on the sex worker angle tonight with Eddie. If I can find him, since the little weasel didn't call me back. Hopefully he hasn't fallen off the wagon."

"Maybe he's shopping for lingerie," Darlene said, which caused Pete to laugh out loud.

"The guy has a thing, lay off. If he didn't have a fetish for women's clothes then his family would probably still be running most of the drugs in the county."

"You have a point. Like we were talking about at the taco stand, people have secrets. I actually think you and your CI are very cute together." I could hear Darlene smiling over the phone.

"You're getting close to an HR report for making me feel uncomfortable in my work environment," I joked.

"Tough titties, Geronimo."

"That's it, you're going to hell. I'll see you in the morning."

I dropped Pete off at his house before driving over to Albert Griffin's where Eddie had an apartment above the garage. Mr. Griffin was the county's unofficial historian and his home had become the repository of thousands of records and documents, including the entire catalog of the local paper, which was now extinct. He'd taken Eddie under his wing when Eddie had to go into hiding to keep him safe from his notorious drug-running relatives. It had been good for both Mr. Griffin and Eddie.

"I'm here to see Eddie, but I wanted to talk to you for a minute too," I told Mr. Griffin as he ushered me into his old Victorian house. He used most of the rooms as archives for local history.

"Eddie should be home from work any time."

My mind had a hard time processing his words. "Eddie

has a real job?" Eddie wasn't known for his work ethic.

"He's been working at the library," Mr. Griffin said. "I heard about the McCune murder. Your dad is going to have his work cut out for him now. Any persons of interest yet?" He threw up his hands. "Never mind. I know you probably can't talk about it."

"I wanted to ask you about Eli Waters."

"I heard that he had an accident and died. That's too bad. Nice guy. We need more vegetable stands. It's not easy to buy fresh food these days."

"What do you know about him?"

"Why are you asking? I thought he just had an accident."

"I'm just doing some background."

"Liar. I won't hold it against you though, and you know you can trust me to keep a secret."

"Honestly, the death is just suspicious at this point."

"Eli was an interesting guy. I was doing some part-time work for the paper back in the '80s when he opened the stand and I wrote an article about him. His parents ran a… I think it was some sort of bookstore or publishing house, something like that. He wanted a job that was more down to earth, literally. New to farming. Bought ten acres and opened the stand. I think he was better at buying and selling than he was at growing. He worked with a number of local farmers to get a lot of his produce. Had a gift for sales."

"Hear anything about him being arrested?"

"Yeah, there was something. Not a big deal. Can't remember what, but I don't think it was anything that was ever included in the paper."

"Soliciting a prostitute?"

"Could be. That's a funny subject these days. You have one group worried about sex trafficking and another group who wants to destigmatize sex work. Seems to me legalizing it would go a long way to solving both of their concerns. Most guys who use sex workers would be more than glad if they could do it in a safe environment where they could be sure the women wanted to be there and were clean and safe."

"Too complex for my pay grade. Do you remember any other issues around Eli or his stand?"

"There were a couple of folks who lived nearby who had a problem with him running a business there. I remember a fear-heated county commission meeting about the zoning."

"That would have been when he first opened the stand?"

"No, about a year later. Wait." He got up and headed for the hallway, leaving me sitting in the front parlor. This was part of his routine. Mr. Griffin would frequently start talking about some subject and suddenly remember an article about it in the paper, so he'd head back to the room where he kept all of the back issues. While I waited, I played with one of his assorted collection of cats.

"Here's an article about it," he said, coming back. "This is a quote from one of the people who complained: 'We didn't worry about it when he opened the stand because we didn't think he'd make a go of it.' That was Kyle Akers. Let's see... the commission decided to make Eli jump through a few hoops. He would have to submit a request for a variance. Comply with congestion regulations. Blah, blah. Obviously he was able to comply. I think Akers still lives out there. Ran for the county commission not long after this. Might have been his fight with the stand that pushed him to run. Don't remember. He didn't do very well. Lost in the primary."

"Kyle Akers... I'll canvass the area first chance I get. That's such a rural area. There isn't a single house that has a view of the stand. Hard to imagine that Akers has held a grudge for this long."

"So you do think it's a murder?" Mr. Griffin said.

"Just going down all the rabbit holes." I heard a sound from the back of the house.

"That will be Eddie," Mr. Griffin said, heading toward the kitchen. "You have company!" he shouted as he went. I got up and followed.

Eddie was poking around inside the refrigerator when we

came in. "What?" he asked without looking up.

"It's your old friend," I said.

Eddie pulled his head out of the refrigerator and looked at me with big eyes. He was surprisingly natty in a polo shirt and slacks.

"Oh."

"You didn't return my call."

"I was going to, but we were really busy at the library. We had a dozen school groups in for ghost stories and a puppet play about the headless horseman. It was really neat."

"That's great. I'm glad to see you're doing well," I said, trying to mean it. I'd found it handy having Eddie as an informant. While I wanted good things for him, I also needed him. "Could we talk about a little inquiry I want you to take on?"

"I don't know," he said, frowning. "Everyone at the NA meetings thinks I shouldn't work for you anymore." He looked down at the floor.

"I really just need to ask you some questions. Not a big undercover thing." I looked back and forth between Eddie and Mr. Griffin. He had become very protective of Eddie's sobriety and had lectured me in the past about using my old CI.

"If you just want to ask questions," Eddie said reluctantly.

"There's a sandwich on the top shelf," Mr. Griffin said. He turned to leave, but not before giving me a warning look.

Eddie got his sandwich and we sat down at the table.

"I want to ask you about a couple of guys who may have used sex workers in the county. The first is Horace McCune. Did you know any prostitutes who might have mentioned going out to his place. Particularly one named Candy?"

"Ha, Candy. They're all named Candy."

"I know that. I might be able to get you a description. And you know Eli the Veggie Man? Did you know that he used prostitutes?"

"No, though I guess I'm not surprised. Lot of guys do.

At his age, he'd have to do without if he wasn't going to pay for it," Eddie said, taking a bite out of the sandwich. I didn't point out that a lot of older gentlemen could still find dates that didn't involve money changing hands. "I heard Eli was dead. That sucks. He was a great guy. I actually worked for him when I was a kid until I realized that my dad wanted me to move drugs using the vegetable stand as a cover."

"Was Eli involved with your dad?" This was the first I'd heard of any connection between Eli and drugs.

"No. Dad thought I could do it under Eli's nose. I quit going to work so Eli would fire me. I didn't want to take the chance of getting him screwed over because I was moving drugs. That was about the last I had to do with Dad. Eli used to hand out fruit to anyone he saw hanging out on the street corners. What happened? I heard he had some sort of accident."

I was always amazed at how fast news traveled in the county. I'd hate to tell Mr. Griffin, but this town didn't need a paper to know what was going on.

"I'm not sure what caused his death yet," I said. "But I think he was supposed to meet someone last night. And he had a habit of using sex workers."

Eddie was quiet for a while as he finished his sandwich. Finally, he wiped his mouth and took a drink of water before he said, "I guess I can ask around."

"I'd appreciate that. And don't forget McCune."

"I guess you've been having it pretty rough," Eddie said.

I felt very weird getting sympathy from him. "It's been tough. Dad's worried about the election."

"Mrs. Drake had a voter registration table sat up in the library a few weeks ago. I filled out the form so I can vote for your dad."

"Thanks, Eddie," I said, touched.

"I've got tomorrow off. I'll hang out and see if I can find out anything."

"Eddie, I don't want you to compromise your sobriety. If this is going to be a problem, I can find out what I need to know some other way."

"I'm working the program. I want to help Eli. I'll look at it like one of the steps. Making amends."

I shook his hand and hit the road for home. It was already dark. I was starving and wanted to have a little time with Cara to make up for all the time I'd been spending on the job lately. I thought about what Pete had said about prioritizing and compartmentalizing as I drove home.

All was quiet outside my house. The Laursens' yurt glowed yellow-orange from lantern light. I walked very softly up to my door and opened it. Alvin ran up and greeted me excitedly, sniffing my pants legs.

"Do you want something to eat?" Cara asked as she got off of the couch to give me a hug.

"Please. Anything. I'm starving. I had to watch Eddie eat a sandwich that looked darned good."

"We have Mom's garbanzo bean soup and French bread."

"You sold me."

Cara let me finish half of the bowl of soup before launching into a mini diatribe about her mother and the wedding.

"I really don't know what's gotten into her. It's worse than I was afraid it would be. She's... obsessed."

"I don't know what to tell you, but I'm fine with whatever y'all decide. Though I'd prefer it if you didn't freak out our friends too much," I said, sopping up some of the soup with my bread.

"I'll figure out something," Cara said with a deep sigh. "How is the McCune investigation coming?"

"There's no real trail. Clues and suspects galore, but no clear forensic evidence. Which I'm afraid means that we'll solve it, but not before the election."

"Can your dad win with that hanging over him?"

I shrugged. "A local sheriff's race isn't like a national, or even statewide, race where people are being polled constantly. Who knows what voters are thinking? Talk to people and they'll assure you they're voting for Dad, but there's no telling what will happen when they get in the voting booth. Those damn billboards are hard to ignore, and McCune's murder is like a huge exclamation point on top of them." I'd been trying not to think about any of this. Talking about it just made me feel like we were in an impossible position.

"When I talked to you at lunch, you said that the veggie guy died?"

"Eli Waters. Yeah, his death looks like it's going to be another investigation for me to deal with."

"You said it might be a murder. I'm sorry about that. He was such a nice guy."

"So everyone says, but he had a few quirks. The odds are about nine out of ten that it's a murder. And you shouldn't be on the table." This last was directed at Ivy, who was trying to grab a bite of my French bread. I pulled off a piece, dunked it in the soup and put it and Ivy on the floor.

As I tried to fall asleep that night, I wondered about the two murders. Yes, they were close together in time and space, but were they *really* connected? I told myself that I needed to strongly resist the temptation to link the cases.

CHAPTER FOURTEEN

I hit the deck running the next morning, filling Darlene in on all the details of the Waters case.

"First you turn an accident into a murder, now you want to complicate the McCune case by tying them together," she said after reviewing the crime scene photos.

"Seriously, I'm trying not to. All I really want is a quick solution to both of them."

"I say we proceed with completely separate investigations. If we both end up with the same suspect at the end of the day, then we'll know there's a link."

"I suppose that makes sense."

Darlene gave me a list of men who had worked on McCune's oil rig crew.

"In one way, it doesn't matter whether there was a cover-up of Ryan's death or not. The fact that Mrs. Pappas *believes* there was gives her a motive for killing McCune. Of course, by talking with these guys, we might find other people who have a motive for wanting McCune dead."

"A part of me really wants to look into the disappearance of her son. McCune was a vindictive ass and hurt a lot of people. From what I've seen, his daughter is only better by comparison."

"It's a dickish move to have a private eye follow you around," Darlene agreed before she was interrupted by her phone. She looked at the number and mouthed: *Lt. Johnson.*

"What's up, boss?" she answered, then listened to him for a minute. "That jerk was tailing Larry yesterday. Followed him from Tallahassee. Larry and Pete were in the car and came up with an excuse to stop him."

Apparently the lieutenant had something to say about that.

"I know Larry and Pete have a bad habit of going overboard when they're together, but it sounds like they did it by the book. I'm sure Larry will submit a report on the stop." She looked at me and I nodded solemnly. "Yes, sir. We'd like to keep the equipment shed off limits. The tractor too. It's possible it's the murder weapon." She paused, listening, then added, "She can get in tomorrow. Text me the... gentleman's number and I'll call when we're done."

"Let me guess. Miss I've-Got-More-Money-Than-You wants access to her father's house," I said after Darlene hung up.

"Bingo. We could stall, but it wouldn't get us anything."

"And would make us look like the bad guys. Besides, we could spend the next six months going through that mansion and not get into every nook and cranny. On the bright side, we already have his phones, computers and other electronic devices. These days, that's where all the action is."

"Amen, brother. Let Cruella de Vil have it."

"The question is, does she want in the house because she's guilty and wants a chance to clean up anything she or her assassin might have missed? Or does she want access to the house so she can get her personal Dick Tracy on the case?"

"I'm sure she just wants to savor the memories of her father and the love they shared," Darlene said with a heavy dose of snark.

"Those two, not so much. Have you finished checking her alibi?"

"She was definitely in Texas at the time of the murder. I wish I could get ahold of her phone to see if she called anyone around here during that time. Like we've said, she's the murder-for-hire type."

"I'll check up on this private dick she has on her payroll. He lives in Destin, so that's only a two-hour drive from here." I had a little bee in my bonnet about Briggs after our meeting on the roadside.

"That could mean taking on hours of phone calls. When are you going to investigate Eli's death?" she asked.

"I've got Julio to help me with that. I think I can handle both. To be honest, if I wasn't working on McCune's murder, I'd spend half my time obsessing over what was or wasn't being done with the case. Better for me to work on it and fit in the Waters investigation when I can."

"We can also still use Tom Horton. He's the one who gave me the names of the oil rig workers," Darlene said.

"Nice to have backup," I said, and left her to call Sean Briggs.

My first thought was to hop on the list of oil rig workers, but Darlene had made me feel guilty about Eli's case. There was one thing I could check on pretty easily.

I headed down to our records section to see if I could get a copy of Eli's lewd and lascivious arrest report. Knowing that there would most likely be some sort of baked goods down there had nothing at all to do with my decision to start with records.

Sure enough, there was a plate of some great tasting butterscotch bars. I ate one and grabbed another while I waited for Beth Miller, our head records clerk, to look up the report number.

"Had to dig through the dust for this one," she said, coming out of the back room. "I'll make you a copy." I looked guiltily at a woman who'd been standing at the counter, patiently waiting for an accident report. I turned my back so she wouldn't see me eat the second bar while I line-jumped.

Back at my desk, I settled back and read the two-page report. I'd called it. Eli Waters and Ginger Jenson had been discovered at night in the backseat of a station wagon without any clothes on. The car had been parked behind the Supersave at the time. Apparently, Ginger worked at the grocery store and had just gotten off of work. Move along folks, nothing to see here. I added the report to a folder with the rest of the Waters case notes.

Next I pulled up the list of guys who'd worked on the oil rig with Ryan Pappas. Cold-calling a long list of numbers was time consuming, but at least these days, with so many people relying on cell phones, the odds were good that they would answer the phone regardless of where they might be.

"I don't really remember anything about my time on that rig," was the response I got from the first person to answer their phone.

"Buddy, I hate cops. Get a warrant or get bent," came from a man who I later confirmed had spent a decade of his life in and out of prison when he wasn't working on oil rigs.

"I'm busy. Sorry," followed by dead air was the result of my sixth call. I was beginning to feel like I was trying to sell folks an extended warranty on their car.

The most promising reaction was, "I… No… I don't… remember him." But I could tell that Bob Pittman was lying and he wasn't very good at it. And the slight hesitation made me think that maybe he *did* want to talk. If I could meet him face to face, then I might be able to get somewhere. I checked his address. He lived in Pensacola. Not impossible. I called him back.

"I told you, I don't remember him. Don't ever call me back."

That was more direct. I'd gambled and lost. Sometimes pushing people worked, but other times it just entrenched them. Pittman had dug in deep. I still thought there was a chance, but I'd have to catch him off guard.

I did a quick search for Pittman online. He'd been only nineteen when Ryan Pappas had disappeared. Now he was a professional dog trainer and handler who had even shown at Westminster. I wasn't surprised that he'd left his time on the oil rig out of his professional biography.

Having exhausted the list of possible witnesses to Pappas' disappearance, I still wanted more information. There had been too much stonewalling for there not to be something ugly that people were trying to hide. Though it was entirely possible the cover-up had nothing to do with Pappas. I didn't know much about oil rigs, but I figured there were plenty of opportunities for them to host some shady dealings. Unbidden, the word *drugs* popped into my head. Wouldn't an offshore oil rig be a great way to land narcotics?

Not drugs, I moaned to myself. I really didn't want to get involved with drug dealers again. The money that was involved when drugs came into play made people crazy. And when you weighed the money against the chance of going to jail for life, you ended up with a carrot and stick combination that encouraged people to kill each other over any whiff of betrayal.

Like I was playing a game of ping-pong in my head, I set the McCune investigation aside for the moment and bounced back to the Waters case. I called Julio and asked him if he wanted to meet me out at the vegetable stand.

"I'll be there in twenty," he said, and I could hear his car starting up as he ended the call.

We decided to divide the road in front of the stand by north and south. Julio would go south and canvass the houses on both sides of the road while I did the same going north. It was such a rural area that, even if we both went a mile, neither of us would have more than ten doors to knock on. I had made sure that the grumpy neighbor, Kyle Akers, was on my list.

Akers's property was the first on the west side of the road. The driveway was about two hundred yards from the vegetable stand. The brick house was set back from the road in the middle of a clearing surrounded by pine trees. The yard was neat and tidy, with a couple of ghosts stuck in a hay bale to acknowledge that it was October. I parked behind a new beige Cadillac.

As I got out of my car, I could hear the sound of a chainsaw from behind the house. I went to the front door and knocked, just to be safe, but wasn't surprised when I didn't get an answer. I followed the noise of the saw around the side of the house. A man wearing ear and eye protection was sawing through a good-size pine tree that had broken off about ten feet from the ground. The man was older, probably in his mid-sixties, with just a ring of grey hair around an otherwise bald head.

I waited until he took his hand off of the throttle to announce myself at the top of my lungs. He turned with a surprised expression on his face before choking off the saw.

"Can I help you?" he said in a tone that implied he didn't want to help me at all.

I pulled the leather case with my badge off of my belt and turned it so he could see my ID. "Deputy Larry Macklin. I'm investigating the death of Eli Waters. Are you Kyle Akers?" I asked.

"That's me. But I don't know anything about it except what I heard from my neighbor."

"I just have a few questions," I said, trying to be as non-threatening as possible.

"Told you I don't know anything about it."

"You weren't happy about Eli's business when it opened," I said.

"That's not a question," he shot back, giving me a disgusted look. "Damn it! Fine." He set the chainsaw down on the ground and took off his gear. "Come on. I could use a break anyway."

I followed him over to a patio table where a couple of bottles of water were waiting. He took a water without offering me one and drank about half the bottle.

"Sit down," he finally said and dropped into a chair by the table.

"Did you and Waters ever patch up your differences?"

"No."

"Care to elaborate? Maybe start with telling me why you had a problem with the stand in the first place," I pushed.

"Jeez. 'Cause his customers parked on the side of the road. It was dangerous. County made him put in a parking lot. That was something. But he never had any consideration for the people who lived around here."

"Did other people have a problem with him?" I asked, and from the look on his face I knew the answer.

"Not really. They were worried about the people parking on the road, but after that everybody else was in his pocket. 'He's charming,' they'd say. Ha! A shyster, more like. Always chatting people up. I'm not going to sing his praises now just because he's dead."

"Did you see anyone around the stand Wednesday evening?"

"What's this, Friday? No. We went out Wednesday morning—I had a doctor's appointment—but we were back by two. I can't see his place from here. Thank goodness," he huffed.

"We? Would that be you and your wife?"

"That's right," he said and then cocked his head. "Wait a minute. I thought he died in some sort of accident. Why are you going around asking questions?"

"Just being thorough," I said.

"Don't try to bullshit a bullshitter. Y'all got enough to handle with the McCune murder and the election. You wouldn't be out here unless you thought Eli'd been killed. I know who you are. How could I not with those billboards? So McCune was murdered less than two miles from here and now the vegetable flogger gets offed. Interesting."

I'd underestimated Kyle Akers. I'd assumed he was just a grumpy old neighbor, but he was proving to be pretty astute.

"Did you hear anything on Wednesday evening?"

"No, the weather was warm enough that we still had the air going."

"When was the last time you saw or spoke with Eli

Waters?"

"Now we're getting down to the nitty gritty. I haven't spoken with him in years. The last time I saw him was when I passed his stand about a week ago and he was standing by the gate. It was in the evening, so I assumed that he was closing up. Not that I care what he does. Or did."

"What about your wife? Has she talked to him or seen him recently?"

"No. She liked him even less than I did. Thought he was smarmy. Her word. You're welcome to talk to her."

"I'll check back," I said.

"Look, if the man was killed then you're barking up the wrong tree here. I speak my mind and when I'm done, I'm done. We got a few concessions out of Waters." He shrugged and started to put his work gloves back on. "That was that. If we're done here, I've still got some work to do thanks to Hurricane Marcy."

I left feeling that Akers may not have been the nicest neighbor in the 'hood, but he was unlikely to have pushed Eli down the stairs. First, I doubted that Eli would have turned his back on the man. And second, Akers was the kind of guy who'd punch you in the face, but he wasn't likely to shove you from behind. He liked conflict.

No one answered at the next couple of houses. It *was* the middle of a work day. But I got lucky at the fourth house. It was a small, old clapboard structure that could have used a coat of paint and a trip around the yard with a mower. An older minivan was parked in the dirt drive beside the house.

"What?" asked the young woman who answered my knock at the door. She was holding an infant to her chest and gently bouncing the child up and down.

I showed her my ID and introduced myself. "I wanted to talk to you about Eli Waters."

She looked back at me with a strange expression, but said nothing. "You know, the vegetable guy."

She still looked nervous, but finally said, "Oh, yeah. Nice guy, what about him? He's not in trouble, is he?" Just when you think that everyone is plugged into the local grapevine, you meet someone who is utterly clueless.

"He was found dead yesterday," I informed her.

"That's awful." From the look on her face, I believed that she meant it. "He was a very nice man."

The way she said it was rather odd and I looked at her more closely. She appeared to be close to thirty, though an abundance of worry lines and a slightly well-worn appearance made it hard to tell. Even still, she was quite attractive with high cheek bones and dark hair that enhanced the bright green of her eyes.

"Your name is…?"

"I'm Nadine Gordon," she said, "and this little cutie is Andy." She placed her head against the child's forehead. The boy couldn't have been more than a couple of months old.

"May I come in and ask you a few questions?"

"Sure, come on in. Though I don't know what I can tell you," she said, backing away from the door. Inside there was an odor of old wood and years of people living close to the edge. "Sorry the place is a mess. I haven't gotten back into my routine since I brought him home from the hospital. My girl is ten. She's at school now. I didn't remember how hard it was to come back after having a baby. Of course, I was younger when I had Maddie." She directed me to the couch.

"How well did you know Eli?" I asked and, for just a second, her eyes darted off to the ceiling.

"We moved in here about six months ago. Eli came by and introduced himself. When he saw that I was pregnant and… Well, I guess it was pretty obvious I didn't have a bunch of money, so he brought me some vegetables and fruit from the stand. I never asked him for nothin'. He was just a real nice man. What happened to him? He seemed healthy."

"We're still investigating. How often would you say he came by?"

"A couple of times a week."

"Who else lives in the house?"

"Just Maddie and this little guy." She smiled down at the baby, who was sleeping through our conversation.

"When Eli came by, did you all talk?"

"Sure. What d'ya think, he just threw the bag at me?" She smiled.

"What kind of things did you all talk about?"

"Oh, you know, just the usual stuff. I guess I went on a bit about my ex."

"You're ex?"

"Gene Lambert. Mean Gene. That's what they called him in high school. It should have been a clue, but I didn't listen to no one back then."

"You were high school sweethearts?"

"I guess. We dated, then got married when I was nineteen. A year later, I had Maddie. Six months after she was born, he was gone. I didn't see him again until last year. And like a damn fool, I took up with the skunk again. Bam! He gets me preggers with this one and disappears again. His momma says he's in Alabama, like I care. Gene likes to make babies, but he doesn't want to be around them." She stopped talking for a moment, smiled sadly, then said, "See, that's the kind of nonsense poor Eli had to listen to. He never seemed to mind."

"When would he come by?"

"Around noon when he'd close up the stand for lunch. He told me the stuff he brought me was too ripe to sell, though I think he was just saying that to make me feel better. It all looked fine to me."

"Did he talk much about himself?"

"Sometimes. Talked about being lonely." I saw her wince a bit as though she thought she'd said the wrong thing.

"Nadine, did he ever seem interested in you? In a romantic way?"

From the look on her face, it was clear that he had. "I don't know what… Okay, he might have had… an interest. He was a nice guy. Never did anything… wrong."

"Did he make a pass at you?"

She carefully shifted Andy to her other side before answering. "I'm a big girl. I've been around the block a few times. He liked to look. I didn't mind… flirting a little with him. I know a nice guy when I meet one. I've certainly been around enough rotten apples, Gene included."

"How far did your relationship go?"

"Mostly just looking. Him looking, that is. He never… you know, pulled out his manly parts or anything. I'd just wear clothes that showed a bit more than I'd wear to church, you know. Sit so he could see a bit."

"But he never made a move to… touch you?" I thought this all sounded very strange.

"You act like this is weird or something. My gosh, men go to strip clubs all the time. I think he liked the girl-next-door-type better. I gave him a little show, and he brought me some groceries." She looked at me like I was the Grinch who couldn't understand Christmas.

"Okay, you say he came over right after you moved in. When was the last time he… brought you vegetables?"

"The last time he came by was Sunday, but he just dropped off some apples and a couple of pumpkins for us to carve. He didn't stay or nothin'."

"Was that unusual?"

"Yes. Maddie was at my mother's so I thought he'd come in, but lately he'd seemed… not that interested in coming in. Still came by, but would just say hi and drop off some apples, tomatoes or what have you." She sounded disappointed. "I can't believe he's dead."

"Did he ever mention any trouble he was having?"

"Like what? He would tell me about some of the customers at the stand. Some of them were pretty rude… he mentioned one or two who'd tried to steal from him."

"Was he mad?"

"No, it was all like a joke to him. He told me he looked forward to this one old woman coming every week 'cause she'd cuss at him then, when he'd turn his back, she'd always slip a couple of pieces of fruit into her purse. He said she'd never steal more than a few pieces, no matter how much of an opportunity he gave her."

"Did he ever mention anyone who was mad at him?"

"I can't imagine who'd be mad at him. Eli was such a good guy. I had a friend come to visit. We couldn't get his car started, so Eli came over and worked for an hour 'til he got it running. Who's going to be mad at someone like that?"

"Maybe Mean Gene?" I suggested. She looked startled at the very idea.

"No. I don't think Gene even knew about Eli." But as she said it, I could tell that she thought there might be a possibility.

"Were you still seeing Gene when you moved in here?"

"Not really."

"What's that mean?"

"It means that I was clearly pregnant and Gene was starting to avoid me. I saw that he wasn't going to hang around."

"But he was still in town?"

"Yeah, he came over here a few times. I guess he might have run into Eli coming or going. A couple of times, Gene stayed here over night. I know for sure that one time I left him here while I went to the clinic for a check-up. Gene wouldn't trouble his fat ass to go with me."

I got Gene's last known address and made a note to follow up on him, then thanked Nadine for her time.

Eli sure had liked the ladies. I wondered if he'd ever crossed the line. No complaints had ever been made to the sheriff's office about him, not that that meant much. Women didn't always report men for assaulting them. Though Eli really didn't sound like the type.

CHAPTER FIFTEEN

I finished the houses in my direction, then met back up with Julio and told him what I'd found out.

"Lot of folks not home," he said. "Did find one guy, Peter Sheehan, who said that he saw a car coming out of Eli's driveway after dark on Wednesday. He was driving home when the car started to pull out in front of him. He said the car suddenly stopped and backed up. The man thought it was odd that the car hesitated and then backed a lot farther away from the road than necessary to wait for him to pass. Sheehan saw it pull out just as he reached his house."

"Did he get a look at the car or the driver?"

"No, just saw the headlights. He was pretty sure that it was a car and not a truck."

"So not Eli's truck."

We grabbed barbeque sandwiches to go from Deep Pit and took them back to the office. I shared the autopsy results with Julio while we ate.

"What do you think?" I asked him.

"He was killed by someone he knew," Julio said with certainty.

"Interesting. What makes you think that?" I had my own

ideas, but I wanted to know what Julio was thinking.

"They were behind him on the landing. I think they were in his home before the attack. He walked out with the person following behind him. I also believe the murder was premeditated," Julio continued. "There are only four steps down to the stone path. You push someone down just four stairs, there's no way you can be sure it's going to kill them. But this killer was ready. Shoved Waters and then moved down the stairs and slammed his head down on the pavers to make sure he was dead."

"I agree. Eli certainly didn't feel threatened if he turned his back to walk down the stairs with the person behind him. But, by all accounts, Eli was a nice guy, if a little bit of a polite lecher. A guy like that might trust someone other people wouldn't."

"Like this Gene guy the woman was talking about?" Julio asked.

"Exactly who I was thinking of. Though why Gene would care since he doesn't appear to want to hang around and take care of his kids, I don't know."

"Some guys are like that. They won't step up, but they don't want other guys hanging out with a woman they consider theirs."

"You're right. We'll just have to hunt the guy down and see if he has an alibi."

"I'll find him," Julio said, glancing at his watch. "I need to get back to my day job."

He called dispatch and told them he was in service. Less than a minute later, his radio crackled and dispatch gave him an address on the west side of the county where a woman had reported a burglary.

"Have fun," I said. "I'll text you Nadine's information and what she gave me for Gene's last known address."

Julio nodded, picking up his trash and heading for the door.

I spent some time working on reports before my phone rang. I glanced at the number and was surprised to see that it was Eddie. "Are you allowed to call me?" I asked.

"That hurts, man. I'm trying here," Eddie whined. "I went out of my way to help you."

"Do tell."

"Buy me lunch."

I looked at my watch. It was three o'clock. "I've already had lunch. Besides, you've got a job now," I reminded him.

"I got expenses," he said. "I pay rent and everything."

I knew that Mr. Griffin barely charged him anything for his apartment.

"You didn't offer me anything to eat when you were chowing down on that sandwich last night."

"Man…"

"Okay, meet me at the taco stand in fifteen minutes." It was a short walk from his apartment.

"Excellent. I'm starving."

Eddie was reading the menu when I pulled up. "This is better than meeting in the cemetery," he said after he'd ordered.

I paid the young man behind the counter. "In the cemetery you couldn't stiff me for lunch… or dinner or whatever this is."

"You'll think it's worth it," he promised.

Ten minutes later, after scarfing two tacos, Eddie told me what he'd found out.

"I figured I'd go check out some of my old haunts first thing in the morning 'cause there'd be less chance of someone tempting me with anything. I used to hang out in those places at night. What they say in the meetings is to avoid the old routines."

"I get it. Was there anyone there to talk to?"

The trouble was that drug addicts and sex workers usually slept in. Even the worst neighborhoods were mostly safe from eight in the morning to around noon.

"I had to wake a few people up, but that worked out too.

They were still a little stoned, so they weren't too suspicious of me asking questions. Most of them just wanted to get rid of me."

"Okay, kudos on a good idea. Give with the info."

"I found Candy. She also goes by Tina and Cindy."

"No surprise there."

"She said she'd talk to you if you didn't try to arrest her."

"No worries. She confirmed that she was paid by McCune?"

"Called him a rich creep."

"That's him, all right."

"I thought you were working for the victim?" Eddie chided me.

"Don't push it. There are victims and then there are victims. McCune is only a victim in this case 'cause he's the one who stopped breathing," I said through tight lips.

Eddie gave me Candy's number. "I also found a couple of girls who knew Eli. Wow, that guy was a real horndog," Eddie said, shaking his head.

"That's what I'm learning. What did the women say about him?"

"They all said he was one of their favorite clients. Wished all guys were like him. I think every one of them called him sweet. Two of them were older and cold as ice, but they both had a soft spot for Eli. Felt bad that he was dead."

"How'd you find them so quickly?" I asked, a little suspicious.

"Not hard. Both guys were known. Eli for being the nice veggie man and McCune for being the rich asshole."

"Are the women being run by someone?"

"Eli's are. He got up with them through their pimp. But the girls said he'd always slip them some extra money and give them some produce. Weird."

"Is their pimp going to be mad that they're talking?"

"He's not the nicest guy, but he gave me permission to talk to them. You aren't going to believe this, but he was sorry that Eli's dead too. Said if you want to talk to the girls it's fine, just keep his name out of it."

I didn't like it. Sex work was one thing. You could argue that, if it was clean and regulated, it was a necessary evil. But I'd never met a good pimp. Even the women who ran other women were mean, greedy people who used every underhanded method they could come up with to control the women working for them. But I wasn't working vice and I needed to speak with the girls, so I put the thought of their pimp out of my mind.

"How do I get ahold of them?"

"Here's the number you can call or text. Their names are Patty, Andi and Gloria. Tell the woman who answers the phone that you have Dan's permission to talk to them. She'll schedule you."

I offered Eddie a ride back to his place.

"Albert and I are cooking up a little surprise for your dad," Eddie said, causing me to turn and look at him as I maneuvered through the city streets.

"What?" I asked suspiciously.

"It's a surprise," Eddie insisted. I thought about pressing him, but since Mr. Griffin was involved, I didn't figure it could be anything that would blow up in our faces.

After I dropped Eddie off at his apartment, I called Darlene. "Conference time," I told her.

It was four o'clock by the time I met her in the conference room at the office. "I want to compare notes and come up with a plan of action." The weekend loomed and I didn't plan to waste it. The election was only weeks away.

"I took Shantel with me and we went through McCune's house again. I told Meredith that we'd let her back in the house tomorrow."

"Shantel have any insights?"

"She did find a couple of things that our friends from FDLE might have overlooked. She took a dozen swabs. Mostly looking for DNA that the killer might have missed. I also asked Tom to check backgrounds and alibis for some of the people that Miss McCune included in the portfolio she handed us the first time we met her. Most of them are in Texas, Louisiana or Mississippi, so it shouldn't be hard to check some of them off the suspect list.

"I also talked to Judge Perkins and the prosecutor to see what we need to do to get a look at Meredith McCune's bank statements and phone records. Maybe that will tell us if she hired someone to do her dirty work. Finally, I started digging into her lawyer's background. I was barely done with the third call when he called me up himself and told me that snooping into his background was a waste of time and resources."

"Which is exactly what the killer would tell you."

"Yep."

"A lawyer and a private investigator. There's not a chance in hell he'd let us interview him. Wonderful," I grumbled.

"I still haven't tracked down Sam Pappas, Ryan's father. I watched an interview that he did with a local news channel on the first anniversary of Ryan's disappearance. He still seemed pretty determined then to find his son, and in the interview he wasn't too shy about pointing a finger toward the people on the oil rig. "

"Celina made it sound like he divorced her because he wanted to move on. The Pappases need to remain close to the top of the suspect list. Which brings up something I wanted to talk to you about. I really want to follow up on their son's disappearance."

"How? You said that all the possible witnesses stonewalled you."

"I've got an idea about one of them. It will involve me driving over to Pensacola and a little subterfuge."

"Subterfuge. You're bringing out the five dollar words now."

I told her my plan. "Of course, it could take a few weeks to schedule."

"I don't consider it a high priority. Like you said, it's obvious that Celina Pappas thinks that McCune had a hand in, at the very least, covering up her son's disappearance.

Whether he did or not is just an interesting side note. Though, if it's true, it could help to develop more suspects… like we need more."

"Let's find a phone and I'll get the ball rolling."

I wanted to use a phone that Pittman the dog handler wouldn't be likely to recognize the area code or number for. I wasn't worried about him recognizing my voice. I probably hadn't said more than a few dozen words the two times we'd talked on the phone.

I knew exactly where to go for a phone. Sergeant Sims, the head of our vice division, kept several phones with different area codes. They'd use them when they were running a sting on drug dealers or sex offenders.

"Mr. Pittman, my name is Jeff Lear. My wife and I want to get into showing dogs. I understand from your website that you give consultations and lessons. I'd like to schedule a consultation. We have a Great Dane we'd like to show. Call me back when you have the chance," I said to Pittman's answering machine.

"Does he show Great Danes?" Darlene asked.

"There's a picture of him with a Dane on his website." I shrugged. "This is just a shot in the dark. He might be booked out months in advance." The words were barely out of my mouth when the borrowed phone rang.

"Hi, Mr. Lear. My appointment for this Sunday afternoon has cancelled. If you're interested, we can meet then."

With just seconds to decide, I blurted, "Sure. Sunday will be great."

"Fine. You'll need to bring the dog that you want to show. I'll evaluate him. Have you shown at all?"

"No."

"Well, the first lesson you'll need to learn is to have thick skin. I'll be honest with you. If I don't think your dog has any show potential, I'll be blunt. But don't worry. If you need to find another dog, I'll be glad to advise you in picking out one with potential."

"That sounds great," I stammered. Darlene just shook

her head as I got Pittman's address and finalized our meeting time.

"I wish I could be there when he sees Mauser," she said with a wicked grin.

"Guess I need to ask Dad if I can borrow his dog," I said, realizing at the same time that I'd need to let Cara know that I wouldn't be around on Sunday. She wasn't going to be happy with me leaving her alone with her parents all day.

Dad was still in his office. His assistant had already left for the day, so I knocked on the door, then let myself in. He was busy working on reports for the department's accreditation. Every few years, the sheriff's office was reviewed as part of our national accreditation and the prep work could be brutal.

"If I lose, I won't miss the paperwork," Dad said morosely. "How are the investigations coming along?"

I gave him the rough outlines.

"So our two victims are the nicest man, if a bit of a pervert, and the meanest man in the county. From the sound of things, neither of these cases is going to be wrapped up easily."

"Not without a bit of luck. Speaking of luck, we're going down one line of inquiry in the McCune case that I need Mauser's help with."

He raised his head and really looked at me for the first time since I'd entered his office, his green eyes curious. "This ought to be interesting," he said, leaning back in his chair.

I explained about Celina Pappas and her missing son. I went on to describe the cold shoulder I'd received from all the possible witnesses. Finally, I told him about Bob Pittman and my hope that, if I could talk to him face to face, I might be able to get him to tell me something about Ryan Pappas.

"Sounds like a long shot."

"I was figuring on tackling it later, but things just fell into place."

"I guess Mauser won't mind the road trip. I've been

spending so much time at work and on the campaign that he could use some extra stimulus."

His idea of stimulus begins and ends with food, I thought, but wisely kept it to myself.

I arranged to pick Mauser up Sunday morning. I'd be able to drive over to Pensacola, meet with Pittman, and be back home by early evening.

Before I pulled out of the parking lot, I called Cara, who should have just been finishing up at the clinic.

"I just have a couple more things to do before I leave," she told me. "When do you think you'll be home?"

"Not long after I spend time with some sex workers," I said, hoping she'd find the humor in it.

"You're a funny guy. Wait… You're not kidding, are you?" I could hear the wariness in her voice.

"It's actually in relation to both investigations. But I've got some other bad news. I have to drive over to Pensacola on Sunday." I didn't see any point in candy-coating it.

"I'm going with you," she said firmly.

"I…" I ran through all the pros and cons, but then decided it didn't matter because Cara wasn't going to give me a choice. "Okay."

I explained to her what the plan was. After she finished laughing, she said, "Then it's perfect. You told Pittman that your wife was interested in showing too, so having me along will be a plus."

"Sure, I guess."

I said goodbye to her, still trying to figure out how I'd gotten to that point. I was just going to talk to a witness. There wouldn't be anything hazardous involved, except for the possibility that Pittman might throw us out on our ears when he found out why we were really there. Then another thought came to mind. I hadn't gotten a price for the consultation from Pittman and, with the way the department's finances were, I didn't see Dad agreeing to pick up the tab. *How much could it be?* I thought.

CHAPTER SIXTEEN

I decided to talk with Eli's harem first. The call was answered by a woman with an accent that I couldn't quite place. I explained what I wanted.

"Yeah, yeah. I was told you would call. Ummmmm, Patty has half an hour free. Get there fast," she said.

She texted me an address that was only five minutes from the office. It was in a seedy neighborhood known as the Ditch, where I'd spent way too much time last month. I didn't have any trouble finding the older duplex. Any deputy who'd worked the streets for more than a couple of months was familiar with the area. The homes had been starter homes decades earlier, but now most of them were rented out to young people, old people and poor people. Most nights there were numerous calls for service to the area, with domestic disputes and burglaries dominating.

I knocked on the door and heard someone on the other side, no doubt giving me the eye through the peephole. "You're daddy sent me," I said, repeating the code phrase that the woman had given me. It made me feel like I was starring in an old movie.

The door opened slowly. "You're a cop," the petite girl with pink and purple hair informed me. "That's cool. Not my first."

She walked into the house, leaving the door open for me. The room smelled of pot and there was a variety of colored bulbs in the lamps. I felt high just being in the room. Patty sat down on the futon and started to pull up a skirt that was already too revealing. She obviously had the wrong end of a very long stick.

"Apparently they didn't explain that I was just coming over to talk," I said. "Please sit up."

She gave me a grumpy look. "Shit! No one ever tells me anything."

"I want to talk to you about Eli Waters," I said, and there was a strange transformation in her features. She went from being a hardened sex worker to a sad woman in the blink of an eye.

"Man, that was such a bummer. I don't know what I can tell you," she said, picking up a vape pen and beginning to puff.

"He was one of your clients?"

"Not so much in the last year. I think he may have been seeing someone else."

"So you haven't seen him lately."

"I didn't say that. About once a month, he'd come by and bring me some stuff. Fruit, mostly. I told him I wasn't really a veggie eater."

"He just came by to bring you fruit?" I was a bit incredulous. How was the man making any money at all, giving produce away to every skirt in town?

"We'd talk and have a laugh, but he never tried nothin'. Sometimes I'd just give him a peek 'cause I knew he got a kick out of it."

"Did he do drugs or engage in any other activities?" I asked what I thought was a reasonable question, but her eyes narrowed angrily.

"Eli was a good guy. He didn't do drugs or nothin'."

"Do you know of anyone who might have wanted to hurt him?"

"Eli?" She sounded floored by the very idea. "There was a little issue years ago when Eli first started using us girls. Our manager thought he might be getting some when he came by without an appointment. Thought he was being cheated out of his cut. But they got that straightened out."

"Did he have any kinks?" I asked and again got the hurt look.

"No. I tell you, he was the best. You don't really think that someone hurt him, do you?"

"I don't know. We're looking into it."

"When are they… you know, going to bury him?" she asked.

"I don't know."

"I guess his family wouldn't want me there anyway," she said. I decided to ignore that comment.

"One more question. Have you ever done business with a man by the name of Horace McCune? An older man, unpleasant, rich." I told her where he lived.

"Doesn't sound like anyone I know. Most of my clients come by right after they get their paycheck, if you know what I mean."

I knew exactly what she meant. Her clients fell solidly between the middle class and the working poor.

There was a knock at the door and a gruff, masculine voice that sounded half-drunk said loudly, "Your daddy done sent me."

"That's my next appointment," she said, putting down the vape pen and standing up.

I thanked her and made a point of glaring at her client as I walked out.

I called Candy next. She agreed to meet with me if I paid for her time. I explained that I would *not* be paying and that she should be bloody grateful I wasn't bringing her into the sheriff's office for a formal interview as a material witness.

I was sitting in her apartment less than half an hour later. She was very attractive. There was just the hint of sex worker in her clothes and makeup. With just a few tweaks, she would have looked fine at any social affair.

"How often did you meet with Horace McCune?" I asked.

For a minute I thought she was just going to stare at me with her cold, flinty eyes. Finally, she said, "He contacted me through my online profile about a year ago. We met every Friday for the first six months. Less often recently. Maybe once a month. I blame that stuck up maid of his."

"Why's that?"

"I could tell she was making snide remarks behind my back. I bet she was telling him it was a sin seeing me or some such crap."

"Was he a good client?"

"He was an asshole, but he paid well and never cheated me."

"How was he an asshole?" The question made her look away from me.

"He liked to call me names and humiliate me. That's not that unusual. But with a lot of guys, it's just a game. He meant every nasty word."

"But you still went back?"

"It's a job. You get good clients and bad clients. Good clients are the ones who pay on time, bad clients are the ones who don't," she said with a sneer.

"Did you ever see anyone else at the house?"

"Just the iron bitch."

"Did he ever talk about someone who might have been after him?"

"He never talked to me. He just did his thing and spit venom while he was at it." She shook her head. "That's not quite true. He always offered me a drink. He'd make some, like, weird small talk before we went upstairs."

"Weird small talk?"

"Yeah, it was like he was talking to someone who knew him or gave a shit. I'd just nod my head and say things like, 'Sure, honey.' He seemed to like that. Then the games would begin. He was rough without being too kinky. Wham-bam and we were done. He let me stay at the house overnight sometimes. I guess that was pretty nice of him. He didn't have to. Paid me for a whole night, even though I only had to spend a couple of hours with him."

My other questions didn't dig up any other information.

Once I got home, I found Cara and her parents sitting around the fire. A breeze had come up from the north and the air was cool. Cara looked relaxed, which was quickly explained by the large glass of wine in her hand. I noticed the bottle sitting on the ground next to her seat. I went inside to change and grab a couple of beers, then sat down on the ground beside her.

"I don't like the cop thing," Anna said, "but this undercover trip to Pensacola pretending to be dog handlers sounds exciting."

I'd decided it would be easier if I was just honest about where we were going and what we were doing on Sunday. It couldn't hurt the investigation and might help to smooth any other issues.

"Man, is he going to be surprised when he sees Mauser," Henry said with a loud chuckle. "That dog is something else. If you can bring him by when you come back Sunday night, I'd love to see the big goof again." Henry was a certified member of the Mauser fan club.

"Do you have to work tomorrow?" Cara asked.

"The only thing I have to do is meet Darlene so we can go out to McCune's place and officially turn it over to his daughter." I could tell that Cara wanted to ask me why I needed to be there, but she didn't. "Darlene is going to text me in the morning when she knows the exact time we're to meet Meredith. It will probably be close to noon. I promise it won't take more than two hours."

Cara gave me a brave smile just before her mother suggested that they should spend the morning considering what aroma the wedding should have. Cara's smile fell quickly.

"If you have time in the morning, I'd like your thoughts on the carving," Henry said to me.

I downed my second beer and Cara and I made our excuses. Inside the house, we found Alvin asleep on the couch with Ivy curled up on the back behind him. I envied them. They were only mildly inconvenienced by the future in-laws.

"Let's go straight to bed," Cara said and I didn't argue.

We enjoyed a little love-making before we both fell into a deep sleep that wasn't interrupted until the sun was well above the horizon. Even then, we stayed in bed a few minutes longer, holding hands and trying to give each other a bit of strength as we faced the new day.

After breakfast, I spent part of the morning staring at Henry's carving, though it didn't have much detail yet. He pointed out different angles of the wood and what they were saying to him. I didn't understand what he was talking about, but there was no doubting his sincerity. I managed to make a few polite comments, though I'd be hard pressed to explain what I'd meant by them.

"Anna seems rather… obsessed with the wedding," I ventured after deciding that we'd worn out the topic of the half-carved piece of oak.

"She's got her reasons. It's not really my place to talk about it. Anna doesn't have many hang-ups, but this is one. I'll see if I can get her to talk to Cara about it."

Darlene texted me at ten-thirty and said that Meredith would meet us at noon. Not wanting to spend any more time than was necessary dealing with the handoff, I told Darlene I'd meet her there.

"You don't have to come," Darlene said, sensing my mood.

"No. I want to see and talk with Meredith again. Also, I think we both need to be there to walk her through the place. It will give us a chance to watch her reactions and emphasize the places that she won't have access to until we're satisfied we've gotten all the evidence we're going to get."

"Agreed. I've got seals and locks for the workshop where the tractor is parked."

With our plans made, I hung up and got ready to go. Cara walked me to the car and I promised her I'd be back soon.

When I got to McCune's place, I saw that Meredith and Darlene were already there. Meredith's rented Mercedes was in front, with Darlene's unmarked parked right behind it. The driver's door of Darlene's car was open, but I couldn't see Darlene or Meredith. However, when I stepped out of my car, I heard Darlene speaking loudly and insistently into her phone.

I jogged around the cars to find Meredith lying on the ground in front of her car with blood all over her stomach. With one hand holding her phone, Darlene was trying to put pressure on the wounds while avoiding the knife sticking out of Meredith's side.

Uncharitably, I thought, *Damn it, this is going to take longer than two hours.*

CHAPTER SEVENTEEN

My first instinct was to rush to Meredith's side, but I realized that time was ticking away for her. I stopped myself and went to my trunk, grabbing a small trauma kit which held items for dealing with stab and gunshot wounds.

Darlene reached for the bag when I joined her and handed the phone to me. "It's Hondo. He's ten minutes away." Alejandro Valdez, known by his friends as Hondo, was one of the best paramedics in the county. He was also Darlene's boyfriend.

"Hey, Larry, glad you're there, pal," Hondo told me. "Make sure Darlene keeps that compression on. Do you have a cuff in the bag?"

It took me a second to realize he was talking about a blood pressure cuff and not handcuffs. "No."

"No worries. Just try to stop the bleeding. And don't move the knife." This was followed by a flurry of Spanish invective hurled at whatever driver wasn't getting out of his way.

Meredith was breathing heavily, but in a steady rhythm. Her eyes were slightly glazed and wide open.

"Her eyes are dilated and she's very pale," I told Hondo.

"She's going into shock. Put a blanket on her legs if you

can. I'll be there in five if this *hijo de puta* will get out of my way," he said and hung up.

I reached into the kit and pulled out a packet with an emergency blanket.

"Who did this to you?" Darlene asked Meredith.

Meredith didn't seem able to focus on the question, so Darlene bent low over her face while making sure to keep pressure on the oozing wound. "Tell me who did this," Darlene said in a slow, firm voice.

"I don't know," Meredith said, her breath coming faster.

"Calm down. The ambulance is coming. You're going to be fine. Try to focus, Meredith. Tell me everything you can remember about the attack."

Meredith's eyes roamed to a spot over Darlene's shoulder as she tried to concentrate. "I don't know. They came up behind me," she said with effort.

"Did they say anything?"

"No."

"Did you notice anything when you drove up?"

This time Meredith didn't answer. In the distance, I could finally hear a siren approaching.

A thought occurred to me and I ran back to my car for an evidence bag. As Hondo's ambulance pulled into the driveway, I quickly took the evidence bag and wrapped it around the handle of the knife, using tape from the trauma kit to secure it.

"Maybe we'll get lucky and get some fingerprints or DNA," I said.

"Good thinking," Darlene said grimly, looking down at Meredith. Her eyes were closed now and her breathing had become ragged and shallow.

"Hey, sweetcakes," Hondo said, jogging over to us. His comment may have been directed at Darlene, but Hondo's attention was fixed squarely on his patient. He set his med kit down and started taking her vitals. Another EMT who I didn't recognize rolled a stretcher up behind him.

Working fast and efficiently, the EMTs had Meredith

stabilized and on the stretcher in minutes. As they wheeled her to the ambulance, Hondo told the other guy, "You drive." Then he turned back to us and said, "I'll let you know how things are once we get her to the hospital."

As soon as they were gone, Darlene and I looked at each other.

"You're a bloody mess. Literally," I told her.

"She was pumping out when I got to her."

I tried to remember where the wounds were on Meredith's body. Both were on the right side. The knife had been left in the wound closest to the middle of her body, but still to the right of her centerline.

"She said the attacker came up from behind her," Darlene said. "Curious… You'd think that if you snuck up behind someone with the intention of stabbing them, then you'd just plunge the knife into their back."

"Maybe she turned around at the last moment."

"Everyone thinks they have a sixth sense about being watched, but I'm not so sure. Maybe when we figure out the sequence of events, it'll make more sense."

"Where did the person come from?" I asked. I looked around for any sign that another car had been parked nearby recently.

"They could have been parked where I am. It's hard to tell how long the attack had taken place before I showed up. Though, considering the fact she was still alive, it couldn't have been long. I know for a fact that no one pulled out of the driveway from the time that I could see it from the road. I was focused on the driveway the whole time, wondering if I was going to be the first person here."

I pulled out my phone and dialed Shantel.

"I'm at home carving pumpkins with my nieces," Shantel said. "I told you I was glad to be able to come out to crime scenes again, but that doesn't mean I want to do it on my days off."

"I can call FDLE and see—"

"Don't you dare! I'm on my way. Nisha is on call. I'll get

her to meet me there with the van," Shantel told me. In the background, I could hear her nieces shrieking and laughing. "Don't throw pumpkin guts at your sister!" was the last thing I heard before Shantel hung up the phone.

Taking a deep breath, I called Cara and, as gently as possible, explained the situation and told her that I was going to be awhile. She accepted it with grace.

Half an hour later, Darlene and I were joined by Shantel and Nisha Branch, another one of our techs. We spent an hour filming and photographing the scene. Once we were done, I retrieved Meredith's phone from the center console of her car.

There were several missed calls. I found where she had called Darlene that morning to confirm their meeting, but it didn't look like Meredith had made any other calls since then.

"Unfortunately, on this gravel drive there isn't any chance that someone left tire tracks," Darlene said.

"There's enough room for someone to have parked beside Meredith," I pointed out.

"Or for Meredith to have pulled up alongside another car."

"You would have thought she would have said something if there'd been another car here."

"She was in a pretty bad way," Darlene reminded me.

"Where was she when you drove up?"

"In front of her car. When I pulled in behind her, I couldn't see more than her head and shoulders from where I parked. In fact, at first I didn't think anything was wrong. I just thought she was standing there waiting for us."

"When did you notice something was wrong?"

"She must have collapsed onto the hood of her car, 'cause she kind of disappeared from view. I got out and when I reached her driver's-side door, I saw her leaning on the hood. Then I noticed all the blood and went over to her. She leaned against me and I eased her to the ground. That's where you found us."

"How much blood was there when you got to her?" I asked.

"You thinking she might have waited until I pulled in and then stabbed herself?"

"I'm only half considering the possibility. I'll admit those looked like some serious wounds."

"It wouldn't be the first time that someone has stabbed or shot themselves in order to deflect suspicion," Darlene allowed.

"I just can't imagine doing it. I'm not a fan of knives anyhow," I said, remembering my own encounter with a knife and Hondo's ambulance.

"We'll see if she pulls through and how serious the doctors say the wounds are," Darlene said.

We started walking the area, tagging potential evidence.

"We'll need to canvas the neighborhood again to see if anyone noticed a car parked here or someone lurking about," I said.

"Evidence first," Darlene insisted. As if to emphasize her statement, we heard a rumble of thunder in the distance. "A front is moving through this afternoon. According to the National Weather Service, there's going to be a hard line of showers coming with it."

I pulled out my phone and called dispatch.

"I need a tow truck out here now. Don't take any of their bullshit about getting here in an hour. We have a vehicle that may contain evidence on the body and we don't want it washed off by the rain. If they give you any crap, I'll talk to them."

Fifteen minutes later, a grumpy old man with a flatbed tow truck showed up. In an ideal world, it would have been best to take the car to the office in an enclosed trailer, but on short notice that wasn't an option.

"Going to charge the county extra for the rush job," the man harrumphed to no one in particular.

"We need to beat the rain," I explained.

"You and everybody else," he complained, squatting

under the car to attach the chain that would pull it up onto the truck. Once that was done, he walked up to Meredith's car to reach inside and shift it into neutral. I took one look at his greasy hands and stopped him.

"I'll do it," I told him.

"Do it right. I'm not paying for any damage caused by your screw up."

"Friend," I said in a very unfriendly way, "a woman was just attacked next to this car. Have some consideration and shut the hell up."

He looked like he was about to shoot me a bird before he reconsidered and brushed his hand over the top of his head. "Whatever," he managed before throwing the lever to start the tow line.

The four of us finished scouring the yard for evidence just before the rain came. Shantel even managed to fingerprint the black metal gates with the thought that if someone had arrived on foot and was standing out there waiting for Meredith to arrive, they might have put their hands on the gate to peer into the property. She picked up half a dozen usable prints. Time would tell if they were also useful.

"Can we test the car now?" I asked Shantel, anxious to see what the vehicle would tell us. I couldn't stop thinking about the chance that Meredith had stabbed herself. We had been able to see smears of blood on the hood of the car, but since it was black it was impossible to see clear patterns or prints.

"While you do that, I'll check out the neighboring houses," Darlene said, getting into her car.

I followed Shantel and Nisha back to the office. We'd asked someone from dispatch to meet the tow truck and make sure that the car was off-loaded into a small storage building located behind the sheriff's office. When we got there it looked like they'd got it right, including surrounding the car with orange cones and crime scene tape so that it wasn't disturbed. Luckily there were no windows in the building, so we could do the luminol test immediately.

"I'm particularly interested in the front of the car," I said.

If Meredith *had* stabbed herself, then doing it while concealed by the front of the car would have been the perfect plan. She would have been able to do it as soon as Darlene drove up, knowing that help was mere seconds away.

After turning out the lights, Shantel brought the luminol and spread it evenly over the front of Meredith's rental car. I felt a little bad for the rental agency. They wouldn't be getting this car back anytime soon, and there was no telling what the paint job would look like when they did. *What the heck, insurance will pay for it*, I thought.

I could barely make out the glow of the luminol. "What do you think?" I asked Shantel and Nisha, as Shantel moved around the car and took pictures.

"There are a few smears here," Nisha said, pointing to glowing streaks on the hood of the car. Nisha had been an intern and had been hired full time partly to fill Marcus's position. Though she was much less experienced, I'd noticed Shantel giving Nisha room to give input and the opportunity to shine and, occasionally, to be wrong. "And I think those are sprays of blood," she said, pointing to a spot that I agreed looked like arterial spray.

"Hard to judge what it means. I think we'll have to leave that up to the blood splatter experts," I said. The interpretation of blood evidence was not as cut and dried as some people thought. You had to judge the damage to the victim as well as the visual display of the blood. In a courtroom, it wasn't unusual to have blood splatter experts supporting both the defense *and* the prosecution.

"We ought to do the rest of the car," Shantel said. I think she was getting some pleasure out of wrecking the finish of the Mercedes.

"Sure, what the hell," I said.

She was right. It could be illuminating, pun intended, to see if there was blood evidence anywhere else on the exterior of the car. If there were blood smears on, say, the driver's door, then that would bolster Meredith's story by showing that she had been attacked before Darlene pulled into the driveway. But while there was some blood on the left front fender, everything else was clear.

"I'm trying to remember exactly where Meredith was lying on the ground," I said, pulling out my phone to look at some of the photos I'd taken. I had shots of the spot where Darlene had been working on Meredith, but nothing that showed its exact location in respect to the car. From memory, Darlene and Meredith had been about six feet from the front of the car and slightly to its left side. "The question is, could the blood have gotten there while Meredith was moving from the hood of her car to the spot where Darlene was tending to her?"

Shantel finished taking pictures and flipped the lights back on. Just then, my phone rang with a call from Darlene.

"She's going to live," Darlene said without preamble. "Hondo just called. She was lucky. According to the surgeon, her only real risks were from shock and blood loss. However, he said that if the knife had gone a little more toward her centerline, it would have done some serious damage to her liver and could have severed an artery that would have caused her to bleed out."

"Interesting," I said, though that really didn't help us much. It didn't rule out the possibility that Meredith had done it to herself, though you'd have to have some nerve to ram a knife into your gut, twice.

I started to tell Darlene about the luminol tests, but she stopped me. "Hold up on that. I've got a couple more doors to knock on and I want to get it done before the heavy rain comes. Call me back in half an hour."

I hung up and called Dad.

"I heard," he said when he answered. Didn't anyone just say "Hello" anymore?

"At least she'll survive. Seems the wounds were bad, but could have been much worse."

"Wonder if she's had any medical training," Dad said, clearly going down the same path as I had.

"Good question. Or if she's recently Googled internal organs. Not that we're likely to get access to any of her electronic devices."

"Are you still going to Pensacola tomorrow?"

I knew that Meredith wouldn't be up to much questioning for a day or two. Since she'd already told us that she hadn't seen the person who'd attacked her, she had every right to expect some time to recover.

"I am. Cara is going with me."

"Great, Mauser enjoys being around her."

"What am I, chopped liver? The big lout had better appreciate all the times I've looked after him."

"Mauser tolerates you," Dad said, and I could actually hear some humor in his voice. He had always been a bit of a hardass, but with the stress he'd been under lately, he'd come dangerously close to losing his sense of humor. It was good to hear him joke around, even if it was at my expense.

"I'm supposed to meet Pittman at noon, so I'll be by to pick up Mauser and the van before eight."

"He'll be ready."

When I got back to my car, I dug out the phone that Sergeant Sims had given me and checked it for messages. Nothing. I texted Pittman and confirmed our appointment for the next day. Within minutes I received a thumbs-up emoji.

I called Darlene back.

"No one heard or saw anything. I've knocked on every door for a mile in both directions. The only thing I accomplished was to send everyone's paranoia sky high into the red zone. Can't say I blame them, what with both a murder and a knife attack in less than a week. What are you up to, Buck Rogers?"

I told her about the results of the luminol test.

"We're going to have to lay it all out. I've been racking my brain trying to remember exactly what I saw when I drove up. Remind me to get a dash cam installed in my car. Not that it would have shown much with her car in the way. But it might have helped with the timing." Darlene was talking to herself as much as to me.

"I'm still going over to Pensacola tomorrow and see if I can find out anything else about Ryan Pappas' disappearance."

"While you're doing that, I'll check up on some of our suspects and see where they were at the time of today's attack. We know exactly when the attack occurred, so if any of the suspects have a rock solid alibi, we can eliminate them."

"I think it's safe to assume that whoever rammed that knife into Meredith McCune is our murderer. Even if that person *is* Meredith."

Once again it was dark before I finally made it home. It had stopped raining, but a few lingering drops still fell from the oak trees. Cara, looking tired and worn, ran out to meet me at the car. I kissed her and she pulled me into a tight hug. I was glad that she would be going with me the next day. It would do us both good to get out of the county for a while.

"I'm sorry about today," I whispered into her hair.

"It's fine," she said, though I could tell that she was crying. "Really, I'm okay. Just feeling a bit overwhelmed."

"We could tell your parents that we need some time alone. I'm sure they'd understand."

"I know, I know. But I don't want them to feel like they've done something wrong. Mom's just being Mom. And I'm also worried about you and your dad."

I put my hands on her shoulders and made her look at me. "Cara, you could have been killed last month," I told her, brushing a lock of red hair from her damp cheek. "You need to think about yourself, love. If you want some time alone, or if you want to talk to someone, you should. You know, if that had happened to me, the department would have insisted that I see a counselor."

"I'll be fine. I swear," she said, wiping the tears away and taking my hand. She led me up to the house. "Mom's inside making grilled cheese sandwiches and soup for dinner. She also made mozzarella and tomato sandwiches for us to take tomorrow."

"Let's enjoy tomorrow," I said. "There's a little bit of business to do, but we'll have almost eight hours away from our troubles."

"Deal. Plus we'll have your four-legged brother along."

"Arrgggh! You just ruined it!" I said, chuckling and smacking myself in the forehead as she opened the door. I heard panting and looked down. "We could take Alvin along too," I offered.

"Are you kidding? He loves my mother. While she's cooking, she drops goodies for him. I need to take him into work to see how much weight he's gained." Alvin immediately wandered off as though he'd heard her threat of a date with the scale.

CHAPTER EIGHTEEN

We got to Dad's just before eight. The front had moved through, leaving the air cool and dry with a strong north wind—Mauser's favorite weather. Dad had already packed his travel bags in the van, so all we needed to do was collect the oaf and load him up.

"I even gave him a bath yesterday evening to help keep up appearances," Dad said as Mauser frolicked around Cara. "You say this guy is a dog handler?"

"According to his website, he's handled dogs in some of the biggest shows in the country."

"Do you really think he's going to tell you anything if you show up lying about wanting to show Mauser?"

"I don't know. What I *do* know is that no one, including Bob Pittman, was willing to talk to me about Ryan Pappas. I don't have anything to lose." *Except for whatever exorbitant fee he charges for his time*, I thought. *Maybe when he finds out why I'm really there and kicks me out, he* won't *charge me.*

"Good luck," Dad said as though he was sure I was going to get the shaft. "Find out what he thinks of the big boy before you tell him why you're there."

We packed the monster into the van and headed for Pensacola. Along the way, we stopped at Falling Waters State

Park for a break. Mauser sniffed up and down the trails, exploring the scents of hundreds of animals, both domestic and wild.

"What do you think?" I said, looking down at the staircase that descended seventy-five feet into a sinkhole. The park got its name from the waterfall that flowed down the side of the sink.

"He'd probably go down there… But I'm not so sure we could get him back out." Cara was right. Mauser was happy to climb down stairs, but he wasn't a big fan of climbing *up*.

"You've got a point. Mauser being the stubborn ox that he is, we'd probably end up stuck down at the bottom for days."

"That's okay. It's nice just watching the waterfall from here," Cara said, taking my hand. It would have been a very romantic moment if my other arm hadn't been almost pulled out of its socket by Mauser trying to lunge for another fascinating scent ten feet away.

"Ready for lunch?" I asked.

"It's early yet. Why don't we wait until after this trainer kicks us off of his property," Cara said with a grin.

"Deal."

We got to Pensacola with time to spare, which was good because we had to hunt around a while to find the dirt road that led out to Pittman's training facility. His property was on the north side of town in a rural area with a mix of homes that spanned the economic scale. Pittman's was on the upper end of things with a fancy gate that reminded me of the one that guarded McCune's estate.

"Nice digs. At least we're going to be booted out of a nice place," Cara said as Mauser hung his head over the front seat, drooling in excitement.

"You're failing undercover show dog," I told him. In response, he shook his head and sent slobber everywhere.

"Terrific," I said, wiping the slime from my face.

Pittman's log home was modest compared to the two steel barns located behind it. I parked near the house and got out.

"I'm up here at the ring," I heard a man shout and looked to see a burly, blond-haired man waving at me from the entrance to one of the buildings. "Come on over."

I walked to the side of the van and opened the sliding door. "Showtime," I said to Cara and Mauser.

As soon as the Dane was out of the van, he stuck his nose straight up, smelling the air and dancing around on top of my feet.

"Fly right or get grounded," I told him.

Cara smoothed back her hair and smiled at me. Her blue eyes were bright with excitement.

We started toward the building, which was about a hundred yards away. Pittman stood in the entrance and watched us approach. I wasn't sure if he was judging Mauser or Cara and me. Probably all three of us.

"Hmmmm, I see," he said, staring at Mauser. After a second he looked up at me. "I… Were you thinking of showing… What's his name?"

"Mauser," Cara said quickly.

"Right, Mauser. Were you thinking of showing him in dog shows in *this* country?" Pittman asked in a tone suggesting that, if this was true, then we were out of our minds.

"Well… er." I looked at Cara.

"We know that he's more typical of European Danes," Cara said. For his part, Mauser had sat down at my side and was looking happily at Pittman, his long tongue lolling out of his mouth.

"He is certainly… husky. Look, I can't encourage you to spend your money showing him in AKC shows. He would never place. Honestly, besides his… um, bulk… his color is marginal at best. Too much white to be a good black and too little white to be a mantle. No. If you intend to show dogs then the first thing I would recommend would be to get another dog. Sorry. I just want to be honest." Pittman's face was sincere and kind. I found myself liking the guy.

"I see," I said, realizing that I had failed to think this through past the point where the dog talk would be exhausted.

"Don't worry. If you just intended to show Mauser and don't think you'd want to get another dog, I understand. I won't charge you for this evaluation. We can just shake hands and call it a day. I wasn't going to have anyone in this time slot anyway." He gave us a wide smile and a shrug.

"We might be interested in expanding our family," Cara said. For a second I thought she meant with a child and my brain froze. But she went on, "Do you know of any good Dane breeders?"

"I hope you won't get rid of this guy," Pittman said, clapping his hands together and leaning toward Mauser, who seemed mesmerized by the man. In the most controlled greeting I'd ever seen him make, Mauser moved forward and laid his head in the man's hands.

It was an awkward moment and one that was completely my fault. I either needed to fess up as to why we were really there or continue the ruse.

"Mr. Pittman, this is my fiancée Cara and Mauser is actually my dad's dog." Pittman looked at me in confusion.

"I'm sorry. I'm Deputy Larry Macklin with the Adams County Sheriff's Office. I wanted a chance to talk with you in person." Either we were going to get kicked out now or we weren't.

He cocked his head and looked at me for a moment, almost like a dog himself, then returned his attention to Mauser, who was still making googly-eyes at him. For a while Pittman ignored me and continued to pet Mauser, then he finally said, "You're the guy who called asking about Ryan."

"That's right. You sounded like you might have something to tell me."

"I should have asked you, but what is this all about? Why's a deputy in Florida worried about a guy from Texas who went missing in Pascagoula, Mississippi?"

"Horace McCune moved to Adams County a few years

ago. This past week he managed to get himself killed. Turns out that Ryan's mother was in town at the time, trying to press a wrongful death lawsuit against McCune. And it's pretty clear she's not upset that McCune was murdered."

"Did she kill him?"

"She hasn't been ruled out as a suspect."

"McCune dead. Not sure that changes much. From the deck of that oil rig, it looked like everyone above my pay grade was corrupt. I'm not sure how anything I can tell you will change things. Honestly, I don't think I'd want to do anything that would hurt her chances of getting off, whether she killed him or not."

"The truth is just the truth. And I'll be honest with you. Having met Mrs. Pappas, I think that if you could give me information that would help to explain what happened to her son, then she wouldn't care if it sent her to jail or not."

"I think you're right. She's contacted me a number of times over the years. Mail, phone calls. She's shown up at my house. She even called my mother once." Mauser leaned into him, staring at him like he was a god, and Pittman seemed to take comfort from the dog.

"Tell your story," Cara encouraged him. "Whatever your reason for holding onto it, this would seem like a good time to get it out in the open."

"If you want, I'll even promise to hold your name back when I tell Mrs. Pappas," I offered.

Pittman looked up at us, took a deep breath and began to tell the story of what had happened to Ryan Pappas.

"I thought it was going to be an adventure working on an oil rig. I was just out of high school and didn't have a clue what I wanted to do. When I got there, I realized it was going to be hard, nasty work. That was okay. I never minded hard work, so some grease and oil weren't going to scare me off."

"What happened?"

"I don't know what other oil rigs are like, but there was a bad feeling on that one. The first couple of months, I didn't notice anything. I was just trying to get a handle on the job. We worked two weeks on and one week off. There was plenty of hazing. I expected it in that kind of environment. What I didn't expect was the way some of the guys seemed to be part of some sort of inner circle. It was later that I realized it had to do with the inspections. Both the inspections that OSHA made and the ones that were done by the EPA. As new as I was, I could see that the bosses were taking short cuts. Dangerous stuff."

"Did you know Ryan Pappas?"

"He started six months after I did. He replaced me as the new man on the crew and took my place as the low man on the totem pole. I guess I took pity on him, 'cause I'd just been through it. Not that he was as green as I'd been. Ryan had been a roustabout on some derricks in Texas. He was a super nice guy. Honest as the day is long and he didn't seem as cynical and hardened as the other men."

"Hardened?" Cara asked.

Pittman looked up at her and shook his head. "When we had that week off, some of the men went home to their wives and families, others didn't. But all of them spent the first day or two on shore getting laid and getting wasted. Not necessarily in that order. One of the sayings was that if someone messed with one of us, then they were going to get messed up. On two separate occasions, I saw drunks screw up and piss off one of our crew. Both were lucky to have survived. Tough is one thing. Mean is another. These guys were mean."

"How long did you know Ryan before he disappeared?"

"Almost six months, maybe. I don't know what it says about me, but I could turn my head when I saw something I shouldn't. Not Ryan. Twice he got beat up for pushing a safety issue. That really pissed off management because they'd lost a couple of guys a few years before and were under a tight watch from OSHA. Whenever there was going to be an inspection, we were given very clear instructions on how to change our ordinary working procedures to ones that met OSHA standards. We were also told not to answer any question that didn't relate directly to the jobs we were doing. Anything else and we were told to play dumb."

"I guess Ryan wasn't good at playing dumb?" I said.

"That's right. Me? I *was* dumb, so it didn't take much acting. But Ryan didn't seem to understand that it wasn't a game. McCune and his crew bosses weren't going to go easy when money was on the line. And there was big money at stake. If we got shut down, even for a month, the company lost hundreds of thousands… maybe millions."

"That's a lot of money to protect."

"That's right. And protect is the right word. But nothing could stop Ryan. He was on fire about all the violations. Like I said, he had a lot more experience than I did."

"His mother said that he disappeared when he was on his way back to Pascagoula."

"He was going to meet me that night."

"She didn't mention that."

"I don't think she knows. We were going to hit the bars before joining our shift for the ride out to the rig in the morning. I liked the buddy system. I always figured that, no matter how drunk we got, one of us would be able to help the other to the dock in the morning. Even though Ryan was a straight shooter, he was good at getting wasted. Maybe all the conflict with the other guys on the rig added to his drinking."

"Did something happen that night?"

"I only know part of it," Pittman said slowly.

We'd come a long way to hit a dead end now. "Just tell us what you know," I encouraged him.

"We hit the first bar and were getting shitfaced. I was lit up pretty good after the first hour and Ryan wasn't much better. We got tossed from that bar. Now, there weren't too many bars that welcomed rig workers. Pretty much only the bars down by the docks. Those were rough joints. Being drunk and looking at two more weeks of hard work, we convinced ourselves that it was a good idea to go to this bar called the End of the Dock. It was literally at the end of one of the docks. Place smelled of stale beer and piss. Most bars discouraged fights, but this place encouraged them. Brawls were an expected part of the entertainment."

"What time did you all get there?" Now that we were narrowing in on the time that Ryan must have vanished, I wanted him to be as precise as possible.

"Eleven. Or close to it. That place didn't even start revving up until one in the morning. Anyway, we showed up and right away I could tell that going there had been a mistake. Inside were five guys from our shift, sitting at a table drunk as skunks and in a foul mood. As soon as we walked in, they locked eyes with Ryan. You'd think Ryan would have been careful around them, but he was almost to the staggering point himself. I think the fact that he was just getting back from spending time with his parents didn't help. He really wanted them to be proud of him. He was always talking about his parents' expectations. Mix that with the alcohol and him knowing that there were all these safety violations on the rig, and he was bound to run his mouth."

"And the guys at the table were people he held responsible for some of the safety violations?" I asked.

"Exactly. I don't remember everything that happened. Once everyone got all worked up, events spiraled out of control fast. I know that the other guys said something about how Ryan was going to screw all of us by blabbing his mouth to the bureaucrats. Or words to that effect. When Ryan heard that, he went crazy and started telling them that *they* were the ones who were going to get us all screwed. He said that the safety regulations were there to keep us from dying like the two guys who'd gotten crushed on the rig. It started with name-calling, then beer bottles started flying through the air. The crowd in that dive didn't help either. They were yelling for a fight. I grabbed Ryan and begged him to leave, but he shook me off. Several of the men—they were all standing now—looked me square in the eye. The message was clear. If I sided with Ryan, then I'd get the same treatment." Pittman stopped talking. I could see his hand shaking a little as he stroked Mauser's head.

"No one can blame you for being scared," I said.

"That's true. But I can blame myself for walking out of that bar and leaving Ryan to face those men by himself."

"Did you ever see Ryan again?" Cara asked, her voice soft and sympathetic.

"I did. I went outside and tried to figure out what to do. At one point I called the cops, but they pretty much ignored me. A fight at the End of the Dock wasn't exactly news or anything that they wanted to get involved with. I'd heard stories before this of cops walking in there and ending up tossed in the bay. But I stayed. I guess it was only ten minutes, but it felt like an hour, when the door opened and Ryan was tossed out of the bar. He couldn't even walk. His face was torn up something awful. Even in the glow of the crappy sodium lights around the dock, I could see how badly beat up he was. Had teeth knocked out. One eye was already swollen to the point that he couldn't see out of it. I half pulled, half carried him over to the car. We had driven his that night. I dug into his pockets, looking for the keys, but couldn't find them. His pants were ripped, so I figured they must have fallen out during the fight. So I found some courage and went back inside the bar to find them. The last time I saw Ryan, he was lying down with his back up against his car."

"What happened to you?"

Pittman reached up and brushed back his hair. A three-inch-long scar ran from his forehead almost to his ear.

"I don't remember anything after opening the door to the bar. Two days later, I woke up in a hospital in New Orleans. According to the hospital records, they found me on the ground outside the emergency room asking when the boat would be leaving."

"Why New Orleans?" Cara asked.

"Distance, I'm sure. I figured they didn't want me found in Pascagoula or admitted to a Pascagoula hospital because someone might put my injuries together with Ryan's disappearance before they had a chance to warn me to keep my mouth shut."

"Did they?" I asked.

"Oh, yeah. They explained to my nineteen-year-old self that I hadn't seen anything anyway and it would be a shame to end up crab food at such a tender age. They meant every word of it too."

"You just walked away?"

"I did for a few years. Then one day I got a call from Ryan's mom. I'd put it all behind me. At least I thought I had. I hung up on her, but that night I cried for an hour. Couldn't stop shaking. My girlfriend had to sit under the kitchen table with me. Funny to be that scared when I couldn't even remember what they'd done to me. The doctors said that it wasn't unusual for a patient with my head injuries to have gaps in memory. Of course, I *did* remember the threats. I'd walked away from the job, never even picked up my last paycheck. I thought once about trying to work as roustabout again and got the shakes. Anyway, after my girlfriend talked me out from under the table, she convinced me to get some therapy. We found someone who used a Golden Retriever to help her clients break through some of their barriers. That's when I started working with dogs. The therapist joked that I was the first person who had actually made her *dog* feel better. Learning that I had a calling went a long way toward rebuilding my confidence. Another thing the therapist suggested was that I do a bit of research into the company that ran the rig. She called it demystifying the fear."

"Did you tell her everything that happened?"

"No, I was too ashamed about not looking for Ryan... or even talking to his mother. I told her that I'd been attacked at the bar by guys I'd worked with on the rig, and they'd threatened me to keep my mouth shut afterward. She told me it might help me if I reported everything that had happened to the police. She also told me that it was a decision I should make only after considering all of the consequences. I respected her for being a realist. She said that we should strive to live in the best world we can, but we should never ignore the realities of the world we live in."

"Did you research McCune's company?"

"Up one side and down the other. When I was done, I wanted to vomit. The whole company was designed to make as much money as it could while getting away with every sketchy underhanded scheme McCune and his cronies could come up with. I spent another year of my life trying to come up with a way to bring them down. Funny. You look at companies that you know are putrid piles of crap and nothing happens to them. Whistleblowers end up in jail or mocked and scorned. My cynicism has grown. Once a decade, the stars will align and some bastard will pay a pittance for all the damage they've caused. But that never makes whole the people they've hurt. I figured out that I would only get crushed in the cogs if I stuck my finger in. So I do what I enjoy. Avoid hurting others. Do a little good. Beyond the show ring, I help therapists find, train and use dogs in their practices."

"What do you think happened to Ryan?"

"I think it's pretty obvious. After they beat the shit out of me, someone high up the food chain was told what had happened. Maybe even McCune himself. Whoever it was made the decision that Ryan should be permanently erased, and they would take a chance on me. I imagine someone on my crew said that they were sure I was a coward and would keep my mouth shut if they told me to. Guess they were right. As to the specifics of what happened to Ryan, that's easy. The boat trip out to the rig would provide a perfect opportunity to drop a package into the Gulf, never to be seen again."

"I appreciate you being candid with me."

"I don't know how any of this is going to help you or Mrs. Pappas. And, yes, I'm still a big enough coward that I'm not going to tell anyone the names of the men in the bar that night. I like my life."

"After this long, I don't know how anyone could go after the men anyway. Maybe if there was a body, or if the car had been preserved and DNA could be obtained from it. Even if it could be proved that a body had been put in the trunk, that would be something. But the testimony of a man who suffered serious head trauma and who, from his own account, can't remember the events of several days afterward, wouldn't go very far in prosecuting anyone," I assured him.

Pittman was quiet for a long time, just petting and whispering to Mauser, who soaked up all the attention. Then his mood seemed to lighten and he said, "Let's take this guy into the ring. You can let him go," he added to Cara, who'd been keeping a loose hold on Mauser's leash in case he got any ideas about escape.

I wanted to tell him that Mauser might follow him into the building, or he might just decide to run off sniffing the grass. But he was the trainer. I nodded at Cara and she unhooked Mauser's leash. Mauser seemed to consider his options for a second, then looked at Pittman for guidance. With Pittman talking to him and maintaining eye contact, Mauser followed right alongside the man.

Inside the building was a show ring that was about sixty feet long and thirty feet wide. There were some metal stands on one side and Cara and I sat down to watch Pittman work. Mauser seemed entranced by him and was soon doing a full range of obedience moves without a leash or treats. After picking my jaw up off the ground, I decided that whatever Pittman charged for his sessions it would certainly be worthwhile, assuming that he could transfer even some of that magic to another handler.

"One of the tricks is to keep his attention. Once that connection is broken, then you have to reconnect. Of course you can use treats, but if you can keep him focused on you, then there's less and less of a need for treats. His reward is your attention," Pittman explained to us without ever breaking eye contact with Mauser.

Ten minutes later, he verbally turned Mauser loose to run around the ring and sniff where dozens of other dogs had been.

"You can't run the sessions longer than ten minutes," Pittman said, watching Mauser lumber around the ring. "Neither the dog nor the owner's attention spans can maintain the required intensity longer than that. He is some dog. Standards only go so far. He may lack the physique required to be successful in an AKC show, but he has the personality."

"He certainly has personality," I agreed.

Cara slapped me playfully. "Mauser's a great dog."

"What do I owe you?" I asked Pittman.

"Forget it. If I charged you for this then you'd have to charge me for letting me lift a pile of baggage off of my shoulders. I wonder where those men are now? Did they pay as heavy a price for what they did as Ryan did… or even me?"

"Give me their names and I'll find out for you."

He looked thoughtful for a moment. "No. If I really thought there could be some justice at the end of the road then maybe, but now… I'll live with the fact that if I had come forward earlier, then maybe Ryan could have been found and the men responsible could have been dealt with."

"You're probably right," I told him. "But let me know if you ever change your mind."

After leaving Pittman's home, we made a quick stop at a city park for lunch before getting back on the interstate. "I asked Pete how he manages to juggle all of his responsibilities," I said to Cara as we drove home. "He told me that he compartmentalizes and prioritizes according to what he's doing at the time."

"You always complained when he was your partner that he spent more time texting his family than paying attention to the job," she chided me.

"There's some truth there," I allowed. "But of all the deputies I know, he seems the most relaxed working the job and maintaining a relationship with his family."

"I think you're being too hard on yourself. In the past month we've dealt with a hurricane, I was abducted and your father is in a battle for his job. Plus now you have a couple of active murder investigations which could have far-reaching political consequences. And, on top of all of that, we just got engaged and we're playing host to my hippie parents. I know how much pressure you're under. I hate to feel like I'm not holding up my end."

"You're fine," I assured her. "I worry about *you*. Look at Pittman. He's still dealing with the emotional fallout from his assault. What I hate is that I can't give you all the attention you need and deserve right now."

Cara reached out and put her hand on my shoulder. "I think we both need to stop putting pressure on ourselves. We'll get through this. And we'll figure out how to balance everything. At least, *most* of the time."

"I guess it *is* unreasonable to think that we can have smooth sailing all of the time. I just hate hitting bumps now when we've just gotten engaged."

"I'll deal with Mom. This too will pass."

"And the important thing is that we're marrying each other. If that means we have to do it hanging by our toes from a live oak tree, then that works for me."

"I think our toes would get tired," Cara said, giving me a light punch on the shoulder. "I should be able to negotiate a better deal than that with Mom… though we may end up in hemp formal wear."

"Hey, that would work. Then when we're old and doddering we can smoke our wedding clothes."

Cara's laughter filled the van and I was glad to hear it.

We delivered Mauser safe and sound home to Dad, who was highly amused to hear about both Pittman's assessment of Mauser and the dog's reaction to the handler.

"You've made a big mistake by letting me know you can be obedient," I told Mauser. "I'm going to expect a higher standard of behavior from now on."

Mauser looked at me like I had lobsters crawling out of my ears, then climbed up on the couch and collapsed on his side. Before Cara and I were even out the door, we could hear him snoring.

CHAPTER NINETEEN

Darlene and I drove to the hospital on Monday afternoon. Darlene had talked to Meredith's doctor on Sunday and was told that she would be leaving the ICU Monday morning, giving us the all-clear to interview her that afternoon.

We didn't need to stop at the nurses' station to get her room number. As soon as we stepped off the elevator, I spotted Sean Briggs standing in the hallway looking vigilant. Darlene must have seen the fire in my eyes.

"Hoss, you need to calm down," I heard her say as we walked down the hall.

"I'm not going to start anything," I said, though I was staring lasers at Briggs.

He saw us approach and stiffened. "Officers," he said by way of greeting.

"Mr. Briggs," I said. "I don't think you've had the pleasure of meeting my partner, Deputy Marks."

"My client still expects to receive access to her house."

"I may just be a hick deputy, but even I know that probate doesn't move that fast. The house is part of her father's estate, and we are investigating his murder. We were willing to grant her access, but now that the property has become the scene of another brutal attack, we'll be keeping it closed until we're sure it's safe for Miss McCune to return."

"She is the sole heir to her father's estate. Probate is just a formality."

"A criminal is not allowed to profit from their crime. At this point, Meredith McCune has not been eliminated as a person of interest in the murder of her father," I said, giving him my best dead-eyed, *film noir* expression.

He bowed up and moved forward, putting us less than a foot apart.

"How dare you? Meredith was savagely attacked and you have the nerve to stand there and suggest that she had a hand in her father's murder?"

"And where were you when your client was being attacked? You had time to follow me around, but you sure did a piss-poor job of protecting her."

His face flushed red and his right hand pumped up and down at his side. "I should…"

"Do it," I told him. There was nothing I would have liked better at that moment than to slam him down and put cuffs on his wrist.

"Stop pissing on each other's legs," Darlene snapped. "The day before yesterday, the woman in that room was bleeding all over me. I'd like to go in and see if she has any information that can help us lock up the bastard who did it."

Briggs and I glanced over at her, then back at each other.

"Are you going to help us find out who stabbed her?" I asked him.

"She's still recuperating. You can talk to her for a few minutes." He paused, then added, "With me present."

I wanted to protest, but there was no point. He *was* her lawyer. Under the circumstances, any good lawyer would have insisted on being present when their client, a possible suspect in a murder, was questioned by the police. Particularly if they were in pain and probably under the influence of medication.

"Of course. I'm sure we all have the same agenda," I said, the sarcasm impossible to ignore.

Briggs stepped out of the way so I could open the door. Inside the room, Meredith was hooked up to several medical monitors and had an IV drip in her left arm. She was reading something on the phone that she held in her right hand.

We had decided before we got there that Darlene would take the lead in questioning Meredith. With Briggs present the idea seemed even better, so I moved out of the way to allow Darlene to stand next to the bed.

Meredith put the phone down.

"I want to thank you for saving my life," Meredith said to Darlene. She sounded sincere, though even if she'd stabbed herself she should have been grateful to Darlene for getting help in time.

"Just part of the job. You should really thank Hondo, the EMT who rode with you to the hospital."

"I will."

I always found it awkward when a victim was also a possible suspect. I had to curb my emotions. Becoming too sympathetic could hamper my objectivity, but so could an assumption of guilt.

"We need you to give us as much information as you can about your attack. Right now, you're the only witness and we were able to collect only a minimal amount of evidence from the crime scene."

I silently applauded Darlene for implying that we had some evidence. Truth was, we didn't have much of anything to go on at this point. But if Meredith had planned her own attack, it would be better for her to think that we *did* have some evidence.

"I don't know how much help I can be."

"Let us be the judge of that. Just concentrate and answer our questions as completely as you can. First of all, when did you pull into the driveway at your father's estate?"

"I was about fifteen minutes early. So around eleven-forty-five."

"Did you see anything unusual?" Darlene asked.

It seemed like Meredith hesitated, but I couldn't be sure.

Maybe she was just thinking hard. "No. Nothing. The only thing I noticed was that you all weren't there yet. So I pulled out my phone to check for messages."

"Were there any?"

"Yes, several. I ignored them. I checked mostly to see if you all had left a message about a change in plans. The messages on my phone were all work-related. Which reminds me, may I have that phone back?" Darlene and I both looked at the phone that she'd set down on the hospital table. "That's my personal phone," she said. "The one you have is my business phone."

"And you don't have her permission to search her business phone. That would be victimizing her for a second time," Briggs said.

Darlene and I looked at Meredith to see if she would override his decision. She didn't.

"Of course we'll return her phone," I said, wondering if we could legally copy the information from the phone before we gave it back. If we didn't access it until we had a warrant, then would we be violating her right to privacy? I decided I'd call the county attorney and see what the legal arguments were.

"You pulled up. Didn't see anyone. Checked your cell phone for messages. Then what?" Darlene asked.

"I got out of the car. The weather was nice, so I thought I'd walk around for a minute. I've spent so much time driving back and forth or sitting in hotel rooms that it felt nice to get out and stretch my legs."

"Think, did you hear anything unusual?"

"No. I heard a car go by. There was a breeze. I could hear the trees blowing in the wind. Nothing really. I walked over to the gate to check what condition it was in. Dad's last wife had insisted on building that house, though he'd hated spending the money. After he divorced her, he didn't put any more money into the place than he absolutely had to. I plan to put it on the market just as soon as the estate clears probate. To be fair, I don't like spending money any more than he did. I'm hoping I can sell it as is."

Her statement struck me as being very callous. I could understand wanting to sell a house where a horrible crime had been committed against her family, but her attitude was more like she was selling a used piece of furniture.

"And how was the gate?" Darlene asked the perfect follow up question. If the suspect—I mean victim—said they went to look at something, then it was important to ask what they saw. Any delay in their response could point to a lie.

"The gates themselves are fine, but the columns where the hinges are attached are showing some wear. If I'm lucky, a buyer won't notice. You have to walk right up to them to see the cracks."

Points to Meredith. I was sure that she was telling the truth about the cracks. If she had hatched an elaborate plan to stage a stabbing with either Darlene or me as a witness, would she have taken a chance of us pulling in the driveway while she was standing near the gate? Of course, she could have seen the cracks some other time.

"What happened after you inspected the gate?" Darlene continued.

"I turned to walk back to my car. I got to within ten feet of it when…" She hesitated again. "I'm sorry, but I've never experienced anything like this. I'm having trouble remembering the sequence of events."

"I think that's enough. You should give her another day to recover," Briggs said. I could have hit him with a two-by-four. We were just getting to the touchy parts.

"I'm sure Miss McCune realizes that the sooner we get her description of the attack, the better our chances are of catching the attacker," I said. I moved between him and Meredith, hoping she would continue talking.

"When a law enforcement officer is involved in a traumatic event, it is standard operating procedure to give him three days to recover his wits and memory. I think Meredith deserves the same consideration," Briggs said. The words were innocent enough, but his eyes were shooting daggers at me.

"Sean, I may as well get this over with," Meredith said. She leaned over so that she could see past me and looked him in the eye. *Interesting*, I thought.

Briggs looked like he wanted to argue, but instead he turned away and held his tongue.

"I think I *did* hear something at that point. Or maybe I just felt the presence of someone behind me. I don't know, but I think I turned to look."

"You think you turned? Did you turn or did you just start to turn?" Darlene asked.

"You know, the reason it's so confusing may be that the guy attacking me was moving to step in front of me at the same time I was turning to see who was behind me."

"The guy? It was a man?" Darlene pressed.

"Oh, yes, I'm positive… almost positive it was a man."

"You said this man was moving to get in front of you at the same time you were turning. Did he say anything?"

"No, absolutely not. I would have remembered that. His silence made it more frightening. He was so close. I felt him push me in the stomach. That's what it felt like, just a push. Now I realize he was stabbing me, but at that moment I just thought, 'He punches like a girl.' Stupid, I know, but that's what went through my head. It just felt like he'd punched me easy, like you would if you were playing with someone." She was looking off toward the window now.

My gut was telling me that something wasn't right with her story, but I couldn't put my finger on it right then.

"Were you looking at his face?" Darlene said.

"Yes, and I couldn't figure out why he was wearing a mask."

"What kind of mask?"

"Woolen, brown I think, the kind that have holes for the eyes and mouth." The cynical part of my brain couldn't help thinking that she was simply describing the type of masks that bad guys always wore on TV. "I guess it was a ski mask.

Again, it all happened so fast."

"Did you have to look up to see the masked face?"

"Maybe a little."

"How long were you standing face to face like that?"

"I can't really say. I felt the punch and then a really strange sensation, almost as though he was pulling my stomach. I guess that was him pulling the knife out. There was another punch that hit me harder. I fell back, which seemed to startle him. I don't know what happened to him after that. I'd noticed the knife and felt the blood all over my stomach. I stumbled to my car and that's when I saw you drive up behind me."

"How much time do you think passed between when you were first stabbed and when you saw me pull up?"

"I have to stop this!" Briggs insisted, stepping toward the bed. I moved ever so slightly to intercept him, but he ignored me. "During such a traumatic attack, a person's sense of time is bound to be subjective."

I hated to admit it, but he had a point. Time does strange things when events are whirling out of your control.

"I think he's right. There's nothing else I can tell you that would help you catch the man who did this."

"Just one more question," Darlene said, holding up a finger. "Do you have any impression of which direction the man went after the attack?"

Meredith seemed to consider this. "I'm not sure. I was facing the road… I'd say, and it's more of a guess, really, that he went that way. He must have gone parallel to the road, or you might would have seen him when you drove up."

"Okay. We'll probably have more questions later," Darlene said. "Don't worry, we'll find the person who stabbed you." The way she said it sounded as much a threat as a promise.

"I'm going to contact whoever I need to in order to get Meredith access to her father's home." Brigg was making his own threats. We just waved and left the room.

When we were walking across the hospital parking lot, I

looked back and tried to find Meredith's window. I couldn't distinguish it from any of the others, but I half expected to see Briggs staring down at me.

"What did you think?" I asked Darlene.

"A good performance, but not really Oscar quality," she answered while unlocking her car so we could both get in.

"My thoughts exactly. It took me a minute to realize what was going on, but then I figured it out. That wasn't Meredith McCune. The woman she was pretending to be was too nice. Too cooperative. The Meredith we met the first day was large and in charge. This one, not so much. I would bet you money that this is her I-want-you-to-believe-me Meredith. I'd bet her father would have recognized this one."

"Two questions, then. What was she lying about and *why* was she lying?"

Most people who want to deceive law enforcement mingle a bit of truth in with the lies. It makes it easier for the liar to remember the details of his story because some of them really happened, and makes it harder for the investigator because he has to spend time unraveling the mix.

"She was definitely stabbed. I believe that much. Everything else, I'm not so sure about," Darlene said. She started the car and we weaved our way through the Tallahassee traffic on our way back to Adams County.

"We need to secure her X-rays," I said. "I don't believe anything she said about her attacker. The mask. All that bit about him sneaking up on her. Where'd he go? Is he some roving, knife-wielding, ski-mask-wearing maniac out randomly stabbing people?"

"I agree, that part was nope-tastic. Sounded like something from a bad horror movie."

"Did you talk to Hondo about the ride to the hospital?"

"I did. He said that Meredith was out of it most of the time. Asked how far they were from the hospital a couple of times, but that was all."

"Maybe one of us should have ridden in the ambulance

with her," I mused.

"That's a coulda shoulda woulda that's out of the barn, Mr. Greenjeans."

"Okay, so how do we break her down?"

"Not going to be easy with her guardian angel hovering near by."

"He rubs me the wrong way."

"Thanks for the news flash."

"Going after her guard dog might be one way to approach this problem. He already warned us off when you were checking his background. Maybe I'll get someone with a few more connections to go after him." I pulled out my phone and dialed Tom Horton with FDLE. I asked him to do the full Monty on Sean Briggs. Tom would be able to check the man's business license and professional certifications quicker and easier than I could.

"I'll dig into his courtroom work too. See what side he plays for," Tom said.

When we got back to the office, I called Celina Pappas. "I talked to one of the last men to see your son," I told her. There was only silence on the other end of the line. "Why don't we meet in person? Then I can tell you everything I learned."

"Please," she finally choked out.

"I can come to Tallahassee if you want."

"No, I'll meet you at your office."

Celina had appointments scheduled with lawyers all day on Tuesday, so we agreed to meet first thing Wednesday morning. I would take the opportunity to ask her where she was when Meredith had been attacked, though I couldn't imagine why Meredith would protect Mrs. Pappas. Circles within circles.

CHAPTER TWENTY

On Tuesday morning, I tried to concentrate on the Eli Waters case. I'd seldom had a harder time coming up with suspects in a murder investigation. With this case there seemed to be only one person with one motive—his brother, who would inherit the property. I scheduled a meeting with him later that morning and was surprised when he seemed as anxious to speak with me as I was with him.

Good as his word, Micah showed up at the office at eleven on the dot.

"The day Eli was killed, I worked until six o'clock at the printing company. There are several people who will vouch for me. After work, I went to Harry's downtown for dinner with my wife and her parents. I guess we were finished around nine. Went home, then went to bed."

"How is your business doing?" I asked him.

"As well as the present economy will allow. We don't carry debt beyond some capital assets. Our building has a small mortgage on it, as do several of our cars. But our assets far outweigh our debts. Personally, my finances are rock solid. I understand why you need to look at me, but you can move on." Micah told me all of this with an earnest expression on his face.

"The trouble is, there isn't anyone else with a motive to hurt your brother," I told him. "Once we rule out robbery and sex, that doesn't leave us with much. Random acts of violence usually involve someone stabbing, shooting or beating someone to death." Mentioning stabbing made me think of Meredith, though I couldn't imagine how she could be connected to Eli's death.

"I can't help you. Like I told you before, my brother and I had been estranged for years."

I thought about the sex angle. Maybe it had been someone like Gene, the baby-daddy of Eli's young neighbor. Maybe the idea that Eli had made a move on Nadine had brought Gene out of the woodwork.

"Maybe someone from his past?" I suggested, hoping to give Micah even a vague idea of possible enemies that Eli might have had.

"Are you sure he was murdered?"

"I am. Was there anyone when he was growing up who could have held a grudge against him?"

"Like I told you before, the only people he ever argued with were me and my parents. He was a bit wild, but he was always a nice guy. He'd help anyone. Even as a kid, he was always looking for a way to help others."

"With some of the women I've talked to, he might have had other motives for helping them out."

Micah nodded. "He loved women. No doubt about that. But from what I heard and saw, he was always polite."

We went around and around a couple more times before I declared the interview over. Neither of us was very satisfied.

After grabbing a quick lunch, I met Darlene in the conference room. She'd laid out pictures of all of the suspects in the McCune murder on the table, as well as notes about each of them, and was trying to find connections and links.

"These are ones with alibis," she said, pointing to a group of enemies and random visitors to the house, such as the pool guy. Also in the mix were Dad and I. "Some of them have pretty good motives, but they all have solid alibis. We're lucky that he didn't live here all of his life. Most of his enemies live in Texas and the states surrounding it. But travel time can eliminate most of them."

"Who are these?" I asked, pointing to another pile.

"Those are people with no obvious motive, but who had the opportunity."

I flipped through the pile. It included the maid Cary Trent, Pops and his lawn maintenance crew, Candy the prostitute and two men from the security company.

The third pile contained Celina Pappas and Sean Briggs.

"I put Briggs in that pile with the thought that he has a motive if Meredith was paying him, or if their relationship is more personal."

"I like him. I like him for it more than Celina Pappas. I don't think she has the killer instinct. Though I've been wrong before," I admitted, thinking of several recent examples.

"Could Meredith and Briggs have staged the stabbing?" Darlene asked.

"That's a hard one to swallow."

"Then this is where we are."

I picked up a couple of names from the pile of folks who had opportunity, but not motive.

"I'll take these. I've been meaning to speak with Pops anyway."

An hour later, I'd tracked Pops Davis down at a Victorian bed and breakfast near the town square. He was supervising several young men as they tackled the flowerbeds with weed trimmers.

"Good kids, but you got to keep your eyes on them," he told me. "Otherwise they'll chop down half the flowerbeds."

Pops's dark skin glistened in the afternoon sun and he wore clothes that Goodwill would have thrown out. But his downtrodden appearance hid a savvy, hard-working businessman. While he still lived in a well-maintained shotgun home in a traditionally black section of town, he'd put both of his sons through college and there was some speculation about how much money he probably had tucked away.

"How long have you worked for McCune?" I asked.

"Too long. That man was a trip. Didn't know nothin' about yardwork, but he'd sure come out and tell me how it should be done. Though he didn't want me to do much more than keep the grass mowed. Cheap bastard didn't really care how the property looked. I quit once, but he found out no else would work for him and got me back." Pops looked at me and winked. "Cost him twenty percent more."

"You ran the tractor?"

"Me or my nephew. I couldn't let anyone else do it. If they'd made a mistake and mowed over the wrong plant or broke one of the other fool rules that man had, I never would have heard the end of it."

"So as far as you know, only you and your nephew ran the tractor?"

"That's right. No one else around there could run it. A little harder then a car."

"Where'd you normally leave the keys?"

"Hanging on the wall. The key has a tag on it. Says 'Tractor' right on the tag."

"Did you ever see anyone have an argument with McCune?"

"When I'm working, I keep my eyes to my work. Doesn't pay to be looking around."

"Can I talk to your nephew?"

"Of course you can. We don't have anything to hide. I've had a bit of trouble with cops over the years, but I think I can trust the boy I taught to drive a lawnmower. Little Mac, you sure thought you was somethin' when you were behind the wheel," he said with a smile.

Pops had taken care of our lawn when I was growing up. One of my favorite memories was of driving the mower across the lawn in a wavy line that had left plenty of grass unmowed. My mom and Pops had been watching me, my mom just shaking her head at the all the spots I'd missed that Pops would have to go back over.

His nephew arrived about thirty minutes after Pops called him. Even in the near perfect October weather, it was clear from the sweat and dirt covering his clothes that the man had been out working hard on another job.

"Hey, Deputy Larry, what can I do for you?" he asked as he shook my hand.

It didn't take me long to bring him up to speed. McCune's murder had been the talk of the county and his personal connection to it had made it a subject of interest for him.

"I just worked the grounds," he said. "Uncle Pops taught me never to look up. We've had a couple of guys get in trouble because they didn't remember that rule. One of our men almost got shot by a woman's husband once 'cause he'd seen a little more of her than he should have."

"You drove the tractor?"

"Yep. During the summer we'd mow the whole place once a month. Big place with some wide open areas. We split it up and did about a quarter of it one day each week." He gave me a funny look. "You know, it's funny you talking about the tractor. I always swept it off before I put it back in the workshop. But a couple of times in the last month I noticed dirt tracks on the cement floor. I wondered who else had been driving the tractor. Didn't make any sense. Anything Mr. McCune wanted, he could ask us to do. I think he liked ordering us around anyway. So why would he let someone else drive the tractor?"

I agreed that it was odd. He said he'd look at his log and see if he could figure out which days he'd noticed that the tractor had been moved. I thanked him, though I couldn't figure out why it was important.

Just to be thorough, I got alibis for both Pops and his nephew for the time that McCune had been murdered and for when Meredith had been stabbed. They both sounded solid and half an hour on the phone eliminated both of them from the suspect list for good.

I spent another hour working on alibis and background checks. Tired of going nowhere with McCune's, I turned my attention back to the Eli Waters case. After reviewing the statements of both Patty the prostitute and Nadine the neighbor, I did find one avenue worthy of additional inquiry. They had both mentioned that his interest in having relations with them had waned. Could there have been a new girl in his life?

I called Julio and asked him to meet me at Eli's house. "What are we looking for?" he asked me as we walked inside.

"Information on anyone who might have worked for him. I know he had a couple of people who worked on a seasonal basis. He kept meticulous records, so we should be able to find some names. I want to talk with someone who might have seen who he was hanging out with."

Julio and I split the papers and books that were piled on Eli's desk. Of course, he might have kept all the information we were looking for in a spreadsheet on his laptop. Lionel in IT had given me a week as his best-case scenario for going through Eli's laptop and phone. With luck, Eli was a paper-and-pen kind of guy.

"Could you tell if there were any rare issues missing?" I asked Julio, referring to Eli's titanic collection of men's magazines.

"I hope you're happy. I am still getting ribbed about that."

"The other deputies are just jealous," I assured him.

"His collection is worth a few thousand dollars at least. Several early issues of *Playboy* and *Penthouse* that are in good shape. Some rarer magazines too. But nothing that's crazy valuable and nothing appears to be missing."

"And I'm sure you looked hard," I laughed.

"Don't you start," Julio said with a frown.

"I wouldn't think of it. Too easy."

"Here," he said, holding out a stack of papers that were

clipped together. "This looks like a record of payments to a Carlos Ruano. His address is in the Sunshine Trailer Park about three miles away."

"Looks like he worked for Eli up until a couple of weeks ago," I said, scanning the paperwork. I looked at my watch. It was almost five. "You want to take a ride over there with me?"

"I can follow you."

"Let's leave your patrol car here. We don't want to upset the whole neighborhood."

Julio and I were both familiar with the park. It was run by a slum lord who rented crappy trailers to migrants and other people who didn't have many housing options. When we drove into the park, it was obvious from the looks we received that no one doubted we were authorities of some sort. Some people gave us tentative smiles, but most looked at us warily. The singlewide mobile homes had all seen better days. Some had old tin tacked onto even older tin in shoddy attempts to repair roofs or walls. The yards were small and almost every one was filled with toys.

Ruano's home was in the middle of the park. There was laundry drying on a line and several cars parked out front. One of them even looked like it might run. Julio walked around the back of the house as I went up to the front door.

My knock was answered by Julio's shout from the backyard. I went around to find him holding on to a man who was hanging half out of a window.

"I'm looking for Carlos Ruano," I said to the man, who stared at me with uncomprehending eyes. The back door was opened by a woman who was crying. She just looked at us without making any attempt to help the man.

Julio started to speak to them in Spanish, then said to me, "They're very frightened that we're here, and that's about all I'm getting. I asked about Carlos, but if they know him they aren't saying."

Another man pushed past the woman and came out of the house. He looked over his shoulder and spoke a flurry of words to her in Spanish and she went back into the trailer, still crying.

"I speak English," the small man said as he approached us. He held his hands out in front of him.

"We just want to talk to Carlos Ruano," I said.

"I am Carlos." He made an effort to smile.

"Let him go," I said to Julio, who was still struggling with the man in the window. Julio let go and man managed to wiggle around and drop back inside the mobile home and out of sight.

"He's my cousin. We are—" Carlos started to say, but I held up my hand and stopped him.

"We don't care about your cousin. We're here to ask you a few question about Eli Waters."

At the mention of Eli's name, the man started to cry. "Such a good man. Sad, sad. My family, we would like to pay our respects," Carlos said, tears streaming down his face. "Mr. Eli helped us out. He gave me a job and sometimes let others from my family help with picking tomatoes or planting. He let me take home fruits and vegetables. We are going to miss him very much."

"Do you know of anyone who might have been angry at Eli or wanted to hurt him?"

From the look on Carlos's face, you would have thought I'd asked him if his children were lizard aliens.

"That is not possible," he said flatly.

"He never got into a fight with anyone? An argument over the price of apples?"

"Maybe a little argument. But he always made it right." Carlos paused. "Maybe one or two left angry, but not because of Mr. Eli."

"Were there any women who hung out at the stand? Or came by often?"

At the mention of women, Carlos looked down with a shy smile. "Mr. Eli, I think he liked the women very much. He would... I don't know the word... made eyes at them. Hand them flowers."

"Did any of the women seem to mind his attention?"

"Mind?"

"Get angry?"

"No, no. A few, they blushed. But anger, no. He wasn't like the men who whistle and make the hand gestures. He was just… special nice. I think some of the older women came by especially because Mr. Eli talked nice and smiled at them."

"What about men? Did he make anyone mad by paying so much attention to the women? Maybe a husband or boyfriend?"

Carlos shook his head. "Never that I saw."

"Any new women come by a lot? Maybe went out to Mr. Eli's trailer with him?"

"There was one woman. I think she was special."

"What did she look like?" I said, trying to hold back my excitement.

"I don't know."

"Then how do you know she was a special woman?" I was disappointed to have such a promising lead jerked away so quickly.

"He say so."

"What exactly did Mr. Eli say?"

"He winked at me and said he was meeting a special woman."

"When was this?"

"A week before I went to work at my church. I help them with the building. Maybe a month ago. One day we were closing and Mr. Eli say, 'I'm going to meet with a very special woman.' Then he winked. That's all I know," Carlos finished with a shrug, swiping at the tears in his eyes.

"You never saw her or heard him say anything else about her?"

"No… wait. Yes, I asked him how it goes with his special woman, and he said he helped her. That might not be the right words. But I did not think much of it because Mr. Eli helped a lot of people."

Carlos couldn't give us any more information. We left the trailer park as the sun was disappearing behind the tree line.

"Who do you think this woman is?" Julio asked as I drove him back to his car.

"Nadine Gordon, maybe? According to her, Eli had been helping her. Now, she also said that their relationship was cooling down, which doesn't jive with her being Eli's special woman."

"Nadine could know something about what happened to Eli and she's *lying* about their relationship cooling off." I was impressed with Julio's astute observation.

"It's possible that Nadine and Eli were going to take it to the next level, whatever that would be, and Mean Gene her baby-daddy found out and made sure that would never happen."

"I like that. Even if Gene has an alibi, bad guys know other bad guys and sometimes they do each other favors."

"Crisscross," I said.

"What?"

"Like in the Hitchcock movie. *Two Men on a Train*. Or *Strangers on a Train*. Something like that. Two men agree to kill each other's wives. The plan is that, if they don't know each other, then they can each kill the other's wife without being connected to the murder. They'd have no apparent motive for the killing. Meanwhile, the husband who *does* have a motive makes sure to have a watertight alibi."

"Oh, okay."

"Putting the pressure on Nadine and Gene should be our next step."

"Stir the pot."

"I think we're mixing metaphors, but, yeah."

"Who do we start with?"

"We'll start with Nadine since Gene lives out of town. Also, if she didn't have anything to do with the murder, then she might be more willing to give up the game."

"Gene might have done it without her knowing," Julio said.

"I believe that he would have killed Eli before telling Nadine, but I don't believe he wouldn't tell her after the fact. The whole point of the exercise would have been to terrorize Nadine so that he could control her."

"I see your point."

"We'll pay her a visit tomorrow afternoon. Try and get her to come down to the office with us. You can bring your patrol car. Riding in the back of a cop car might help her to understand we're serious."

CHAPTER TWENTY-ONE

When I got home, there were giggling sounds coming from the yurt, which I chose to ignore. Inside the house, Cara, Ivy and Alvin were all curled up on the couch. Cara was reading a book, *Behind and Beyond the Badge*, that Pete's wife had given her when she'd heard about our engagement. Ivy was going through her evening cleaning ritual while Alvin snored next to her, though, to his credit, he did raise his little smooshed face and gave me a brief *huff* before falling back to sleep.

"Mom made a salad. It's on the counter," Cara said.

"I think I just feel like a sandwich," I answered, heading into the bedroom to change. Once I'd made my sandwich, I joined her on the couch.

"Do you want to watch something?"

"No, I'm good reading." I was enjoying the peace and quiet and having our little family together. For a moment we could ignore what was going on in the yurt and our fears for the future.

"How's the book?" I asked.

"It's interesting. The author was a homicide investigator with the Tallahassee Police Department. The book's a collection of different first responders' perspectives on their careers. I think Sarah's trying to warn me." Cara must have seen my face. "Don't worry! Actually, it's kind of reassuring to see that everyone in the law enforcement… family has the same worries and problems." She lightly kicked my thigh with her foot.

I smiled at her and opened my own book. I was re-reading *'Salem's Lot*, a Stephen King classic I'd enjoyed as a kid.

After Cara went to bed, my stomach made it clear that the sandwich hadn't been enough. Browsing around the kitchen, I found the bowl containing the salad that Anna had made. It looked pretty good, with crumbled cheese, olives, spinach and other rabbit food. I was a little disappointed that there was only one mushroom in the mix, which I finally found at the very bottom of the bowl.

I read a little while longer, then joined Cara in bed. I was feeling particularly relaxed after our quiet evening and fell asleep quickly.

The things I dreamed that night were terrifying and bizarre. Cara told me later that I had been thrashing around so much she'd considered waking me up, but instead she'd decided that even restless sleep was better than no sleep. So she'd taken her pillow and a blanket and spent the rest of the night on the couch.

I opened my eyes with a start and grimaced at the light flooding in through the window. My head was a scramble of strange images from the night before. I lay in bed for a few minutes, trying to remember not only where I was but *who* I was. A single phrase—*Do not resist*—was going around and around in my head.

"What in the ever-loving hell?!" I exclaimed, rolling over and falling out of the bed as I tried to get up. I was drenched in sweat.

Cara came in from the kitchen. "Are you all right?" she asked with concern.

"I don't know yet. My head feels funny. The dreams I

had last night…" *Do not resist*, I could still hear a voice telling me. I think it was Pete's. Or Cara's. Or maybe both of them. "What did I have to drink last night?" I asked, trying to make a joke out of it though I knew I hadn't even had a beer.

I stumbled to the bathroom and managed to shave myself without cutting anything off. My mind was still a whirl of thoughts and crazy images. The hot shower helped. By the time I'd dried myself off and put on some clothes, I was finally thinking more clearly.

Then I remembered the salad I'd eaten. The salad that Anna had made. In that big bowl where I'd found one lone mushroom at the bottom. A mushroom that had looked a little different than what I usually put on my salad, but with Anna and Henry everything was a little different… a little more hippie. Anger came rolling up from deep inside of me.

"Cara!" I yelled as I stalked out of the bedroom. "Your mother put a friggin' psychedelic mushroom in my salad!"

Cara just stared at me, trying to make sense of what I was saying. My fury decided to bypass her and I went to the front door and flung it open

"Anna! Get in here now!" I screamed at the top of my lungs. I turned and started pacing between the kitchen and living room.

Anna came hesitantly through the door, followed closely by Henry. "What's the matter?" she asked, fear and worry in her voice.

"What the hell do you think is the matter?" I yelled. "You put a psychedelic mushroom in my salad and have the nerve to ask me what's the matter?"

Anna's face flushed. "I… I…"

Henry just stood by the door, looking panicked. Then his flight response kicked in and he said, "I'll be outside," escaping through the door before anyone else could say anything.

"How dare you?" I said, staring at Anna angrily.

Out of the corner of my eye, I could see that Cara was stuck in an indecisive loop. She would start to move forward and say something, but then just stand there, looking back and forth between her mother and me.

"I didn't mean to," Anna stammered and dropped onto one of the kitchen chairs. She looked very vulnerable, which triggered a sympathetic response from me. It couldn't put out the inferno of my rage, but it threw a good-size bucket of water on it.

"I could have been called out last night! People's lives might have been put at risk." My tone was still harsh, but I wasn't yelling anymore. The way Anna was sitting there, staring down at the table, made my voice soften. "What were you thinking?"

"It was an accident. I used the same bowl to collect the mushrooms that I used for your salad. I promise you, I didn't realize there was still one in the bowl." She didn't look up. Anna was the picture of shame.

"Look, I know you didn't mean it. We're just... Why have you been so crazy about us getting married?" I decided to take advantage of having the high ground to deal with the issue of her wedding mania.

"I..." She looked up for the first time since sitting down at the table and locked eyes with Cara.

"You *have* been acting like a crazy woman," Cara said softly.

"I'm sorry. I... There was a... thing that happened a long time ago. I told you about how I followed in Peggy's footsteps to find myself. Well, when I got back, I was like, 'Okay, that's out of my system. It's time to settle down.' I know that doesn't sound like me, but at the time my parents'... expectations... Well, I met a guy... Actually I'd known him in high school, but we hadn't dated or anything. When I came back, I ran into him and one thing led to another. We started seeing each other. It was a whirlwind. He really was a nice guy..." Anna spoke with a deep melancholy.

"Wait. Where was Dad?" Cara asked, confused.

"This was about a year before I met Henry. Travis was

his name. Terrific Travis the other girls called him. Travis and I set a date for a wedding. My mother was so excited. I was finally feeling like I was a part of… the world around me. I'd never quite fit into our small town, not much more than Peggy had, but now everyone was being so nice, helping me pick out invitations and flowers. The minister actually smiled at me. I think that was a first. It took us three months to get everything ready." She stopped talking and wiped at her eyes.

"What happened?" Cara asked. My guess was that her fiancé must have been killed.

"He left. Three days before the wedding, his brother came over to our house and told me that Travis had joined the Air Force. He never even had the guts to write me a letter or call me. We spent two weeks getting deposits back and undoing all of the planning that had gone into the wedding. Mom told me that it was my imagination, but I swear everyone in town, all those people who had started to be nice to me, now they were looking at me like there was something wrong with me. I left a month later and didn't go back for years. But soon after I left, I met your dad and we had you." Anna gave Cara a glowing smile.

"That must have been awful," Cara said, sitting down and putting her arm around her mother.

"It all worked out," Anna said, wiping her eyes and leaning into her daughter. "But ever since then I get a little looney at the thought of a wedding ceremony."

"I guess that explains why you and Dad have had so many vow renewals."

"I know that Henry loves me and would never run out on me, but deep down… I get scared sometimes. I know it's a crutch, but whenever I'm feeling insecure, standing next to your father and recommitting ourselves to each other makes me feel better. When I heard that you all were engaged, I just wanted to make sure that nothing happens to spoil your happiness."

I raised my right hand. "I promise you that, as long as

Cara will have me, I'll be there when the minister, Voodoo priest or whoever says that we're married."

Anna reached out and took my hand. "I know you're a good man. I've seen your aura in the moonlight."

With our emotions purged, I finished getting ready for work. Before I left, I texted Darlene that I was running late and asked her to meet Celina Pappas if she got there before I did.

As I expected, Darlene and Celina Pappas were waiting in the lobby when I got to the office. I thanked Darlene and took Celina back to the conference room.

"We can talk in here." Then I filled her in on everything I'd learned from Bob Pittman. I tried to deliver the news as gently as possible to a mother who was still grieving, even after so many years.

"I knew something like that had happened to him. Hearing the details, though… it's still difficult." For the second time that day, I watched a woman wipe away tears.

"I wish I had better news," I told her, knowing there was no way I could have made the information hurt any less.

"I'm grateful," she said, trying to give me a smile. "The sad fact is that so many people were hurt by that pig." The smile was gone, replaced by a healthy dose of vitriol.

"He paid a price for the way he lived his life," I reassured her. *Could she have been the one to make him pay?* asked the voice inside my head.

She choked a little as she continued wiping at her tears. "Could I get a glass of water?"

"Of course. I'll be right back."

I stepped into the hall and, out of habit, checked the messages on my phone. There was one from Cary Trent, McCune's former maid, asking if she could get into her apartment on the McCune estate. I wasn't about to let her go there on her own, so I texted her back that if she could come to the office in half an hour, I'd escort her to the house and let her get whatever she wanted from her room. Before I'd finished fetching the water for Celina Pappas, Cary had responded that she was on her way.

Celina and I talked for a little while longer. She told me that she would be in the area for a few more days and would continue to be available to answer any questions. I thanked her and started to escort her back to the front when I saw Dad coming out of his office. After Celina assured me she could find her own way out, I went to have a quick word with Dad.

"Who knows?" was his answer when I asked him how the campaign was going. "We've got that candidates' rally at the courthouse on Saturday. Hopefully, we can get some supporters out to it. Sam's daughter, Emily, has stepped up to coordinate the folks who have volunteered to help."

"Parks certainly has a strong personal interest in seeing you reelected."

Major Sam Parks was in charge of most of the day-to-day administrative responsibilities of the sheriff's office. Though he'd often threatened retirement, I knew he enjoyed working for Dad. If Chief Maxwell won the election, he'd do what any sheriff would do and replace the top administrative officers with his own choices to run the departments. I didn't doubt that ninety-nine percent of the employees in the department would be voting for Dad.

"The investigations?" he asked me.

"Do you want the truth or something that will make you feel better?"

"Hit me with the truth," Dad said, a grim smile on his face.

"If we knew of someone who wanted Eli Waters dead, that would help. As it is, everyone loved the old letch."

"The business and his farm must be worth some money. Doesn't he have some family?"

"His brother runs a book publishing and distribution company in Tallahassee. According to the brother, he has no money problems, but that is an avenue we're looking into.

It's going to take time to dig into his finances and know for sure whether he's telling the truth."

"And McCune?"

"Everyone on the planet wanted McCune dead. Unfortunately, not many had the opportunity. There's also that business with his daughter getting stabbed. Darlene and I think she's playing coy with the truth."

"Great." Dad sighed. "Didn't you say there was a chance that the Waters and McCune murders could be connected?"

"That's a big fat maybe. I'm resisting the urge to connect them right now. Darlene and I figure it's better to investigate them separately until the evidence makes it clear whether they're connected or not." As soon as I said I was resisting the urge, the strange phrase from my nightmares popped back into my head—*Do not resist*. Now it seemed that I could remember a vampire version of Cara who'd kept repeating that phrase as she came in to take a bite out of my neck. *Do not resist.*

"If you run into any roadblocks, let me know," Dad said and walked away, snapping me out of my thoughts.

Cary Trent was waiting for me in the lobby. She seemed a bit confused. Through the glass door behind her, I could see a car leaving the parking lot at high speed. *Must be a hot lead or someone needing backup ASAP*, I thought.

CHAPTER TWENTY-TWO

I went back to grab my keys from my desk, then asked Cary to follow me out to McCune's property.

"I'm sorry, but after the stabbing the other day, we don't want to take the chance of another attack," I explained to her as I unlocked the front door.

"You had the locks changed?" she asked.

"We do on some crime scenes. Just an added precaution. We aren't naïve enough to think that crime scene tape is going to keep people from entering a house when they have a key."

I followed her through the mansion. It was dark and quiet. The over-the-top furnishings and large empty spaces made it seem foreboding. I shook off the feeling, deciding that I was still on edge after the magic mushroom-induced nightmares.

Cary confidently made her way to the small apartment that was at the back of the house over the kitchen. It had two rooms and a bathroom.

"Nice," I said, looking out the windows. The angle wasn't quite right to see the shed where the tractor was stored.

"I'm going to miss the apartment and the salary," Cary said as she packed a couple of suitcases.

"Meredith McCune is going to need a caretaker until she sells the house."

"I don't think she's going to be interested in keeping me on," she said with a smirk.

"Did McCune hire you?"

"A service hired me."

"Had you ever met McCune prior to working for him?"

"No. Where would I meet a man like McCune?" she said with a rough laugh. I watched her clean out the small desk that sat in one corner of the room by a window.

"We ran a background check on you. Sorry, but it's just standard operating procedure. You're from Texas?" I remembered that the background check hadn't revealed anything of interest. It sounded like the woman had led a pretty quiet life.

"Yes, that's how I got hired. McCune uses… used a company out of Texas. I guess it was the one he'd used when he lived out there."

"Never married?"

"No. Close a few times. And, as you should know from your research into my background, I've never had a child."

Cary could have been considered attractive if she didn't have a perpetual frown on her face. I'd taken some of that as a disapproval of McCune's lifestyle and the general anxiety of having a murder take place in close proximity to her. However, the look hadn't gone away. Now, as I studied her face, I could see that some of the worry lines were deeply ingrained. No husband, no children… *What does she have to worry about*, I wondered.

"Sorry about the questions and the prying. I'm afraid it's all a part of the job," I said, not sorry at all. I was curious by nature. Being able to be nosy was one of the perks of the job.

"I'm ready," she said. "Would you mind carrying one of the suitcases?"

I grabbed the larger of the two and let her go first down the staircase. Once outside, I helped her load the suitcases into her older model Cadillac.

"Nice, solid car," I said.

"My last employer let me have it for a song. It's a real pleasure to drive."

"What are your plans? We'll need you to stay in touch since you're a material witness."

"I'm not leaving town yet. I'll be at the motel another night or two. I've spent the last few days filling out online employment applications."

I made sure she got out of the gate safely, then decided to take a walk around the grounds. If the person who stabbed Meredith hadn't parked in the driveway behind her, then maybe they'd come onto the estate another way.

I didn't find any sign that anyone else had been there. I even drove to the other gate at the rear of the property and found it still securely chained and locked with one of our locks. And I didn't believe that the mad stabber had walked down the road. They had to have pulled up behind Meredith, which made her one big fat liar. I called Darlene.

"She's lying to us," I said.

"No shit, Sherlock," Darlene shot back.

"I know we both figured that, but the point now is that I'm positive she had to have known who stabbed her. I think we need to find a way to put some pressure on her."

"All we need to do is find a way to call off her attack dog. I went by the hospital a little while ago, and he was standing outside her room looking like the best dressed Rottweiler in town."

"I've got Horton on it. I'll give him a call tomorrow and see if he has anything we can use. I wish I knew how involved Briggs is in whatever the hell she's involved with."

"Maybe the stabbing has to do with some other person she pissed off and has nothing at all to do with her father's murder. The McCunes seem to have a knack for making people hate them."

"I hadn't thought about that. You've got a point. Someone followed her over here from Texas, figuring it would be a good opportunity to take a stab at her, pun intended, when she was out of her element. Whoever the attacker is could represent some dirty laundry of hers that she doesn't want to air."

"How did it go with Celina Pappas?"

"It was tough relaying Pittman's story to her."

"She must have been pretty upset. She almost hit me leaving the office," Darlene said. I remembered the car that I'd seen recklessly leaving the parking lot.

"I didn't think she was that upset when she left. Strange."

Back at the office, I intended to map out some of the information that had been coming in fast and furious. I looked at the different reports and suspects spread out on my desk. I'd barely had room to organize both cases the way I wanted. *Tough to keep the two cases separated*, I thought. *Do not resist* immediately popped into my head. Then my phone rang.

"What's up, Julio?"

"I went back out and talked with Carlos. I thought he might remember something else in a more relaxed situation."

"Did he?"

"We went over what Eli had said about helping the girl. And Carlos remembered that Eli had said something about teaching or lessons. He wasn't sure exactly what Eli had meant."

"Anything else?"

"No, sorry."

"Every little bit. Thanks, Julio."

I went back to my layout.

"You need a bigger desk," Pete said, coming up behind me.

"Thanks. I expect a big promotion when Chief Maxwell takes over. Maybe I'll get it then," I said in my best *woe-is-me* voice.

"If Maxwell wins, we won't need desks. We'll all be walking a beat."

"No one walks around here."

"Maxwell has a couple of his cops who ride bikes around the courthouse square. He might create a bike squad for us. It'd be great. I could lose a few pounds," Pete joked.

"Let's hope it doesn't come to that. With that as the goal, why don't you solve these two murders for me." I waved at the papers.

"Why didn't you lay all of this out in the conference room?"

"Major Parks is having a budget meeting with some of the department heads in one, and some of the assistants are setting up for a birthday party in the other," I said, moving pieces of paper around.

"Have you decided on one case or two?" Pete asked.

"Let's look at it as one case," I said, deciding to listen to that strange voice in my head, at least for the moment.

"Sounds good. I'll start. McCune was murdered. Call him the primary. That would make Eli Waters the secondary crime. Does that make any sense?" Pete asked.

I furrowed my brow and tried to see the sequence of events.

"Actually, that would solve one of the main problems with the Waters case. No one had a motive for killing that man. I take that back. There *could* be one jealous ex out there. But, ignoring him for the moment, there's no obvious motive for killing Eli. But if he's the secondary target, then the motive can be covering up the first murder. Did Eli see something or hear something? Here was a man who was moving from his farm to his house to his stand all the time. He had lots of friends, especially women. He's the perfect person to have been in the wrong place at the wrong time."

"McCune is murdered. Eli knows something, so the killer has to take Eli out," Pete said.

"In that case, then the person who killed McCune was known to Eli."

"How do you figure that?"

"Eli was dressed—" I started, then realized something.

"Eli was dressed to meet a woman. If we're assuming the person who murdered Eli was the person he was meeting—and I think that's a safe assumption since no one has come forward to admit to being his hot date for the night—then the person who murdered Eli is a woman. If her motive was to cover up her participation in the murder of McCune, then the person who murdered McCune was probably a woman." I thought this cleared the air a little, but I still wasn't sure what I was seeing.

"Name your female suspects," Pete instructed.

"Celina Pappas. Her alibi is good, but not air tight," I said grumpily. "I don't like it." I thought about her tearing out of the parking lot. Had I let my sympathy for her blind me to the possibility that she could have committed the murders?

"Did she know Waters?"

"Unlikely. Though she's the type of woman you could trust pretty easily. But I don't think she's quite… sexy enough for Eli to be excited about dating her."

"Other women?"

"Meredith McCune. Her alibi is tight. However, she has enough money to buy a hit squad of mercenaries. She even has her own legal eagle attack beagle by her side. I can't see her being Eli's date. Not that he wouldn't consider her a very hot date. I just can't see her lowering herself to flirt with him. Besides, that would have required her to be in the local area for longer than she was. And I don't think Sean Briggs was Eli's type.

"Then there's the maid, Cary Trent, but she doesn't have a motive. She had the opportunity. But the means?"

"What do—" Pete was interrupted by my phone. It was dispatch.

"Some one just called 911 and reported that Cary Trent has been hit by a car. When I put her name in the system, it was flagged with your name," the dispatcher told me.

"Where was the accident?" I asked, getting to my feet.

"At the Roads Best Motel."

"Have you sent a car? An ambulance?" I asked, already

knowing it was a stupid question.

"They're both in route."

"I'll be there in ten," I said, hanging up. "Want to ride along?" I asked Pete.

"I've got some reports to write so… Yeah, let's go," he said with smile.

"What were you saying?" I asked as I pulled onto the road and flipped on the lights in my grill. I kept the siren off since I wasn't going to be the first on scene anyway.

"I was asking what means you were talking about?"

"McCune may have been hit in the head with the proverbial blunt object, but the killer used a tractor with a bucket on the front to apply the killing blow. According to Pops, no one at the house could drive the tractor."

"Where is Cary Trent from?"

"Houston. Born and bred. City girl. She has that look."

I quit talking, giving my full attention to my driving as I had to do a little weaving in and out of traffic. I made good time and pulled up in front of the motel only minutes after Deputy Sykes and an ambulance.

"I don't need an ambulance. I can't afford one. I just want to get in my car," Cary was saying in a loud voice to Sykes and a couple of EMTs.

"You could have a head injury," one of the EMTs told her.

"I wouldn't have even called 911," Cary said, sounding exasperated. She glanced at Pete and me as we walked up. "Jeezus! Is every first responder in the county going to show up?"

Tarek, the motel owner's son, was standing about twenty feet away. "I called 911. You were knocked down. That car came barreling through here."

"I told you I was fine. I need to get going," she said and headed toward her car. Suddenly, she stopped and turned to look at us. "If that's okay with everybody."

"I'd like to ask you about the car that attempted to hit you," I said, thinking about Meredith McCune's stabbing.

"I've already told everyone else. I didn't see anything. I had my back turned when the car bumped me," she said. "And that's all it was, a bump. I've got a dinner date. Okay?" Her brazen attitude had all of us buffaloed for a moment. It was long enough for her to reach her car and drive off.

I turned to Tarek, "What did you see?"

"I swear, the car came in fast. Ms. Trent was walking away from the office when the car came from the back of the motel. I thought it was going to run her down and kill her. Only at the last second did she throw herself out of the way," Tarek stammered.

"Wait, she threw *herself* out of the way?" I asked as the EMTs packed up their stuff and headed to their next call.

"That's right."

"But she said she didn't see the car coming."

"I saw her look up."

"What kind of car was it?"

"Some sort of sedan, probably a rental. White, very nondescript."

"Was a man or woman driving it?"

"A man maybe? They had a baseball cap on, pulled down over their head. So I couldn't really see their hair or face."

"Did you see which way they turned when they left?"

"Sure. Toward the interstate," Tarek said.

Before I could ask anything else, my phone's text alert went off. I read the message, then turned to Pete. "Let's go." I knew where some of the puzzle pieces fit now.

Back in the car, I called Darlene. "I think I know who our killers are. That's the good news. The bad news is that I don't know where they are now," I told her.

"Killers, plural? So the two cases *aren't* linked."

"No. They are. One's a murderer and the other person conspired to commit the murders. Or at least one of the murders."

"Celina Pappas is gone. She checked out of her motel and she isn't answering her phone. I wanted to check on her after seeing how she left the office," Darlene said.

"Don't worry about her. I think I know why she skedaddled too."

"Aren't you the man with all the answers?"

"Problem is, now that I know who they are, I don't know how to catch them. Wait! Damn!" I spun the car around. "I know what I would do if I was in their shoes."

"What are you talking about?" Darlene asked. Even over the phone, I could hear her confusion.

"Head to McCune's place now."

"What are you talking about?"

"He's gone manic," Pete shouted loud enough for Darlene to hear him over the phone.

"I've always liked him better when he's in a depressive phase," Darlene said.

"Screw both of you. It's Meredith and Cary. Both of them could be headed for McCune's house with the intent of burning the place down."

"I'm on my way. But I think you're crazy," Darlene said.

"Look, it's their only chance to muddy the waters. They both have to realize that they're about at the end of their rope. Before I called you, I got a message from Tom Horton that Meredith had checked herself out of the hospital and Sean Briggs has resigned as her lawyer. That should give you some idea of the thin ice she's walking on I'll meet you at McCune's." I disconnected the call and flipped on the siren. I was on a two-lane road now and I wanted everyone out of my way.

I hoped I wasn't making a fool of myself. If I had my facts right, both women were smart, ruthless and determined. I knew what I would do in their shoes, but maybe they were smarter than me.

CHAPTER TWENTY-THREE

About two miles out from the McCune property, I killed the siren and glanced at Pete. "Call Darlene back and tell her to do the same."

Pete did as instructed, then put the phone on speaker and put in on the dash.

When we got to McCune's driveway, I knew I was right at least about one of them. Someone had plowed through the gates, leaving them bent and half off their hinges.

"Damn, I can't wait to see the car," Pete said we drove past the damaged gates.

"Darlene, the gate is smashed open. Pete and I are going in."

"I'm right behind you," she said. "What exactly are we looking at?"

"Two homicidal women. Cary stabbed Meredith and Meredith tried to run Cary down at the Roads Best about forty-five minutes ago."

"I suddenly wish I had my gear in the car," Pete said. He took out his Glock 21 and checked to make sure there was a round in the chamber. "I see smoke."

Sure enough, there was a column of smoke rising from the direction of the house. As we got closer, I saw a Chevy

Malibu parked at a crazy angle near the front steps. From the damage to the front of the car, it was obviously the one that had smashed its way through the gate.

I blocked the car in and got out. Keeping one eye on the building, I went to the back of my car where Pete was already waiting.

"I want the rifle," he said. "I hope you've sighted it in sometime in the last year."

I popped the trunk open and grabbed my tactical vest and shotgun. Pete pulled out an extra vest that I kept in the car and put it on, though it was too small for him to do up all the straps. I grabbed a handful of extra buckshot.

"Looks like something's on fire at the back of the house," I said.

I heard a car pulling up behind us and whirled around to see Darlene slide to a stop and jump out.

"I called for backup, but we may have this to ourselves for a while. There's a big pile up on the interstate and most of patrol is there," Darlene said while strapping her own gear on.

There was a loud crash from the back of the house.

"What the hell was that?" Pete asked, then looked a both of us. "We go together. Left side of the house."

"If we split up and—" I started, but Pete cut me off.

"Sign up for the SWAT team and I'll listen to you. We aren't taking a chance of one of us getting caught in the crossfire. We stay together," he hissed. "Our only responsibility here is to make sure no bad gals get loose to wreak havoc on anyone else."

Darlene and I weren't going to argue with him. We started around the left side of the house as a loud explosion, accompanied by a big puff of coal black smoke, came from the direction of the tractor shed.

We were going wide around the back corner of the house, using clumps of azaleas for concealment. We reached a point where we could see both the back of the house and the tractor shed, which was now engulfed in flames. One of the roll-up doors was halfway open and smoke billowed out from it. Cary's Cadillac was parked between the shed and the house. I could see movement on the other side of the car.

"Let's move to—" Pete began when there was a crack of rifle fire from a balcony on the second floor of the house. We dropped and hugged the ground. The azaleas might provide concealment, but they weren't going to stop a bullet.

"Wasn't aimed at us," Darlene said.

"I'll kill you, you traitorous bitch!" I recognized the voice as Meredith's.

"Your father killed my son!" With that, a bottle of flaming liquid came flying over Cary's car and fell a dozen feet short of the house, but in line with the balcony.

"Ranging shot," Pete commented. From our prone positions under the bushes, we had a pretty good view of the playing field. A couple more rifle rounds were fired from the balcony and we saw them punch holes in Cary's car.

Darlene had called for the fire department to respond as soon as she saw the smoke. Now she radioed dispatch and told them to hold the engines at the gate. It wouldn't help anything to have our firemen gunned down.

"That's a hunting rifle. Big caliber. We definitely don't want to attract her attention," Pete said.

"I'd sure like to take at least one of them alive," I said, pondering the situation. Then another Molotov cocktail came flying from the far side of the car. At almost the same second, another rifle shot rang out and the back windows of the Cadillac blew out.

"Who do you want, the fire breathing dragon or Annie Oakley?" Darlene asked, sounding like she had little enthusiasm for taking on either one.

"I say we let them fight it out," Pete suggested.

"Apart from our moral obligation to save lives, if they die at each other's hands then there will always be suspicions about Dad and his part in getting rid of McCune."

"Not many people are going to believe that kind of garbage," Pete said dismissively.

"This is Florida. A dozen votes can easily sway an election," Darlene said.

"Bingo! Do you want to end up as one of Maxwell's minions?"

Pete sighed. "Okay, here's the plan," he said, looking through the scope of my rifle. "The building is stucco. I can probably keep Meredith out of the window by shooting around the frame. Unless she's wearing eye protection, pieces of stucco and cinder block flying into her face will make it hard for her to take aim with her hunting rifle."

"What's the rest of the plan?" I asked as I watched Cary chuck another Molotov cocktail at the house. This one went a little wide and hit the concrete deck around the pool, sending fire rolling into the flower beds.

"Sorry, that's all I have. You all can take care of the firebug."

"Fine. If you can keep Meredith from popping up and shooting us, I'll go around the back of the tractor shed and come up on Cary's right. Darlene, you take her from the left."

"You realize that if she's got one of those Molotov cocktails, then she can just kill herself and there isn't anything we could do to stop her," Darlene said.

"We'll just have to chance it. On your mark, big guy," I said to Pete.

"Meredith's been sticking her head up about every twenty seconds by my count. There she goes." He paused. "Damn, she's gone again. Apparently she decided not to take a shot. Next time, be ready." Pete started to count. It seemed like a lot longer than twenty seconds to me, but finally he said, "There she is," and squeezed the trigger of the rifle.

Darlene and I didn't hang around to see the result of his shot. I cleared the side of the building and saw Darlene take up position behind a stack of firewood by the shed. I kept going around the back of building. The wind was blowing away from the house, so the smoke from the burning shed was wafting around behind it. The mix of burning plastic, rubber and who knew what else had me gagging as I made it to the other side of the shed.

This was where things got tricky for me. This side of the shed would be visible to Meredith in her sniper's nest. I heard a shot and started to duck, but from the sound of the shot, it had come from my smaller caliber AR-15 rather than McCune's big-bore hunting rifle. Pete was keeping me covered.

I looked frantically from left to right, seeking not just concealment but also cover. Now that Meredith and Cary both knew we were there, we were going to become targets in their pissing match. There was no stacked firewood on this side of the building, but a six-foot harrow for the tractor was parked off to the side. I dove behind it and took a minute to catch my breath. I counted to thirty without hearing any more shots. My radio cackled.

"I think she's retreated back into the house," Pete said. "She's probably looking for a different window or balcony. Keep behind your cover until I can find her."

I thought about the fact that Pete was still behind the azaleas, which wouldn't provide him any protection if Meredith got the upper hand.

"Pete, get to some cover."

"Second that," Darlene's voice came through the radio.

There was a brief hesitation. Then Pete said, "Roger that. Cover me on my mark."

I tried to get in position to watch the house around the steel harrows while exposing as little of myself as possible.

I heard a *whoosh* from in front of the workshop, followed by a couple of gun shots. Handgun this time, not rifle.

"I'm okay," I heard Darlene say over the radio. "The witch threw one of her hot toddies at me, but I sent her running. She's behind her car."

"I'm going on three," Pete said. He counted down and I started scanning all the windows, balconies and crevices I could find. A rifle barrel appeared through a set of French doors on the third floor.

Nice, I thought. I squeezed off three rounds from my shotgun that blew glass out of both the doors. I wasn't trying to hit Meredith, just make her take cover. But as I fired the first round, she managed to pull off a shot. I said a little prayer for both of my partners.

"Close but no cigar," Pete's voice came over the radio. "Found good cover, but it has a limited view of the rear of the house."

"Roger that," Darlene said.

"Stay put," I instructed.

I looked around, trying to figure out how to deal with our firebug and fast. The workshop fire was getting way out of hand. I was thirty feet from the steel frame building and could feel the heat coming off of it. I wondered at what point the steel would give way and the building would collapse.

"Ideas? Anyone?" I asked over the radio.

I'll be damned if Cary didn't lob a fire bomb around the corner in my direction. She must have heard the shots I'd fired at Meredith. The bottle fell short and landed in the grass. It didn't break, so the fire just oozed out over the ground. Not terribly threatening, but I now had fire in front of me as well as the heat from the burning workshop at my back.

"None that don't end up with fireface getting shot," Darlene answered me.

"She just threw a bomb at me. I'm caring less and less. If she'd gotten a little more lift on her throw, it would have hit the concrete slab to the right of me." As I said it, I looked at the ten-by-ten-foot slab. There was a drain in the middle of it. Slab plus drain equaled water. I saw the spigot nearby attached to an upright four-by-six, with a garden hose next to it on a metal wheel. There was a low wall of cinderblocks on that side of the slab. I needed to get over there and see how much hose there was. Could I keep my ass low enough not to get it shot off by Meredith? It was worth a try.

"Friends, I need a little cover. I may have found a

solution."

"I've got a bead on Miss Red Ryder. She's at the small window on the first floor. I think she figured out she didn't want to be stuck in a burning building." When Pete said this, I noticed that one of Cary's earlier firebombs had fallen close enough that the fire had walked its way to the house and was now crawling up the side of the structure.

Meredith on the first floor worked for my plan. It would be much easier keeping my ass out of range.

"I'm going… now!" I said and dashed toward the cinderblocks. I banged my shoulder dropping down behind cover, but I didn't have a bullet hole in me so all was good.

There was at least a hundred feet of hose rolled up on the wheel beside the spigot. I reached up, trying to keep my hand behind the post that the spigot was attached to. I didn't want to end up with less fingers than I'd started the day with. As soon as I turned the knob, water gushed out of the spigot.

"I've got a plan," I said into the radio, attaching the end of the hose to the spigot. "This relies on Pete keeping Meredith from shooting us."

"I've got your back right now. But move quick before she decides on changing location," Pete said.

"Darlene, I've got a hose. If you'll come at dragon breath about five seconds behind me and jump her, I'll keep her attention and spray her down with water so you all won't go up in flames."

"You better know what you're doing with that hose. Burning to death is numero uno on my list of one hundred ways I least want to die."

"Just make sure I'm spraying her before you jump on her."

"Go fast. My turkey could flush any minute," Pete said.

"I'm going." I just hoped that I had gauged the distance right. Also, I prayed that the hose wouldn't get a kink in it. I'd already tested the wheel to make sure it moved freely.

I got up and made a dash for the front of the shed, while

at the same time staying as close to the building as the heat would allow me in order to use it as concealment from Cary. Finally, I had no choice but to come around the edge and confront whatever was waiting for me on the other side.

It was just my luck that she was ready to light the next bomb when I appeared. I squeezed the pistol-grip nozzle on the hose. Nothing happened. My brain, coming late to the party, scolded me for not having cleared the air out of the hose before running toward the maniac with the fireballs.

Cary didn't hesitate, hurling the flaming glass bottle. I had no time to react as the bottle smashed in front of me, splashing gas and burning fumes at my feet. Mercifully, water started to squirt from the hose. Instead of squirting Cary, I proceeded to water myself and the puddle of flames in front of me.

I was aware of Cary crashing to the ground with Darlene on her back. They fell behind Cary's car, which she'd been using for cover in her battle with Meredith.

Then I heard a couple of shots ring out and remembered that, unlike Darlene and Cary, I was still exposed to gunfire from Meredith. I ran forward, still holding the hose and squirting it in the general direction of Cary and Darlene, who were wrestling on the ground. I threw myself on top of them. I could hear Darlene instructing Cary to submit, which she seemed reluctant to do until she felt the added weight of my body.

In less than a minute, we had her handcuffed and shouting invectives at us. I'd dropped my radio, but Darlene pulled hers out. "Dragon is down!"

"Good thing, 'cause I've lost Top Gun," Pete said, not sounding happy at all.

"Let us know what you need us to do," I said, taking Darlene's radio while she read our prisoner her rights. "We're going to need to move soon. The heat from the workshop is getting pretty intense."

I was going to have to start spraying the ground behind us with water to protect the five-gallon can of gas that Cary had been using to make her cocktails. I could see the paint on the shed doors curling up and smoking. We were only fifteen feet from it.

"Shit, I hear a car out front. Damn!"

"What?"

"Sounds like a demolition derby in the front of the house. Must be Meredith making a run for it."

Using Darlene's radio, I switched channels and told the firefighters and the deputies who'd finally arrived to block the road out and to be ready for a mad woman in a car.

As we dragged the cursing Cary toward the front of the house, Pete joined us. We were halfway around the house when we heard the roar of a car coming back our way.

"I could take her out," Pete said, holding my rifle at the ready as we moved up against the house.

"Let her try getting out the back." I knew the gate was chained, but Meredith might be able to drive through that, so I called for a deputy to go around and block that road out of the property. "Try hard not to shoot her, but be aware she is armed and crazy," I said.

"On it," I heard Julio's voice on the radio.

Ten minutes later, I flinched when I heard shots from the direction of the rear entrance.

CHAPTER TWENTY-FOUR

It turned out that Meredith had surrendered, but not until she'd exchanged a couple of rounds with Julio.

"Nice!" Dad said a couple of hours later when I called to tell him that we'd rounded up the female desperadoes. "What the hell is their story?"

"I've figured out some of it. Meredith and Cary were working together up to a point. I think that, somehow, Meredith helped arrange for Cary to get the job with McCune. She managed a company that her father used to vet hires and do payroll for his employees."

"You said that Eli's murder *is* connected?"

"Yes, and that might have been where the falling out started. I think Cary talked Eli into coming out to the house and giving her tractor lessons. McCune traveled enough that she could have arranged times when she could do it without him knowing."

"So Eli was killed as part of the cover up?"

"Yes, but I'm not sure who murdered him. Either Meredith pressured Cary into doing it, or she did it herself. I'm leaning toward the former. From the murder scene at Eli's, it looked like he was ready for a date with Cary. Also, he seemed to be very comfortable with the person who killed him."

"Did Meredith hire Cary to kill her father?"

"I don't think so. I have my suspicions, but… I'll get back with you later on Cary's motive. First, I suspect that Cary isn't her real name, but it would have been easy enough for Meredith to fabricate Cary's ID when she was hired. We ran a standard background check, but looking back, I remember it was thinner than most."

"This all sounds very convoluted," Dad said, clearly hoping for a standard murder-for-money ending.

"Darlene and I are going to question the suspects now. I'll fill you in when we have all the details," I said.

"Remember the candidates' rally on Saturday," Dad reminded me. His voice had a bit more spring to it.

"Cara and I'll be there," I assured him.

I ended the call and waited for Darlene to get back from changing her clothes. We had booked both suspects into the jail an hour earlier, and I hoped that Cary's fingerprints would come back with her true identity. As soon as Darlene was ready, we were going back over to talk to our murder suspects. At this point, they had only been charged with an arm's length of charges related to their firefight. We could take our time and work with the State Attorney when it came to charges in the deaths of McCune and Waters.

"You were hoping to spray me and the suspect down for your own sick purposes, weren't you?" Darlene said with a sad shake of her head as she came up to my desk.

"Good job tackling her."

"Somebody had to. You were too busy doing your fire and water dance."

"I'd thought everything through, too. Who would have thought about the air in the hose?"

We walked over to the jail, enjoying the fresh October air and the knowledge that the murderers were locked up.

"We'll talk to Cary Trent first," I told the sergeant at the desk.

Ten minutes later she was ushered into the interview

room wearing her new orange jumpsuit and handcuffs. Oddly, she was wearing the same self-satisfied look that I was sure I had on.

"You look happy with yourself."

"I am."

"Cary—" Darlene started, but the woman held up her chained hand.

"Sorry about that. I should have told you when you were booking me into the jail. I was still a little worked up. My real name is Regina Broussard. My son's name was Duane Broussard. He died on the same death trap rig that Ryan Pappas worked on."

"Did you see Mrs. Pappas when you came to this office this morning?" I asked.

"I did. I think she recognized me."

"Did she have anything to do with your revenge plot against McCune?"

"No. We met several times after her son disappeared, but I haven't seen her for a couple of years."

"You seduced Mr. Waters into teaching you how to drive a tractor?" Darlene said.

"Is that a question or a statement? He was drooling when he saw me. I'd already decided that I wanted to use the tractor to crush McCune's skull. That's what happed to Duane. His head was crushed in a piece of machinery because it lacked the proper safety features. All of the equipment on that rig was junk."

"Did you approach Meredith or did she approach you?"

"That conniving witch approached me. She looked me up after she'd done some research on her father's old companies. Told me she was trying to make amends. Ha! She was sounding me out. Looking for someone she could use as a weapon against her father. The perfect murder. She set it up so that I didn't look like I had a motive. Unlike hiring a killer, there'd be no money trail. Plus, I'm smarter than your average hired killer. Win, win."

"Who met with Eli the night he was murdered?" I asked.

"We both did." I saw an angry blush come to her cheeks.

"Tell us what happened," Darlene encouraged.

"Meredith and I had gone 'round and 'round about how to deal with Eli now that McCune was dead. She was hot and heavy that he had to be killed. I… he wasn't such a bad guy. I thought if I could explain to him about my son, then he might understand. He'd met McCune a couple of times and didn't like him. I told Meredith that we could work it out. Anyway, she insisted that if she came along when I went to talk to him, then he might be more cooperative. Meredith said she'd back me up and tell Eli what a shit her father had been." She grew quiet.

"Go on."

"I don't… Why don't you ask her? She's the one who killed him."

"You're right. And I'm sure we can trust Meredith to give us the straight story on what happened that night," I said nonchalantly. I saw Regina grit her teeth.

"We showed up and Eli was all dressed for a night on the town. He knew McCune was dead, but he hadn't heard that the tractor was involved. He thought we were going out on a date. He was a little surprised when he answered the door and saw Meredith. But it wasn't a problem. I think he was giddy, thinking he was going out with two ladies."

"Did you go into his house?"

"Just for a minute. Meredith and I had talked beforehand and the idea was, we'd take him out and give him food, booze and cleavage, then come back and talk about McCune. That was the plan. Or so I thought."

"Meredith didn't stick to the plan?" Darlene said.

"No. When we got ready to leave, all three of us stepped out onto the porch. I went down the steps, but Meredith waited on the porch while Eli locked the door. I turned and saw her rub up against him and tell him to go first so he could catch her if she fell in her high heels. He laughed and turned to go down the stairs, then she reached out and shoved him. I should have done something, but…"

"And then?"

"He landed hard. I just stood there when she came down the steps. She stood over him, reached down and slammed his head against the stone walkway. I'll always remember two things. The sound of the bones cracking in his head and the look on her face. She enjoyed it."

"What did you do then?" I asked.

"I cussed her out, but there wasn't anything I could do to save him. I knew that from the sounds he'd made afterward. His breath made a rattling sound while his eyes glazed over. I won't lie, I'm ashamed about my part in Eli's death. All the rest I can live with. But Meredith was cold as ice. She told me to pull myself together, went over and got a pumpkin from the stand, then dropped it in front of poor Eli. She said everyone would think he fell coming down the stairs with the pumpkin."

We went over the murder of Horace McCune, which had happened pretty much the way we'd envisioned. She'd told him that there was a problem in the garage. When they got down there, she'd hit him on the back of the head with a pipe. He still managed to crawl out the door.

"Which was fine with me. I didn't want to have to drag him outside anyway. Once he was out, I hit him again. I was afraid he might get up again while I was going for the tractor, so I used some duct tape to bind his hands and feet."

Then she had used the tractor's bucket to smash his head.

"After he was dead, I rolled him into the bucket, hauled him out to the road and dumped him like the trash he was." There was no remorse in her words.

"You stabbed Meredith," Darlene said

"Damn right I did. When I saw what she did to Eli, I knew she'd figure a way to get rid of me the first chance she got. I decided to strike first. So I followed her out to McCune's and pulled in behind her. Meredith asked why I was there and I just walked up to her and stabbed her. She told me you all were on the way, so I got in my car and got the hell out of there. I really thought that I'd killed her."

"She didn't tell on you."

"I knew she wouldn't. If I was caught, she knew I'd give her up in a heartbeat. Why wouldn't I? I guess you've figured out her next move."

"She tried to run you down at the motel," I said.

"Almost got away with it. I turned just in time to see her coming and jumped out of the way."

"You could have ended it then. You could have told me what had happened."

"I still thought there was a chance I could get away with it. I just needed to destroy the evidence. I was going to burn the whole wretched place down. Unfortunately, Mad Meredith had the same idea."

"Why wait all these years?" Darlene asked.

"I used to think about it all the time. Duane had told me about the lax safety procedures on the rig. I told him to quit. But who listens when their parents tell them something is too dangerous? I didn't beg him to quit or demand that he quit or give him some ultimatum. I should have. I should have done everything I could to stop him from going back to that rig.

"Anyway, after he was dead and buried, I couldn't decide who I hated the most, myself or the people who'd operated that rig and allowed it to happen. I wallowed in self pity for a decade. Then for a while I thought I'd moved on. I got remarried, had a job I could tolerate, didn't hate the place I lived. The American dream. As long as I didn't think about my son lying in his grave. Then... Then one day about two years ago Meredith showed up at my door with all of her talk about making things right. We spent more and more time together, until one day I realized that she was talking about killing her father. It all happened so slowly."

Regina stopped, a perplexed expression on her face. "I think it must have been like getting sucked into a cult or being drawn in by a master con-artist. One minute we're talking about ordinary things and the next we're plotting how to kill the man I'd hated for eighteen years."

We spent another half hour talking about various aspects of the crimes before letting her go back to her cell. She'd be arraigned in the morning with the charges already pending against her. Darlene and I confirmed her real name and updated all the paperwork.

"You ready for the queen bee?" I asked Darlene.

"Bring her on. Though I think I know what we'll get out of her."

Darlene nodded toward a guy sitting patiently in the lobby of the jail. From the cut of his suit and shine on his shoes, it was obvious he made more in a month then I did in a year.

Sure enough, Johnathan Pratt joined us when we interviewed Meredith. "My firm is representing Ms. McCune," he said after introducing himself. Meredith's face was as calm and relaxed as if she were sitting in a boardroom.

We went over the preliminaries and got down to business. "When did you first contact Regina Broussard?" I asked.

"My client has no comment," Pratt said while Meredith smirked.

More questions were answered with more no comments and more smirks.

"You might think this is clever," I said. "You might think that paying Mr. Pratt and his firm millions to represent you gives you some advantage. In a normal case, I'd agree with you. It's true that a high-priced lawyer can sometimes get a person off on a charge of murder. There's no question that can and does happen. Juries can be swayed by a slick argument and a lot of smoke and mirrors. But none of that is going to work in this case. You want to know why?" I paused and got bored looks from both Pratt and Meredith.

"There are simply too many charges. Murder, attempted murder, attempted murder of a law enforcement officer three times over, reckless endangerment, conspiracy to commit murder, etc. etc. And that doesn't even get into the federal charges that could be lodged against you since some of the plotting took place across state lines. Oh, yeah, and you helped Regina get a fake identity. The list goes on and on. No matter how good your lawyer is or how bad the prosecutor is, some of these charges are going to stick and most of them carry a lengthy sentence. A first-year law student could prosecute you and you'd end up with at least twenty-five years without parole. So smirk away, but the writing is on the wall." I stood up.

"I wish I'd shot your ass," Meredith said, looking me square in the eye. Her lawyer looked like he'd just swallowed a rock.

"Honey, you sure are a piece of work," Darlene said with a smile as she also stood. "I wish all the crooks we nailed were as unpleasant as you are. It's been a joy putting you in here." Darlene turned to me. "Regina gave us plenty. We don't need to sit in here with this piece of filth."

Meredith couldn't stand it. She wasn't going to let us get away without hearing her side of the story. We sat back down and listened. Most of what she said was true, but she put such a crazy spin on every word that it blurred the lines between truth and fiction. The only real thing we got out of the hour we spent listening her was confirmation of the facts that Regina had already sworn to.

The rest of the week went well. Everyone from Dad to Cara was in a better frame of mind. On Saturday morning, we packed up the car with campaign signs and stickers. Cara and I had even talked Henry and Anna into wearing "Ted Macklin for Sheriff" T-shirts before we headed down to the courthouse for the candidates' rally. We took Alvin along for the trip.

Outside the courthouse, candidates for various local and state races had set up tables and had their glad-handers passing out flyers that mostly ended up in washing machines and trash cans.

"Wow, this is quite the turnout!" Henry said.

"For good or ill, it's become a tradition in Adams County to ignore local politics most of the time, but then once every two years, you come down to the square to meet the candidates. You shake their hands and stare into their faces and decide who you'll vote for," I said somewhat cynically.

"There are worse ways to decide," Henry said, and I couldn't help but agree with him.

"Special addition. First paper in a decade." Albert Griffin proudly handed us a copy of the *Adams County Times*. "Endorsing Ted Macklin for Sheriff."

I looked at the paper. A banner headline announced the endorsement, while the other four pages contained stories detailing various successful investigations that the sheriff's office had conducted since Dad had taken office. Right under the headline was a short, breaking news headline about the arrest of Regina Broussard and Meredith McCune.

"Wow! That's nice," I said sincerely.

"Eddie helped me get a small press I had in the garage up and running again. He's actually a pretty good typesetter."

"Is Eddie here?"

"He's on the other side of the square handing out papers."

We found Dad's table set up underneath one of the four oak trees on the square. There was a crowd of a dozen people by the table, including Shantel. When we got closer, it was clear who the real star was, as people formed a queue to get their picture taken with Mauser. Jamie, Dad's dogsitter, was acting as Mauser's road crew.

Dad worked the line, talking with everyone.

"Careful or Mauser will get elected sheriff," I joked.

"Luckily he's not on the ballot." Dad smiled. The crowd, the good wishes and the closure of the Waters and McCune cases had him feeling more optimistic than I'd seen him in months. "I really appreciate Albert doing that," Dad said, pointing to the newspaper in my hand.

"Eddie had said they were working on a surprise for you.

I admit I was a little worried."

About that time, Mauser noticed his little buddy, Alvin, and dragged Jamie over so the two dogs could sniff butts. This went on for about five minutes before Mauser's head shot up and his floppy ears canted forward. He was so focused that we all followed his stare and the mystery was explained. Cleo, a female Great Dane friend of Mauser's, had shown up with Bernadette Santos in tow. The two Danes romped and played while a circle of people formed around them and watched, many of them taking pictures and video. Eventually, the leashes were untangled and the dogs laid down in the grass in the shade of the oak tree, both panting heavily.

Henry and Anna, who had walked off to look at some of the other tables, came up to shake Dad's hand and wish him well.

"I never would have thought I'd have a deputy for a son-in-law, let alone a sheriff as a fellow father-in-law," Henry told him with a good natured smile. "I've got something for you in the car. I'll go get it."

I asked Henry if he needed any help and he waved me off.

"We need to wait around to see his reaction to this," I said with a wink at Cara. "I insisted that Henry put a bag over it so there could be a big reveal."

"Hey, Mr. Larry!"

I turned to see Jerome Martel and his friend, Mrs. Peters. Jerome was a young man with developmental issues who Dad and I had helped get out of jail back in June. He'd done a very nice YouTube video thanking Dad that had gotten tens of thousands of views.

"Jerome, it's great to see you," I said and, before I had a chance to react, he pulled me into a bear hug.

"Good to see you too."

"He's enjoyed being a big star," Mrs. Peters said with a smile.

"Sheriff Ted is the big star," Jerome insisted.

"People asked for your autograph," Mrs. Peters reminded him, causing him to blush and look down at the ground.

"I'd be in jail if Sheriff Ted and Mr. Larry hadn't saved me."

Henry came back, carrying a big, bulky object covered in a garbage bag clutched to his chest. I helped him lower it to the ground near Dad's table.

"Henry took part of our oak tree that broke in the hurricane and did a little carving on it," I told Dad. "Henry, you want to do the unveiling?"

"Took me a while to see him in the wood, but he was there," Henry said and awkwardly lifted the bag off of the carving. It revealed quite a fair likeness of the conceited Lord Mauser himself.

"I'll be damned," Dad said, clearly impressed. "Jamie, bring Mauser over here."

Jamie tore Mauser away from his fans and brought him over to stand next to the carving. Mauser gave it several sideways looks, sniffed it a few times, then gave it a good lick.

"He recognizes himself," I kidded.

"Wow, who did that?" Genie Anderson, Dad's girlfriend, walked up with her son, Jimmy. Both of them were carrying a large pile of flyers and buttons in their hands.

It went on for several hours, friends and well-wishers coming up to talk with and encourage Dad. Cara and I broke away for a while and walked around the square, looking at the other tables. I couldn't decide whether to stop and talk to Chief Maxwell when we passed his table, but the matter was taken out of my hands when Maxwell saw me and excused himself from the supporters he was talking to.

"Larry, I want to congratulate you on closing the Waters and McCune cases," he said, holding out his hand. I hesitated for a moment, wondering how it would look if someone got a picture of me shaking hands with Dad's opponent, but in the spirit it was offered, I reached out and shook hands with him.

"Thank you. But you'll understand when I don't wish you luck with the election." I said it with a smile and he took it well.

"No problem. It pains me to say it, but the county will be well looked after, whoever wins. Though I think I can offer some fresh and needed new ideas."

"We'll agree to disagree on that one."

"I also want to assure you that, no matter who wins on election night, you're guaranteed a position as investigator with the sheriff's office."

I was taken aback. I hadn't thought too much about it, trying not to jinx the election, but whenever I did I figured Maxwell would send me back out on the road… if I got to keep my job at all. We'd had a few rough times in the past when the city police and the sheriff's office had clashed.

"I appreciate that. And I respect your professionalism," I said, glad I could say it honestly.

The weather remained beautiful and the atmosphere of the rally maintained a cordial feeling. The only thing that marred the day was concern over the real test to come. Like they say, the only poll that matters is the one on election day.

EPILOGUE – ELECTION NIGHT

It rained heavily on Election Day. Genie, Cara and I spent most of the day waving signs between downpours or making phone calls on Dad's behalf. He drove from one polling place to another, greeting people and encouraging his volunteers. The rain didn't help, but Pete and Darlene managed to rustle up a dozen awnings and set them up across from different polling places.

Cara and I arrived at the Palmetto, where we'd be holding our watch party, at the same time as Genie and her son.

"I hope this isn't too close," I said, feeling concerned. Maxwell had also had a good number of volunteers out working the corners.

"This is Florida. Of course it will be close," Genie said, sounding equally worried.

"I'm going to check on the food," Cara said.

"I'll go with you. At least your parents finally went home," I said as we made our way to the back where one of the waitresses had told us we'd find, Mary, the owner.

"They had half a dozen candidates in Alachua County they'd promised to help. And, yeah, I'm glad that no matter what happens tonight, we can go home to peace and quiet." Cara took my arm and hugged it.

"We're going to close at eight, though there might still be a few customers in the restaurant when we do. After that, it's all yours," Mary said.

"We really appreciate you letting us use the Palmetto for this," I said.

"Glad to do it. Not that I'm taking sides. Maxwell and his officers are good customers, too," she said.

"Right now there's no hard feelings between the two camps, so I think you're good."

We went over a few more details with Mary before letting her go back to supervising her kitchen. I looked at my watch. The polls had been closed for twenty minutes. The supervisor of elections was competent and meticulous, which meant that we wouldn't be getting any results until nine at the earliest.

"There's Pete, Sarah and the girls," Cara said.

"I dropped off the TV earlier," Pete said. I followed him to a corner of the restaurant where we set up a monitoring station with a flat-screen TV and a large computer monitor that Lionel hooked up to a laptop so we could display the real-time election results.

"What are you misfits up to?" Darlene asked, walking up to find the three of us passing cables back and forth.

"Men's work," Pete joked.

"Listen, buster, no matter who wins tonight I'm going to see about getting you a crossing guard position," she shot back.

Despite the jokes, I could feel the tension in the room. If Maxwell won the election, it wouldn't be the end of the world for most of the department, but it would mean change. Who wants change?

By eight-thirty, the party was in full swing. Only a dozen volunteers who had offered to be poll watchers were still missing, as they observed the transfer of ballots and machines from the precincts to the office of the supervisor.

Dad held a tight smile as he mingled and talked with everyone. Now and then he glanced at the monitor to see if any numbers had begun to appear.

At a table in the center of the restaurant, Lilly Parks, the major's wife, was holding court. Lilly had always reminded me of Ethel Merman whenever I saw her at sheriff's office functions. Major Parks sat next to her with a spreadsheet that listed all of the precincts and the percentages he'd decided that Dad would have to win to get reelected.

"Okay, everybody. I've got a little game. There are eighteen precincts. My analytical husband, who rethinks retirement every time he remembers that it would mean spending more time with me, has figured out what numbers Ted needs to win this thing. I'm going to take a shot of vodka for every precinct where he underperforms. Think of this as a public service. If I can walk out that door at the end of the night, then everyone here will know that we've won this sucker! Who's with me?!"

Her craziness was infectious and turned knotted stomachs into smiles and jokes. Major Parks occasionally hushed her or put a hand on her arm to restrain her, but more than once I caught the worshipful looks he gave her—the quiet man who had married the life of the party.

"Numbers! We've got numbers!" Lionel shouted as he refreshed the supervisor's web page where a few precincts had begun to report votes and percentages.

With everyone watching the first numbers come up, I was finally able to talk to Dad. "What do you think?"

"We had a good turnout," he said, then turned to me. "But no matter what happens, we'll be fine. Two years ago, losing this election might have been a bitter pill for me to swallow. Today, though, I've got Genie and Jimmy. I can even bask in your glory," he said, giving me a nudge and a crooked grin.

I realized just how much Dad had changed over the last year. Thinking about it, I realized all of the milestones that had passed, including solving an old case that had haunted him for years. He'd watched me mature into my job and he'd found a new relationship that promised a future outside of work.

We spent the next two hours closely watching Lilly. At midnight, she might not have been able to pass a field sobriety test, but she could walk out of the Palmetto without bumping into the door frame.

At twelve-thirty, Cara and I walked over to where Genie and Dad were saying goodnight to the last of his well-wishers. Two of the last ones out the door were Shantel and Marcus, both with big grins on their faces.

Cara gave Dad a warm hug while I did the same to Genie. Then I grabbed Dad's hand in a firm grip. "Congratulations! You've got four more years!" I said, and he pulled me into a bear hug.

Larry Macklin returns in:

Spring's Promises
A Larry Macklin Mystery—Book 13

ACKNOWLEDGMENTS

I admit to taking literary license for one scene in this book. Florida is one of only four states where texting is *not* a primary offense. There have been several bills before our state legislature to fix this problem, but we're still waiting.

As always, thanks to my wife, Melanie, for her editing skills and support; to H. Y. Hanna for her inspiration, assistance and encouragement; and to all the fans of the series. Larry never would have come this far without all of you!

Original Cover Concept by H. Y. Hanna
Original Cover Art by Carmen Design & Photography
Cover Design by Florida Girl Design, Inc.
www.gobookcoverdesign.com

ABOUT THE AUTHOR

A. E. Howe lives and writes on a farm in the wilds of North Florida with his wife, horses and more cats than he can count. He received a degree in English Education from the University of Georgia and is a produced screenwriter and playwright. His first published book was *Broken State*. The Larry Macklin Mysteries is his first series and he released a new series, the Baron Blasko Mysteries, in summer 2018. The first book in the Macklin series, *November's Past*, was awarded two silver medals in the 2017 President's Book Awards, presented by the Florida Authors & Publishers Association; the ninth book, *July's Trials*, was awarded two silver medals in 2018. Howe is a member of the Mystery Writers of America, and was co-host of the "Guns of Hollywood" podcast for four years on the Firearms Radio Network. When not writing, Howe enjoys riding, competitive shooting and working on the farm.